FAT MONSTER

Gevera Bert Piedmont

Nightmare Press
Shepherdsville, KY

NIGHTMARE PRESS

Cover Art by Christy Aldridge at Grim Poppy Design
Edited by Jacob Floyd

To Aunt Bert, who never thought I was fat. I miss you every day.

And to my husband, who lets me stay home and write because he loves me and believes in me.

Other Works by Gevera Bert Piedmont:

Airesford, with Carole Urban
The Maw and Other Time-Traveling Lizard Tales
The Mickey Crow Series: Shiver, Formless, Metal, and the *Murder One Omnibus*

Editor of:
Horror Over the Handlebars, with John Opalenik
Necronomi-RomCom, Cthulhu Mythos duology
The Atlas of Deep Ones (forthcoming), with Elizabeth Davis

Her story "Toad in the Hole" in the anthology *Wicked Sick* was on Ellen Datlow's recommended reading list.

FAT MONSTER

Gevera Bert Piedmont

Mycosis: any disease caused by infection with a fungus.

Newhaven, Quinnitukqut, in a slightly askew world one step from ours…

CHAPTER ONE

The bus knelt, groaning, as Becca inched down the metal stairs, right foot, right foot, right foot, dragging her left leg behind her, the unsympathetic stares of those still on the bus heavy upon her. *Being fat isn't an actual disability; it's a choice*, their impatient faces seemed to say.

A newly finished pyramid loomed over her, matte black against the cloudy sky. What religion was this one for? Becca pushed her dark-red hair from her chubby face. Stepping from the air-conditioned bus into the humid air was like appearing under a hot, wet blanket. Heat mirages danced above the parking lot she had to cross. She wished she hadn't had to sell her car, which had fit her perfectly. She had already spent that money, so had it even been worth it?

Her knees ached as she hobbled across the baking asphalt toward the diner. Becca's stomach growled. She pressed her hand to her hanging belly, wondering about the cheapest menu item. She remembered the joy she had felt the few years in her life she had ordered anything she could afford, as much as she wanted, and not be hungry. Just a few short months ago.

Now Becca was losing everything. Except weight.

Sweat pooled on the small of her back, behind her knees, on her elbows. Her baggy black clothes fit like a prison.

The diner entrance offered a long, shallow wheelchair ramp or a short set of steep steps. Becca's knees screamed. Either choice seemed awful. She grabbed the handrail to pull herself up the steps, right foot, right foot, right foot.

She was twenty-six years old. Everything shouldn't hurt all the time.

The diner's interior was as chilly as the bus. The sweat turned into cold slicks under her clothes. Wet fabric clung to Becca's body. She scanned for Leila and didn't find her, so she evaluated the seating situation. How would two big people fit? Her mind whirled. Someone needed to design a restaurant app with accessibility details for disabled people's wheelchairs and large people's bodies—the tall and the broad. Becca added it to her "brilliant ideas" mental file.

Chairs with arms. That wouldn't work. Unmovable booth tables were attached to the walls. But tucked in the back corner hid a horseshoe booth with a moveable pedestal table.

A server wandered over to Becca. "Table for one?" She looked as if she wanted to be somewhere else, chewing the inside of her cheek.

Becca shook her head. "Can we get that corner booth?" She pointed.

The server's eyebrows thickened. "That's for big parties."

Becca huffed and waved her hand across her body. "I'm a big party, and so's my friend."

The woman's smile tightened, and her eyes slid sideways. "Big as in lots of people."

"My friend will order enough food to satisfy whoever made that rule." A mukbanger who gorged herself on food for money, Leila didn't always eat like that off-camera.

The server walked across the dining room toward the curved booth, never turning sideways or deviating from her path.

Becca plotted a route between chairs filled with diners. Restaurants wanted to cram as many customers in as small a space as possible, but they never accounted for larger people moving among them. That was probably why all the servers were always so damn skinny.

She pulled her messenger bag close and wove through the maze. Inevitably, there was a section where she didn't fit, even when lifting her bag and wiggling sideways between two occupied chairs, sucking in as much as she could, which wasn't much. No one eating ever wanted to scoot in their chairs, even an inch, to let someone by.

She detested people who ate with their chairs pushed way back.

Becca knocked into a bony guy with a lank, blond ponytail. He whipped around to confront her. "Bitch! You made me spill my soda!"

She crept past, eyes almost closed. If she could have, she would've closed her ears.

The woman with Ponytail crowed, "Oh my gods, look how fat she is!"

Ponytail exploded with cruel laughter. "What a fat monster!"

Becca kept going, face hot, eyes wet. She wished she was brave enough to say something rude back, that the earth would open up and swallow them.

"I hope you choke to death on your food, fatty!" the woman called. "You're disgusting!"

The server waited by the corner booth, gnawing her cheek.

Becca rubbed her eyes with the side of her hand. "Did you hear that?"

The server chewed. "Hear what?"

"Oh my gods!" the woman shrieked. "That fat thing's British! Listen to that accent!"

Becca attempted to slide into the curved booth. She had to push the table out of the way. She wanted to return home and watch her betta fish swim. Fish didn't get fat. Fish didn't torment other fish about their looks.

The server dropped two silverware bundles on the table, pointed to the menu code, and walked off, slim as a reed, past the loudly laughing Ponytail. Becca scanned the sigil with her phone and studied the menu, closing her ears against Ponytail and his horrible cackling companion, who continued to catcall insults in an exaggerated British accent. No one intervened.

How much money did she have left in the bank? The rent was past due. Becca's mum, no surprise, had not returned her calls or answered her messages asking—begging—for help. *You don't have to see me. Just please, mum, help me with some money. I lost my job. Or help me get a new job.*

"What fresh hell is this?" Ponytail exclaimed as a shadow fell across Becca.

She flinched, thinking Ponytail had approached, ready to attack, but from across the room, he continued to swear, throwing out slurs, including loudly wondering what gender Leila was and commenting on the dark color of her skin.

Leila towered over Becca, wearing a complicated orange wraparound dress with one of her signature corset belts. She had piled her hair high. Black ringlets curled around her brown face against an orange headscarf with a tiny black design. "Darling!"

Becca scooted sideways. Leila mushed herself beside her, smelling like strawberries. Her huge, red purse had long knotted fringes, and her fingernails were also long and orangey-red.

Becca leaned her head on Leila's big shoulder, and Leila kissed her sweaty hair. "What's going on? What happened to your job?"

"*Fast Fashion*'s parent company hired a stupid bitch of a consultant who met with everyone in person to 'evaluate' them." Finger quotes. "I didn't make the cut. She claimed to know my mother, which made it worse. I felt like she was punishing me for being Willow LeNoir's daughter."

Leila patted Becca's arm. "Who else got laid off?"

"All the overweight people."

The server appeared, a small tablet in hand. "Ready to order?"

"I haven't even opened the menu." Leila glanced at the red-faced Ponytail, who continued to rant. "What's wrong with that guy?"

"What guy?" The server flicked a glance at Ponytail. "I'll come back."

"It's as if his rudeness is invisible to her. He was screaming at me from a foot away, and she ignored it."

"Obviously, he's a valuable customer who can do no wrong." Leila scratched her neck. "If I owned a restaurant, I would definitely want someone like him eating there daily. Especially throwing insults at other diners."

"What if another diner is fat, though? And one is a tall, manly-looking woman."

"Hmm. That's a hard call." Leila pretended to weigh the choices on her hands. "Fat people eat a lot, which is good for the bottom line, but look at them. They are ugly and gross. It brings down the room, and him, well, he's such a fine specimen." She raised her perfect eyebrows.

They gazed at the ranting man: red-faced, with long thin hair, tall and skinny to the point of boniness. His female companion had a potbelly and uncombed hair. As the server left them their check, she glanced at Becca and Leila.

Leila inspected the menu on her phone, tapping the screen with a fiery nail, and returned to the earlier topic. "Your work can't fire just the fat employees. That's not legal."

Becca shrugged. "*Fast Fashion* put on my record that they sacked me for doing a poor job—even though I had commendations in my file—so I can't collect unemployment. Obviously, I don't have access to that file to prove the commendations. I'm behind on rent, and I had to sell my car. My mum isn't speaking to me."

"It's bad?"

Becca nodded, staring at the menu. If she made eye contact with her friend, she would cry. But in her peripheral vision, Leila's cheekbones seemed more prominent than usual below all the makeup.

Ponytail stood. His loose-bellied companion glanced over her shoulder with bright eyes, sneering at Becca, and flashed her middle finger.

Becca's cheeks flamed, and she focused on her phone. Her stomach growled.

"What do you want?" Leila's face was oddly intent, one thickly lashed eye squinting.

"A bacon cheeseburger with tots, I guess?"

Leila's hand slapped over Becca's phone, knocking it to the table. "Not to eat, Beck."

Becca remembered having a similar conversation during their college freshman year when Leila had been an unhappy, ungainly girl faced with too many choices. Leila eventually embraced all the things, being bi and appearing masculine.

Becca shook her head. "I don't know. Money would solve all my problems. Or being thin. Money is easier and quicker to get." Especially if she kept eating bacon cheeseburgers with tots. "You always have money." That sounded more accusing than it was.

"And you have a rich, famous mother." Which was true.

"Who hates me." Becca poked at the menu. "I guess I should say what I want is for her to talk to me. But we all know she won't until my appearance is 'acceptable.'" More finger quotes. Becca's mother was a famous British fashion model, deeply ashamed of the fat creature she had adopted. Becca was a plump cuckoo in her slim nest.

The server returned and waited beside the table, tablet and stylus in hand, eyebrow raised.

Leila said, "I will have one large glass of water and one smaller glass of crushed ice. My friend will have whatever she wants. I'm paying." She raised a hand to shush Becca.

Becca added an onion rings appetizer and a bottomless soda to the cheeseburger and tots platter.

The server slanted an angry gaze at Becca, who recalled her promise of how much food Leila would order. Becca widened her eyes and micro-shrugged one shoulder. *Oop*s.

"Water?" She turned to her friend.

"Yes, water." Leila rummaged in her giant bag and pulled out a long black tube, like a fat straw. It had neon mushrooms printed on the wrapper and a "MYCO SYSTEM" logo, which rang a faint bell in Becca's memory. Next to the straw, Leila placed a small, fancy glass bottle with a rubber eyedropper stopper. It was pretty, with an embossed logo Becca couldn't quite read, but no label.

The server plopped three glasses on the table, ungently. Water splashed.

A muscle jumped in Leila's jaw. She peeled the wrapper from the straw, popped the end off it, and poured the powdered contents into the water, adding a few drops from the bottle. She popped off the other end of the straw and stirred the water with it.

The water changed colors, looking like a glowing nebula.

"What is that?" Becca cocked her head. The rotting fall leaves smell was unappealing.

Leila sipped and added ice. "It's better cold, but hard to stir with the ice already in the glass."

"What is it?"

Leila wrapped her hands around the glass. The black straw stuck up. Her long nails had an expensive-looking orange-to-red gradient. "I lost weight." She tapped her nails on the sweating glass.

"I thought so."

"I'm sick." Leila sipped the autumnal drink and added more ice.

"Is that medicine?" Becca had never heard of medicine packaged in straws or fancy bottles, but her specialty was fashion advertising and writing, not pharmaceuticals.

Leila sucked at the straw, wincing. "Ooh, brain freeze. In a manner of speaking. My kidneys are going. I need to lose weight. I don't want to give up mukbanging permanently because that makes me a lot of money, so I refuse to get surgery restricting my stomach size, even if that's what the doctors advise." People paid not only to see Leila eat vast amounts on camera, but also for the food itself.

"Kidneys? What does that mean, Lee? You aren't dying or anything?" Becca put her hand on her friend's arm.

"We're all dying, Beck." Leila drank and added more ice. The scent of strawberry shampoo and the rotting leaf odor of the drink permeated the surrounding air. "Here's your burger."

Becca ate, but she barely tasted anything. She imagined what her late grand-mère would have said, seeing her eat a plate of fried food and bread, items rarely passed between her grand-mère's or her mum's lips.

Becca had no health insurance. What if she got sick? Kidney disease sounded expensive and complicated.

When the server removed Becca's cleaned plates and Leila's empty ice glass, Leila paid the check. "We are going to sit here and talk," she told the server, whose mouth twisted as she nodded.

Becca stared at the faux-wood table, eyes wet and hot. What if Leila died? Leila was her oldest friend, her only friend, her best friend. The scannable menu code looked like a square labyrinth, something to trap her inside. She could never get out alone.

She became aware that Leila was talking.

"I won't die, Beck, and I lost weight. I'm fixing the problem." She licked her full, glossy lips and pushed the galaxy glass toward Becca. "This is a weight-loss drink called Black Gill-Tea Pleasure, an advanced bioceutical mushroom tea meal-replacement drink. And this,"—Leila pointed an ombre nail at the glass bottle, "is Red Fun Gi-Up anti-obesogenic fungal protein drops."

The closer the glass got, the stronger it smelled. The Black Gill-Tea smelled awful, like overturning a rotten log. *Please, don't make me drink it.* "Is it special for your kidney disease?"

Leila's brown eyes widened. Her lips curved. "No. I want to talk to you about it."

"Hmm."

"Don't be like that. I'm not saying you're fat or need to lose weight."

But I am fat, and I do need to lose weight. Becca fixed her eyes on her friend and waited to see how Leila would dig herself out of that hole.

"I'm selling this. Well, shakes similar to this. From MyCo System. And I think with the marketing stuff you did at *Fast Fashion*, you could also use those skills to sell it."

Becca pursed her mouth. "Who would buy weight-loss drinks from a fat lady?"

Leila raised her arms and pointed toward herself. "They buy from me. This stuff sells itself. It's amazing." She scratched a red mark on her neck.

It made little sense to Becca. She studied the drink, the black straw, the galaxy of powder, the glass vial.

That *smell*. She couldn't imagine drinking something that stank like that. It must work great if people could overcome that stench.

“Look, I’ll front you money for a start-up kit of Shromshee smoothie shakes and Cosmic Cleanse Caps. It wouldn’t cost you anything. I’m not supposed to do that, but I will, just for you. Then you make twenty percent on every sale. If you want to drink the shakes, you can buy more at a twenty percent discount.” Leila leaned forward, too eager. Her breath smelled of rotten leaves.

“I don’t think I want to sell diet drinks.” Becca scrunched her nose, trying to avoid the odor. “I’m not a salesperson.”

“Just until you find a proper job. You post stuff on your social media that other people write for you. Trust me; this diet is the next big thing.”

The stench made Becca dizzy. She scrubbed her nose with her knuckles. “I don’t want to keep cases of shakes in my flat, and I can’t afford the postage to mail it around.”

“No, no, it’s not like that. That was the old way of doing this kind of business. Now, it all gets sent directly to whoever orders. You don’t touch their products at all. If you want to have some extras in stock at your place, you can, but you don’t need to.”

“It’s not me. It’s not my thing. I really don’t think people would buy from me. I’m not charismatic like you.” Becca thought of Ponytail screaming at her that she was a fat monster. “What if I sell candy bars?”

“This isn’t fifth grade.” Leila frowned and scratched her cheek. “Adults don’t sell candy bars to other adults. These are innovative dietary supplements. Not sold in stores. People are going wild for them. Opal Knox has been talking them up.”

“Opal Knox.” Becca rolled her eyes. She wasn’t a fan of the television psychologist, or the nutraceutical crap she peddled.

“You want to sell a product that she shills,” Leila insisted. Her full lips curved around the straw as she finished the galaxy drink. “New products are being added all the time. Supposedly, a test will tell you exactly which supplements to take to lose weight soon."

"If I want to lose weight, I'll buy the shakes from you." That seemed obvious.

"Exactly, but I want you to be able to offer the same opportunity to other people."

Becca shrugged. "I would tell them to just go to you?"

Leila seemed blind to all the arguments Becca was making. "I want you to make money, my friend. I'm looking out for you. Three months ago, when you told me you lost your job, I had just started on this journey. I thought of you immediately, but I wasn't sure it was a good fit. Now I know it is. Losing your job was a sign."

"I'm not sure it's a good fit." Becca rubbed her nose again. "What do you get out of it? Some kind of credit for signing me up?"

Leila waved her nails. "Yes, but that's not why I'm doing it. You need help, and I'm in the perfect place to help you. You can make money and lose weight. It's a no-brainer."

It seemed obvious when she put it that way, but something about the whole thing was off. It literally smelled terrible, for one. "I really don't think so." Becca wanted to pinch her nostrils shut. "Thanks for the burger."

Leila slid from the booth. She really had lost weight. The design of the dress, a Leila original, Becca assumed, hid the weight loss with bright colors and complex folds.

Leila drove a cute electric SUV not much different from the one Becca had sold, except it was brand new, bright red with black seats. She didn't offer Becca a ride home.

Becca felt like she had killed their friendship by refusing to sell the stinking drink.

MyCo System Product Listing

Weight Loss That's Out of This World
Your Weight Loss Journey and Financial Future Starts Here
(For Body Management Partner Use Only)

Starter Level:
Chocolate Shroomshee™ smoothie shake
Strawberry Shroomshee™ smoothie shake
Vanilla Shroomshee™ smoothie shake
Mint Shroomshee™ smoothie shake
Nutraceutical mycoprotein meal-replacement diet shake

Cosmic Cleanse Caps™
Adaptogenic mushroom-based dietary supplements, oil and powder capsules
*Body Management Partners only

CHAPTER TWO

A delivery waited on Becca's welcome mat when she exited the elevator carrying her mail. She hadn't ordered anything. Had Leila sent some weight-loss shakes before they even spoke?

She lifted the box. Not heavy, not light. About half the size of the mat, from Pink Power Fitness, who she hadn't heard of, not MyCo System. She checked the address label. Yup, addressed to her. Weird.

Still worrying that she had lost Leila's friendship with her flat refusal to drink and sell the stinky shakes, Becca brought the box inside her cozy studio. Usually, she liked her flat. Perfect for her and her betta fish, Apep. Today it felt like too much. Something she couldn't afford. What would she do with Apep if she got thrown out?

She flipped through the envelopes. One was from the landlord corporation, labeled FIRST NOTICE in red letters. Her throat clenched. She stuck her index finger under the flap. Eviction notice. Non-payment. Well, she hadn't paid in months. She threw the paper on the bed along with the unopened credit card statement. She couldn't afford the minimum payment anymore.

"Apep, I don't know what we'll do." The spiky orange betta swam back and forth in his little tank. "You are going to be living in a one-gallon plastic bag," she warned her fish. "Not even one with a zipper; they cost more."

She kicked the unordered package, removed her shoes, and threw them toward the closet. Throwing things accomplished nothing but felt good. She grabbed a butter knife from the kitchen drawer to open the box.

On top of the packages inside sat a computer-printed gift message from her mum.

Becca sat on her bed, crumpling the past-due bill and the eviction notice beneath her wide ass.

Willow LeNoir stiffly explained she was not immune to her adoptive daughter's pleas for help. But obviously, *Fast Fashion* had dismissed Becca for cause, since she was grossly overweight and attempting to work in the fashion industry, a place for slim people. All Willow could do was help Becca lose weight and give her an incentive: this smart scale and fitness tracker, already programmed. "I will pay you to lose weight," the letter ended. "You must wear the fitness tracker and weigh yourself daily."

Humiliation complete.

Becca cried.

She opened the inner packages: a smart scale and a watch-like object with a hideous girly pink strap. She hated her mum, who had never understood her lumpy, perpetually hungry child. Willow LeNoir was effortlessly model-thin, as Grand-Mère before her had been. Eating just a few bites of green food satisfied them. Becca was always starving, even as a baby; Willow even had doctors evaluate her for Prader-Willi syndrome, a genetic disease that causes out-of-control eating.

Baby Becca ate as if she had a black hole inside her. If she didn't eat, it physically hurt. A few bites didn't placate her. She could devour an entire layer cake by herself at age ten, when she already outweighed her mum and was a walking, jiggling embarrassment.

Tears dripping from her soft chin, Becca followed the charging instructions for the tracker. She carried the awful scale, a clear-glass square with black rubber feet, into the bathroom and stared at it with loathing. Finally, she stepped onto it. Three hundred and seventy-eight horrible pounds. One hundred seventy-two kilograms.

If she had a hammer, she would have smashed the glass. In the other room, the fitness tracker beeped as it synched with the scale. She nudged the thick glass aside with her bare toes and left the bathroom. The tracker's tiny LCD recorded her BMI as 65 in red numbers. That seemed alarming. Wasn't it supposed to be around twenty? The tracker was charged, so Becca tried to strap it on, but it was too small for her plump wrist.

She wailed. Apep swam faster, sensing her agitation. Becca threw the fitness tracker box onto the floor, stomped on it, and kicked it.

Extra packaging fell out, along with a strap extension. Feeling embarrassed, she attached it and put the hateful thing on. The tracker itself was black, square, and ugly, with that horrid pink strap. Even with the extension, it cut into her wrist and made her forearm appear even plumper than usual. She swung her arm a few times to see if it would make her hand swell and marched the circumference of her flat (one hundred thirty steps).

She waited in vain for Willow Lenoir to acknowledge she was using the fitness tracker. But it didn't matter. No matter how much her mum was willing to pay, Becca would have to hack off a limb to lose enough weight to pay her past-due bills. This would not work. And Willow LeNoir could easily blackball her in the fashion industry.

Becca wiped her nose with her hand, smelling forest loam. She dug out her phone to message Leila.

Ok, I will sell the drink. What do I need to do to sign up?

MyCo System: Your Roadmap to Financial Freedom!

This five-tiered system offers you almost unlimited growth opportunities and leadership experiences. You can

earn deep discounts and access to exclusive advanced products—while losing weight and gaining health!

Level 1: Quartz Body Management Partner

Your team: Yourself

You sell: Shroomshee™ smoothie shakes and Cosmic Cleanse Caps™

Your nutraceutical program: Shroomshee™ smoothie shakes and Cosmic Cleanse Caps™

Your headscarf: None

Your meeting location: Quartz Auditorium

Your perks:

- First access to new Shroomshee™ smoothie shake flavors (free at meetings)
- 5% discount on MyCoLysis™ and SporeCode™ testing
- 20% discount/commission on Shroomshee™ shakes and Cosmic Cleanse Caps™

My friend "Lee" was dying of kidney failure! She started drinking MyCo System's unique adaptogenic formula meal replacement Shroomshee™ weight loss smoothie shakes and taking their specially formulated supplements and she lost enough weight to reverse the damage to her kidneys. Her doctor said it was a miracle. Lee had never been able to lose any weight and keep it off before. Now she is almost unrecognizable!

To celebrate Lee's success, for today only I'm giving you 20% off your first order of a starter pack of shakes and supplements. Just click the MyCo System link below and use the code Becca20.

CHAPTER THREE

Becca twisted the cap off the small square Shroomshee smoothie shake carton and sipped the pasty "chocolate" brown mushroom smoothie, grimacing at the genuinely awful flavor. The starter kit, paid for by Leila, contained enough Shroomshee shakes and supplements to feed her for several weeks. Technically, she was supposed to have an in-home party and give it all out as samples.

"I live in a studio apartment with one chair," she reminded Leila.

Everything in the starter kit was beginner-level, perfect for Becca, with none of the advanced Black Gill-Tea Pleasure Leila drank for every meal.

Becca lacked a vast social media following, but she knew about makeup and fashion, with her famous fashion model mum. *Fast Fashion* magazine had liked her well enough until the bitchy consultant had come along and ruined everything. Although she didn't want to be on camera, Becca leveraged her knowledge to gain followers looking for makeup and fashion tips—and then bombarded them with information on the MyCo System diet.

She never mentioned her mum. She didn't follow Willow LeNoir on any social media or tag her. Leila was one of the few who knew Becca had a famous rich mum and who that mum was. Too many questions arose. Such as, *if your mother is so rich and famous, why do you live in a shitty studio apartment with a fish?* Or, *you look nothing like her*—since Becca was three times the size of her beanpole mum and had different skin coloring. Nature versus nurture; Becca was sure that she was the case that proved nature always triumphed over nurture. Nothing her mum and grand-mère had done ever changed her innate hunger.

She wondered about her birth family. Did she have siblings, and were they fat? Did another grandmother or two lurk somewhere, plump and cooking pies? Even, perhaps, a father, a grandfather, an uncle? She had minimal male influence growing up. Her unmarried mum had kept Becca far away from her famous and beautiful boyfriends.

The thick drink stuck in Becca's throat, making her gag. Leila couldn't understand why Becca didn't find the shakes scrumptious. Maybe Becca just needed to get used to the taste.

Leila insisted the Shroomshee shakes were filling, and Becca shouldn't still feel hungry after finishing one.

Mushroom smoothies! Shroomshees! Delicious.

All lies.

Mushroom smoothies tasted like dirt in which an animal had died. No, dirt in which an animal had shit and then died. Everything MyCo System made was mushroom-based. It all tasted like shit to Becca. Not that she had ever eaten shit, but she knew the smell. Everybody knew that smell.

Becca walked the perimeter of her flat at least once an hour. She played her favorite VR mystery game, but it burned hardly any calories, and she couldn't advertise MyCo System inside the vibrant artificial world. But in-game, all the character bodies she inhabited were thin, and no one ever made fun of her for her appearance.

She tapped her screen, searching the MyCo System forums for new scripts to post on her social media while waiting for Leila to arrive. She hadn't had many sales and had only lost three pounds.

Her mum sent no money or messages.

Becca hadn't gone to her mailbox in a week, knowing there had to be another eviction notice. She still didn't have the money for back rent, much less current rent. The corporate landlord wasn't some Mr. Nice Guy who would listen to her sob story and let her stay a few more weeks if she gave him a partial payment. Might as well keep all the money unless she got enough.

Even Apep seemed agitated because Becca kept pacing the perimeter past his tank. He fought constantly with his reflection in the hanging mirror toy.

Bottles of MyCo System adaptogenic nutraceutical supplements sat on the nightstand, one full of powder-filled capsules and the other full of oil-filled ones. Both left a hideous aftertaste, like unwashed snails coated in dirty beach sand. Becca took one of each with each meal, three meals a day, of the soil shake-in-a-box. Shroomshee smoothies came in "flavors" (finger quotes); the difference was the color. Pink, cream, or brown. Fake strawberry, vanilla, or chocolate. What a joke.

CHAPTER FOUR

Becca kicked the litter of mail across the floor as she answered Leila's knock. Next to the door sat a giant black trash bag spilling over with MyCo System Shroomshee containers. The bag stank of curdled milk and shitty dirt. Her flat stank.

Leila waved a hand at the mess. "What is going on in here?"

"These shake things are gross." Becca would have kicked the bag, but she was afraid it would explode.

"You still think they are gross?" Leila examined the overflowing bag. "You've drunk that many? How much weight have you lost? At least thirty pounds, right?"

Becca snorted and plunked on her bed. Her soft belly sat on her quivering thighs. "A tenth of that. Three pounds."

Leila's immaculately drawn brows came together. She scratched her cheek. "What else are you eating? You know you aren't supposed to mix these drinks with regular food. It messes up how they work metabolically and will make you sick."

"I can't afford to eat anything else." She found the crumpled eviction notice under her butt and flipped it toward her friend. "I'm about to be out on the street as it is."

Leila lowered herself into the only chair and read the notice. Her nails today shaded from green to blue, and her clothes matched. Teal leggings, blue knee-high boots, and an aqua sari that left her slab-like arms bare. Blue and green extensions in her black hair completed the mermaid look with an aqua headscarf wrapped around her forehead. She tapped her mermaid nails on the pages. "You have a little over a week to get out."

"I know." Becca eyed the papers littering the floor. She usually wasn't such a slob, but she was leaving soon. Why bother cleaning?

"How much money do you need?"

"Thirty-three hundred in back rent, plus whatever stupid penalties, plus this month's rent of eleven hundred." Becca stared at Apep in despair. "I'm worried about my fish."

Apep fought his reflection in the mirror ball toy.

"I'm worried about you, Beck. You haven't made enough selling MyCo System shakes and supplements to pay this rent, have you?"

Becca shook her head. She wished she could hug her fish. Instead, she grabbed a pillow off her bed. The pillowcase needed washing, but the scent comforted her.

Leila dropped the eviction notice onto the messy floor and scratched her scalp with both hands, getting under the extensions and making them dance. "Listen, I could just give you the money. I have it. But I have a better idea. Come move in with me. I have enough space. I can help you build your business. Once it gets going, it's basically turnkey. When you get another job, the MyCo money will be a bonus. I need to level you up. I need to level myself up." Her voice trailed off, and her hands dropped.

"Level?" Becca leaned forward.

"Well, yeah, there are levels. Like, I use the Gill-Tea and the Fun Gi-Up drops, and you use the premixed shakes and the capsules. Didn't you read any of the papers when you signed up?"

Becca waved that away. "Is that why I'm not losing weight?"

Leila's face scrunched. "No. You should be. MyCo products work really well. I lost weight right away with Shroomshee smoothie shakes. There is a meeting next week if you want to come. You can learn something, and you skipped your first one. Anyway, yes, there are levels—you're at Quartz level. You just started. You only sell to a few people. None of them want to sell MyCo System products. Yet. It's your job to get them interested in doing that."

Becca licked her teeth. They tasted like dirt. She craved actual food. "I don't get it. Why would I want someone who is buying from me to stop buying from me and start selling to other people? Wouldn't they become my competition?"

"You would think that, but no, because they know different people from you. You would lose them as a customer, but they will open a new market you would never reach. And you get a percentage of their sales."

Becca dropped her head to the side. "You get a percentage of my sales?"

Leila raised her hands and dropped them. "Well, yeah."

"I turn my customers into my competition, and then I get their sales, so I don't have to sell anymore?"

Leila grinned with fierce blue mermaid lips. "Yes. Eventually. If you have enough customers turned salespeople."

"And that is a level?"

Leila nodded.

"Then I get the black straw drink?"

"You are eligible for Gill-Tea at the Rainbow Obsidian Level, the next level up from where you are. The Gill-Tea Pleasure drink is more powerful and concentrated."

"And are there levels above that?"

Leila nodded again. "The person who signed me up is on that level, which is Red Diamond. Opal Knox is one level up from there, Black Sapphire level."

"I saw a video of Opal on SeenIt yesterday. She's thin again, except her ass." Opal's big, bulbous ass was impressive, like a creature living on her backside. Men lost their minds over it.

Her ass had made her famous as much as going on daytime talk shows and peddling pseudoscience.

"It's possible she might be at the next meeting. She appears on video usually. But we aren't that far from New Amsterdam, and she lives there."

Opal may have known Becca's mum. Willow LeNoir knew many famous people. But Opal wouldn't know of Becca. It might be nice to talk to a psychologist who understood being fat and the problems with weight loss. But something about Opal turned Becca's stomach. Her shilling MyCo System products was a count against MyCo System, not for it, although in her posts, Becca talked about Opal as much as possible, linked to Opal's social media accounts, and tagged her.

"You make more money the higher you level up." Leila cocked an eyebrow.

Leila didn't need the money. She made custom clothing, did private mukbanging, and was a BBBW (Big Black Beautiful Woman) model.

Becca scrunched her face and buried it in the smelly pillow. "Isn't this a pyramid scheme?" Didn't people invest their life savings into pyramid schemes and end up broke and homeless? Becca was halfway there, broke and almost homeless, with no savings. Could it get any worse? People filled their garages with pallets of powdered soap that cost fifty dollars a box because it was "concentrated." Becca didn't have a garage, only the parking space that came with the flat.

There was a catch somewhere with MyCo System. They would require her to rent a storage facility packed with pink, cream, and brown Shroomshee smoothies. Because she'd lost her flat, she would live in the storage facility, using the drinks as furniture. She laughed into the pillow, but it was more like a sob.

"It isn't a pyramid scheme. Those are illegal. MyCo System sells actual products, and the products work great. They have patents and trademarks with scientific research behind them. The only pyramids at MyCo System are their buildings."

"Wait—that new black pyramid next to the diner? I thought that was a Mexican church!"

"People who lose weight and regain their lives with MyCo System products might feel like it's a religion, but it's not. The owner, Milo Cobalt, likes pyramids for some reason. He's built a bunch across the country. If you can grow your business into a new city that doesn't have a pyramid, you can petition him to build one there. Imagine that! Just find customers in cities with no pyramids and get them past Quartz level."

Becca couldn't imagine influencing some guy she had never met and never even heard of before a minute ago to build a freaking pyramid. Her fitness tracker whirred against her wrist, and she climbed from the bed and started her hourly circumference.

Leila stared. "What are you doing?"

Becca held out her wrist. Her soft flesh bulged around the tracker's bright-pink band. "Once an hour it buzzes me if I haven't moved. If I walk around in this pattern, it's about a hundred fifty steps. There's another that's a hundred thirty."

"You have no money, and you bought a step tracker?" The immaculate brows came together.

"Oh. Did I not tell you?" Still clumping around, Becca explained her mum's last communication.

Leila was aghast. "She is paying you to lose weight and tracking your steps and your weight remotely? Throw that shit away now!"

"I lost three pounds. In seven more pounds, I'll get a payout, I hope." Willow hadn't said how much or how often she would pay.

"I'll give you a hundred right now to throw away that shit right into there." Leila pointed at the trash bag of shake containers.

"I don't know what she'd do if I did that." Stubbornly, Becca kept walking. Her bare feet swished through the past-due and eviction notices on the cold tile floor.

"Your relationship with that woman is pathological."

Advanced Level:

*Black Gill-Tea Pleasure™ drink**

*Red Gill-Tea Pleasure™ drink**

Advanced bioceutical mushroom tea meal replacement drink

*Red Fun Gi-Up™ drops**

*Black Fun Gi-Up™ drops**

Adaptogenic power-up fungal protein drops, anti-obesogenic

*Black BubblyBoost™ drops**

*Red BubblyBoost™ drops**

Adaptogenic power-up fungal protein drops with organ support

MyCoLysis™ testing

Unique, non-invasive biometric testing by a specially trained Body Management Partner

SporeCode™ Testing

Unique genetic blood test to discover your MyCoType™

FungiFuel™ custom MyCoType™ supplements

Custom supplementation based on your SporeCode™ testing results

ShroomSlim™ custom formulated supplements

Custom supplementation based on your MyCoLysis™ testing results.

*LipoGest™ spot reduction treatment**

Free spot reduction treatments for qualified Red Diamond Body Management Partners

*Body Management Partners only

"The Devastating Loss of Hall Lake"
from *History of Nature* magazine, online edition

Once one of the world's largest artificial reservoirs, Hall Lake is a puddle of its former self. The increasing effects of climate change have caused its water level to drop precipitously in the last year. Evaporation and overuse are revealing new and bizarre discoveries almost weekly. One website has even started a wiki listing interesting items, plotting on a map where each object was discovered and by whom.

Up to now, the most significant finds have included the rotted, rusted hulks of cars, some with the unfortunate drivers and passengers still inside. Not to be ignored are the dozens of leaking 55-gallon plastic and metal drums filled with trash, toxic waste, and body parts, plus hundreds of shopping carts, e-scooters, and bicycles. Local and federal police have been busy searching DNA databases to identify the human remains. The smallest, most minor finds are the thousands of empty drink cans and bottles and layers of trash, especially plastic, creating pockets of strata across the lakebed and giving it the appearance of an archeological dig.

Most important, however, are actual, historic archeological finds. Hundreds of years before engineers built the great Kimi Dam to hold back the Kimi River, Desert Bloom Natives lived in the valley. Now that Hall Lake has almost disappeared, stone ruins poke from the shallow water. These never-before-photographed relics had been underwater for over a hundred years. That's how long it's been since the Kimi Dam turned this empty valley into what engineers projected would be an inexhaustible reservoir of drinking and irrigation water for the western and southwestern region, or what we now affectionately call the Compass States.

Archeologists have mixed feelings about investigating such finds. There is little funding. Any grant money that would have gone into archeology has instead been funneled into research seeking solutions to the water crisis. Winter snowfalls, spring runoff, and summer rains no longer replenish the vast basin at the rate they once did. Losing the millions of gallons of water Hall Lake once held is a catastrophic blow to an area already reeling from drought, heat waves, and fires.

But now, as the water dwindles and farms and cities gasp with thirst, something even more remarkable has arisen from the trash-strewn mud.

At first, the archeologists from Compass University North thought the stone block to be another Desert Bloom artifact, perhaps a building of some sort. It is a red stone sarcophagus-like object that would not have been out of place in Egypt, although the carved hieroglyphics on its surface are not Egyptian. Nor are they from any known New World language. Whoever built the sarcophagus sealed it tightly….

CHAPTER FIVE

Floodlights lit the black pyramid imposingly, casting a reddish glow upward along the sides. Leila was dressed in red and black. Becca always wore black because Willow had told her it was slimming, although that was a lie. Everyone wearing it sweated so much in the sun that they lost weight.

The MyCo System pyramid was not at all slim. It loomed close to the Newhaven harbor, looking like something transported from Mesoamerica. Most pyramids Becca had seen were smooth-sided Egyptian-style ones dedicated to worshipping Egyptian gods. Those tended to be white and gold, not black and red. Cat ladies and dog lovers frequented the pyramids of Bast and Anubis. The temple of Bast in Newhaven, where Leila worshipped, was a square building retrofitted with a pyramid on the roof. Like all temples of Bast and Anubis, the place of worship doubled as an animal shelter and pet cemetery.

Now that she was paying attention, Becca noticed the MyCo System logo was prominent in red neon near the pyramid's point on all four sides. A nearby billboard overlooking the highway read, "What are you starving for?" with a MyCo System logo and web address.

Her stomach growled at the frying food odor drifting from the diner next door. The Shroomshee shakes weren't working for her. She had finally sold a few over the last week, but no one was interested in selling them alongside her. Or under her. She didn't really understand how it worked. When she thought about it too deeply, it stopped making sense, and she felt hungry and drank a shake that tasted like dirt. That discouraged her from thinking about anything except trying to brush the taste from her mouth, which didn't work either. The whole thing was exhausting.

Although the interior lighting was reddish, Leila's dark skin appeared pale and ashy. Usually she walked confidently, taking over the room between her height and her bright colors, but tonight she seemed subdued. She even stumbled a few times, although the heels of her red boots were not too high. Becca took her friend's arm.

Leila slanted a glance at her. "Are you nervous?"

"I don't want to get separated."

"For now, I'll stay down here with you, but as we level up, we'll meet on the higher floors of the pyramid."

The building was hollow, and the overhanging balconies were crowded, primarily with women. The auditorium had generously sized, padded folding chairs set into rows. Along the edges, under the balconies, were tables piled with shakes. No snacks, no carafes of water. One side of the great hall held a big screen hovering above a stage set up with chairs and a lectern for guest speakers. A black thermos sat on every chair on the platform.

Becca would have preferred to sit in the back, but Leila dragged her forward. The auditorium smelled like wet dirt with a sharp undertone of shit. Did MyCo Systems grow the mushrooms here? Was that odor the substrate? She tried not to gag at the thick aroma; no one else seemed bothered by it; maybe they were used to it. Along the slanted walls hung posters advertising the weight-loss products with various social media hashtags.

Leila pulled her into aisle seats in the third row. Way too close. Becca estimated the crowd was about ninety percent women, most overweight. She could not see who was on the balconies above them.

"You need to meet with my mentor." Leila looked a little livelier now. Her color was better. "I should have set that up right away when you joined."

"What mentor?" Becca, hardly listening, was doing the thing. The thing fat women do. Probably all women did it; she didn't know. She was checking whether she was the most overweight person in the room. Horribly, she appeared to be, by a wide margin. Leila was the tallest, as always. Leila used to complain about being so tall even though it helped her carry her bulk, although now Leila appeared deflated after her MyCo System-assisted weight loss.

"I call her my mentor. She brought me into MyCo System, like how I brought you."

Becca arched her brows. "You are my mentor now? My savior maybe, but mentor?" Mentors were wizened old men in fantasy films, not six-foot-tall, extremely fashionable Black women.

"Salome taught me so much. She saw some of my videos and contacted me, thinking I would be a good fit."

Becca crossed her feet and turned her body toward her friend. "Explain this. Some random woman saw your mukbanging videos where you consume thousands of calories at a sitting and thought, 'great, that person would be perfect for pitching weight-loss products'?" She used finger quotes.

"No, not my mukbangs. One of my fashion videos, where I explain how to drape fabric over a rotund body attractively." She indicated her own body. "Salome contacted me over that."

The name Salome made Becca's eye twitch. She had recently met a very unpleasant woman with that uncommon name. "And said what? Seems weird."

"Just that she had a business opportunity for me."

"Seems fishy. I would've marked it as spam."

"I almost did. But there was the kidney thing happening just then, and I was worried about losing my income, and Salome mentioned weight loss and making money…." Leila trailed off. The same thing she had sucked Becca in with. Lose weight *and* make money at the same time!

"It seems so against your personal message, though. You're into body positivity, doing your own thing, being your own person. Fat is fabulous. Eating is awesome. Then you start pushing weight-loss shakes, and that thin is good…."

"Fat for me was getting to be bad."

People were staring at them. People stared at androgynous Leila and at obese Becca. The two together were like a circus sideshow. Plus, fat positivity as a subject might be verboten at a meeting for weight-loss supplements.

"Shouldn't we be networking?" Many women stood by the tables, taking advantage of the free Shroomshee smoothies.

"Theoretically. But I'm waiting to see Salome. She's all the networking we need."

"It's crowded in here; what does she look like? Wouldn't she be on the balcony?"

Leila tilted her head back and scanned the first level. "Yes, but she'll come downstairs. She's as unique as I am, in her own way."

Becca felt that eye twitch again. "Unique?"

"She's got this amazing face, all cheekbones and jawline. I would love to do her makeup. And she obsessively vapes."

Becca's mouth flooded with dirt-flavored saliva. "She got me fired."

"The Black Pyramid" from *TheDailyDose.com*

…Tourists, illegally trespassing in a restricted, dangerous area close to where the Red Sarcophagus appeared last week, have discovered a small black step-pyramid. Several SeenIt users have posted photos of what appears to be the same pyramid to the social media platform, reporting that it was not there previously. Past images from the same area seem to confirm this assertion.

The pyramid is about a meter high and made of dull black stone. It has no openings and appears to be carved from a single piece of stone, with clusters of strange mushroom-like fungus growing around its base. Unlike the red sarcophagus, the pyramid bears no hieroglyphics….

CHAPTER SIX

"Salome got you fired? What? How?" Leila demanded. "She's the consultant *Fast Fashion* brought in. She met with everyone individually, and then everyone fat got fired."

"That can't be true." Leila's dark eyes widened and then narrowed. "That makes no sense. She wants to help fat people."

"She made us all unemployed, so now we are desperate to make money and lose weight and we'll all sign up to sell stupid shakes for MyCo System. Brilliant plan." Becca uncrossed her feet and set her heels. Although this wasn't a church, the pyramid felt like one, with a hollow echo and weird smell. Although churches usually smelled nicer, like incense. Or flowers. Or animals. Not like shitty dirt.

Salome. Now Becca felt like evil had joined the meeting.

Those gathering by the tables took their shakes and sat as others climbed onto the platform. Those on the stage all wore red and black, like Leila. Becca noticed how many people wore that color combination. Becca, in all black, accidentally matched without meaning to.

A woman with a red headscarf took the microphone and launched into statistics, such as how many shakes had been sold and how many people had signed up to sell them since the last meeting.

Becca wondered how many shakes they had sold just to people inside the pyramid.

Almost everyone greeted her words with yelling and cheering. Becca sat silently. Leila clapped and shouted with everyone else. When Becca's stomach growled, Leila shot her a side eye as if Becca had made noise on purpose.

The woman in charge of the meeting—Becca hadn't cared enough to register her name—kept shouting like a preacher. It was more of a rant than anything. Becca didn't think anyone was listening to her. This felt too much like church. Becca hated church. Her mum had brought her to synagogue a few times, even trying out some other monotheistic religions, but neither had enjoyed it—possibly the one thing they had in common.

The screen behind the woman, which had been showing a floating, bouncing, color-changing MyCo System logo, flashed to black.

Opal Knox appeared, peering into the camera.

The crowd screamed as if they were at a concert, getting to their feet, howling. Opal wore a black headscarf and a formfitting black bodysuit with a fabulous red corset belt, much like one of Leila's designs. Becca glanced at Leila and raised an eyebrow, and Leila grinned back and raised a thumb.

Opal twisted her hips toward the camera and slapped her generous, round ass. "We should only have fat where we want it!" she yelled.

Everyone howled like demented wolves. It was creepy.

How did that work? Becca wondered. Spot reduction of fat was a myth. Everyone knew that. Leila was melting, all parts of her getting smaller. The neck fold she was developing was the worst. Becca would rather have a nice, soft double or triple chin than a big old turkey wattle. Hmm. The ends of Opal's headscarf cleverly hid her neck and throat. Did Opal have a wattle? She was in her forties, wasn't she? Based on how long she had been vamping her big tits and bigger ass and her shitty nutraceuticals on TV, she had to be at least that old.

But for a woman in her forties who had lost and gained weight repeatedly, her body appeared tight, except for her famous round ass. Which could have been full of silicone implants. No one knew for sure, except, maybe her doctor and longtime rock 'n' roll boyfriend Ted, lead singer of HaunTED.

Opal started a pep talk about selling more Shroomshee smoothie shakes, leveling up in the organization, and getting access to the Gill-Tea Pleasure drink.

Leila elbowed Becca. "You need the Gill-Tea," she murmured. "We gotta work on leveling you to Rainbow Obsidian once I level to Red Diamond, which I intend to do soon."

"The shakes don't work on me." Becca tried to concentrate on what Opal was saying. Some ideas made sense to her from a marketing standpoint. MyCo System lacked a central repository for marketing materials. This word-of-mouth message-board method wasn't the greatest. Becca had been a professional (in her mind, she still was, because being fired didn't remove her knowledge), and she wasn't doing very well selling these miracle shakes using her expertise. It really was all in who you know. Leila had more followers, so she was getting the message to more people, that was all. It was a numbers game.

"We'll figure it out. I'll level up and then put new people under you until you can level up and move from shakes to Gill-Tea."

"I don't think that's allowed." Becca had barely skimmed the documents when she signed up; she had been that desperate and that trusting in Leila. She supposed there was a copy online somewhere she could read at leisure.

Leila waved. "They also didn't allow me to pay for your starting kit."

Audience members yelled and stamped their feet as if Opal were a stripper. The TV psychologist wasn't even physically there, yet the energy was quite high. Becca craned her neck, but she couldn't see the reactions from those in the higher tiers. It seemed excessive. It was just diet shakes that tasted awful and didn't work. The people losing weight were probably doing something extra and lying about it to make sales.

So much foot stomping happened that the slanted walls seemed to undulate.

Becca sighed and smelled her own foul breath. She had a bad attitude.

Opal signed off. A woman with a black headscarf took the podium, and she talked about exactly that: attitude, and how if you weren't selling and weren't signing people up and weren't losing weight, it was because you needed to cultivate a positive attitude. Great, thought Becca; in other words, it was all your fault for not trying. For not working the program properly, for not following the system, for not talking to enough people about how great the shakes were.

Becca felt intensely seen. She didn't really care that much about losing weight. Other people cared about what she looked like, people like her mum and that ponytail asshole in the diner. She was fine. Probably. She wasn't sick like Leila. She couldn't afford lab work without insurance, but when she had last had some in college, she had been okay. Not great, not terrible.

The woman with the black headscarf kept talking. "I'm so excited to be here today to speak with you about the incredible weight-loss products at MyCo System. We are revolutionizing the weight-loss industry. If you're drinking our Shroomshee smoothie shakes, you know firsthand how effective they are at helping people shed extra pounds and feel great."

She paced the stage, sipping from her black thermos. "But I know you're not just satisfied with the success you've already achieved—you want to level up and help even more people reach their weight-loss goals." She pointed into the audience.

"First, let's talk about the science behind our truly out-of-this-world products. We make our Shroomshee smoothie shakes and Gill-Tea Pleasure drinks with adaptogenic fungi, which help your body adapt to stress and while supporting healthy weight management. They contain nutraceutical and bioceutical ingredients that support healthy digestion, nutrition, and weight loss."

The mesmerized crowd nodded.

"But it's not just the ingredients that make our products so effective—it's also how they combat the obesogenic factors in our environment that can make it hard to lose weight. With our shakes, you can finally break free from the cycle of yo-yo dieting and achieve sustainable weight-loss success that's out of this world!" By the end, she was shouting and waving her free arm.

"So, how can you tap into this amazing opportunity and help even more people experience the benefits of our products? It's simple—ask yourself, 'what are you hungry for?' Are you hungry for success? Are you hungry to make a difference in the lives of others? If the answer is yes, then there's no limit to what you can achieve with MyCo System." Now her voice dropped, and everyone leaned forward.

"Our products are in high demand, and people are always looking for ways to lose weight and improve their health. By sharing your success story and offering incentives to your customers, you can help even more people join the MyCo System family and achieve their weight-loss goals."

The crowd stamped and hollered until the walls seemed to slither again. As usual, Becca was thinking instead of listening. Another problem she had, going off into her own head instead of paying attention to her surroundings. The meeting broke up now that everyone was exhausted. People headed back to the refreshment tables for more Shroomshee shakes.

Becca needed to drink more than three of the foul drinks a day for excellent results. At least, that's what she was thinking.

Was it the exceptionally low calories that helped more, in which case she should consume less of them (her poor ever-hungry stomach!), or was it some additive in the shakes that helped boost metabolism, in which case she should drink more (her poor sad taste buds!)? She didn't know.

Becca had signed on to sell a product that she knew nothing about—except that it tasted horrible, and it made most people lose weight, but not her.

Becca turned to ask Leila those questions, since Leila was her—what did they call it? Upline? What did that even mean? She should be able to explain—but Leila, standing, towered over Becca with a grin, looking down the aisle. Becca turned to see a skinny woman with a chiseled, skull-like face. A vape pen, its end glowing, hung from her lip.

Salome was indeed the same woman who had interviewed Becca at her magazine job and then had her fired, supposedly for cause, but in reality, for obesity.

"That's Salome." Leila elbowed Becca's shoulder. "My mentor."

"That's the woman who fired me from my job." Becca pressed her lips together. "For being fat."

Leila shook her head. "That still makes no sense to me. I can't see it."

It made all the sense in the world to Becca. She set her back teeth and vowed not to bring it up. She didn't stand, leaving her butt on the padded metal folding chair as Leila moved in front of her, hands out to Salome.

Salome was razor thin, her straight black hair in a fashionable asymmetric cut across her pale skin. Vapor puffed from her vape pen with every breath, as if she had a tiny dragon poking from her mouth. Becca did not smoke or vape, but she wanted to rip the pen from Salome's perfectly outlined, plump lips (the only plump part of her body) and suck in that sweet smell. The chocolate mist was the most delicious scent Becca had been near in weeks. It reignited her fierce hunger.

"My favorite protégée." Salome's lips barely moved around the sleek stainless-steel pen. She grabbed Leila's big hands in her small, thin ones and pretended to kiss her cheeks, almost poking Leila's mouth with the pen's glowing tip. "Your numbers are good, my dear, but they could be better. Should be better. We must talk." She blew a delicious cloud at Becca in a way obviously calculated to be rude. "Is this one of your girls?"

Becca squinted a fake smile at the skinny bitch. "Excuse me." Becca brushed by Leila, heading for a table of dirt shakes, stomach growling. She would not go for a brown shake because the lack of actual chocolate flavor next to that delicious scent would be a killing blow. After sitting in a cloud of Leila's scrumptious strawberry shampoo for the whole meeting, she wasn't going for pink either. Cream, then, the fake vanilla. How hard would it be to add actual vanilla to the shakes? She would buy premium vanilla extract and try it. Although the instructions explicitly warned not to add anything.

"Perfectly balanced and mixed," the label claimed, in what should have been a sarcasm or finger-quote font. Yeah, right. The flavor department should get on the stick and make it a little more appetizing. Becca inspected the boxes and saw a green one. New mint flavor. Oh.

Becca grabbed at it. Mint wasn't among her favorite flavors, but the other three bored her. Green would be a welcome choice. She shook the carton and twisted off the top. Chalky, as if someone had squeezed toothpaste into the vanilla cream flavor. Sipping and grimacing, Becca meandered toward Leila, hoping that Salome would have left by now.

No luck; the skinny woman with the skull face was still there, breathing smoke, watching her approach. Salome wasn't much taller than Becca; her heels were ridiculously high, so much so that her skinny ankles wobbled.

"Leila tells me you aren't losing weight or selling very much."

If only Salome knew the rude clouds of smoke in her face were delicious to Becca.

Becca inhaled chocolate, drank the green smoothie, and tried not to gag. Toothpaste mixed with dirt when it could have been fabulous mint chocolate.

"You look familiar." Salome did the trick where the smoke drifted from her mouth and into her nose in twin streams.

Becca sipped again. When exactly would she get used to drinking milky dirt? Her stomach growled audibly. She could satisfy it with a good milkshake made of ice cream, so the problem wasn't that these meal replacements were liquid. They just weren't food, not to her body.

Salome turned to Leila. "Your friend is very rude. No wonder she isn't selling."

"You fired her," Leila explained.

Becca's throat stopped. She tilted up her face. Seriously? She didn't want to talk about that.

"I fired no one." Salome blew out a gigantic chocolate cloud. Her cheekbones really were terrific. Even as she had been interviewing Becca at *Fast Fashion*, Becca had wondered if Salome had ever modeled, especially since she knew Willow LeNoir. In the fashion world, there wasn't even six degrees of separation between Becca, a random stranger, and her mum.

"From *Fast Fashion* magazine," Leila explained further. She scratched the mark on her neck.

Becca would have kicked her, but Leila's boots were thick, as were her calves underneath.

"Oh, that little job. The consulting gig." Salome blew smoke out her nostrils and tipped her head, studying Becca. "Yes, perhaps. They have a certain look to uphold, and you don't fit it."

"I mostly worked in layout and marketing," Becca said through her clenched teeth. "I wasn't customer-facing. Much of the time, I worked from home."

Salome pointed, vapor trailing from her nose. "That's another reason. People who work from home are slackers. No way to measure their productivity. No dress code." She wagged the pointing finger at Becca's loose black outfit.

"Hm." Becca took a big drink of wretched liquid toothpaste. She wanted to throw the shake in Salome's face. But with that bone structure, she would still look beautiful even with green goo dripping off her.

"As a MyCo System Body Management Partner, you've landed on your feet since losing the position at *Fast Fashion*. It's a great opportunity. You were lucky to meet Leila, and that she took pity on you and helped you. How did you meet her?"

"I met her years ago at uni. Leila and I have been friends for a long time."

"It seemed a perfect fit," Leila interjected. "When Beck lost her magazine job, right away I thought she might make a good MyCo System Body Management Partner, but it took a bit to talk to her into it."

"You may have been wrong." Salome frowned. Smoke leaked from the corner of her mouth. She pulled a small tablet from her pocket and reviewed it. "Her numbers are extremely poor, and you say she has lost no weight?"

Three pounds, Becca wanted to say, but she knew that at her starting weight, three pounds was a rounding error. And she did not want to argue with this fire-breathing dragon bitch who talked over her like she wasn't standing right there.

"I have faith in her," Leila said. "I'm hoping to level myself up soon to Red Diamond."

Salome tapped the screen. "Hm, yes, you're ready, but then you'll have to leave the lesser functioning behind." She tucked the tablet away and reached out to touch Leila's belly in a gross invasion of personal space. Leila recoiled as Salome palpated the softness above her corset belt. "Yes, you're ready. Recruit a few more. Bring them up to speed properly." She spoke with a slanted glance toward Becca, implying that she was anything but proper. Trailing a chocolate vapor cloud, Salome moved to her next victim.

"What was she doing to your belly? That was gross."

"The upper levels are eligible for special spot-reduction procedures called LipoGest treatments. And advanced-formula drinks."

"A drink that spot reduces?" Becca scoffed.

Leila touched her belly and then scratched it. "Having less around here might help my kidneys."

"I thought you were getting better."

"I am, I am." Leila glanced away. "We should pack your things tomorrow."

"I messaged my mum again, just in case."

"She won't come through with the back rent."

"I know, but it's so much to ask of you."

"You didn't ask. I offered."

Becca watched Salome, skinny dragon bitch, working the crowd. A chocolate cloud followed her. "Why does a skinny bitch like that represent a company that sells weight-loss products?"

"She's been part of similar companies; makeup ones and the legging one, and I think a fitness one. She moves around at the top level of direct sales companies. They ask her to come in, give her all kinds of bonuses, and she brings her people from the previous company. Me getting in under her is an enormous deal because if she leaves MyCo System for another company, and she likes me, she will bring me with her, and I'll be at the top. And I'll bring you."

Becca sipped the green smoothie. She hoped it would have morphed into tasting like a minty dream in the last two minutes. Nope, muddy toothpaste. She followed her tall friend from the pyramid out into the hot, dark rain.

"I'm not understanding any of this. You joined this company at the bottom under Salome, hoping she would bail on it and move to another company and like you enough to bring you along and move you to the top?"

"That sounds mercenary." Leila lifted one hand to scratch her scalp. "I believe in the product, and it's working for me. But once I'm thinner or at least healthier, I could move on. And many of these direct sales companies don't mind if you work for more than one."

Since Becca had sold her car, she had also lost her disabled parking permit. They stumbled through the dark rain toward Leila's little SUV. The area around the pyramid smelled of damp unpleasantness, as if animals had been living there until recently and no one had cleaned it. Becca allowed herself to get wet. She didn't mind warm rain; icy rain was awful. Leila had temporary red hair dye, and her boots were not made for walking on bumpy, wet pavement. The night steamed.

Level 2: Rainbow Obsidian Body Management Partner

Your team: Quartz Level Body Management Partners

You sell: Shroomshee smoothie shakes and Cosmic Cleanse Caps™

Your nutraceutical program: Black Gill-Tea Pleasure™ drink and Red Fun Gi-Up™ drops

Your headscarf: Any color except red, black, or gray

Your Meeting Location: Rainbow Obsidian Balcony

Your perks:

- 30% discount/commission on Shroomshee™ smoothie shakes and Cosmic Cleanse Caps™
- 20% off Black Gill-Tea™ Pleasure drinks and Red Fun Gi-Up™ drops
- 15% of your downline's sales

- 10% discount on MyCoLysis™ and SporeCode™ testing
- First access to new Shroomshee™ smoothie shake flavors (free at meetings)

From SeenIt s/anti-MLM

RE: MyCo System and Shell LLCs

Hello, fellow anti-MLMers. I've been looking into that new weight-loss MLM, the super culty one from the Compass States, MyCo System. I made an AI web spider with basic information on the owner, Milo Cobalt, and his wife Melissa/Missy, with the address of the main pyramid and some other info, and sent it to crawl the internet.

And it found something, well, interesting. Not only does MyCo System own plots of land big enough to build their black step-pyramids in every major city under various shell corporations, but they also own the Chow Compound Corporation, which operates several brands of all-you-can-eat American and Asian-style buffets across the country. That's a strange thing for a weight-loss company to sink its money into, isn't it? Almost like they don't want people to actually lose weight? So, unless you want to support this horrible MLM that preys on women, especially stay-at-home moms, stop eating at the following restaurants …

CHAPTER SEVEN

Leila rearranged her large condo to give Becca a bedroom. "This was my video room, but I combined it with my sewing room. They don't really need to be separate. Do you want Apep in your bedroom or the living room? Because at home, everything was all one room. Your former home, I mean."

The college-aged discount movers put Becca's few things into the newly emptied room. Apep's small tank and accessories sat in Leila's spacious living room. Apep swam in a gallon bag, one with a zippered top, despite Becca's threat. Leila's black Sphynx cat, Nyx, sat before the bag, her green eyes and soft dark ears huge, watching the fish.

"Do you like Apep?" Becca asked. "I would like him to be out here if you don't mind. But the cat…."

"Once Apep is in the tank, Nyx won't be able to get him. The fish would look nice here. The bright orange and red would match the décor."

Once they set up the tank, Becca dumped in the extra bags of water she had saved and added Apep, who seemed happy enough to be back in his old house with a new view.

Leila sprawled in an oversized ruby-colored chair with her tablet, bare feet on a sapphire-blue ottoman. The living room was a blaze of jewel colors that almost hurt Becca's eyes. She retrieved her laptop, an older single-screen model that always needed to be plugged in, and checked her sales. Zero. Frustrated, she logged in to the MyCo System message boards and searched out new memes to post or scripts to follow. She felt funny having her bare feet on the emerald couch.

Leila whooped. “I’ve leveled up! I did it!” She sat up, waving the tablet.

“What?”

“I signed four more people as Quartz Body Management Partners, and one of my existing Quartzes signed another Quartz Body Management Partner, finally leveling me!” Leila tossed the tablet onto the red chair and did an erotic victory dance for which she could have charged money. Becca didn’t know if she should look away. Nyx stayed perched on the big green cat tree by the window, seemingly unfazed. “Spot reduction, here I come!”

The tablet Leila had casually dropped had probably cost three times what Becca’s laptop had when new. The disparity in their financial outlook became clear, and Becca had only been there a few hours. Another thing penetrated her mind. “Those four people, are they all in Newhaven?”

“Three of them are!”

“And the one the Quartz signed up, is that one in Newhaven too?”

“Um, I don’t know.” The last was over her shoulder as Leila headed into the kitchen. “I wish I could drink! This is cause for a celebration!” The refrigerator’s ice machine rattled.

Becca’s wet eyes tightened. She stared at her social media stats. Few hits, engagements, likes, or clicks. Meanwhile, her supposed best friend signed up more people to be her direct local competitors. But that skinny dragon bitch who had gotten her fired complained that Becca wasn’t doing enough work? The amount of work barely mattered. Her slice of the Newhaven pie got smaller every hour.

Leila strutted into the living room, crossing her feet in a catwalk, a large glass in one hand with a black straw peeking out, in the other a square pink shake box. “Let’s celebrate!”

Becca accepted the horrible shake. The only reason she could find any strawberry taste in it was that she could smell Leila's strawberry shampoo. Foul.

Leila sucked on the black straw like it was ambrosia, her eyes closed. Her red-tipped lashes were as long as centipede legs. She must spend hours on her makeup. "Spot reduction," she murmured, licking the straw.

Becca put down her pink monstrosity. "Can you please help me?" she whispered. "I am failing hard here. I'm going to get kicked out for lack of sales."

"No." Leila moved to her side. "They actually don't kick anyone out. They might not let you sell anymore, but you can buy at your discount forever."

Becca choked. The chalky pink drink flooded her mouth from below. That didn't improve the taste. "I thought I was supposed to make money at this and lose weight. My mum watches my every step and pound. I'm a loser and not in the way I need to be."

"I have a plan," Leila declared. "Once I'm officially a Red Diamond, I will put my next few Quartzes under you. I don't care if it's wrong. You will at least have that income. I might start you on the Black Gill-Tea too." She sucked the straw deeply. Her eyes bulged prominently, and she was constantly scratching herself. Just how sick was Leila?

"Is that allowed?"

"Fuck what's allowed. You're my bestie. You've always been there for me. I'll schedule a meeting with Salome about leveling up and what that entails. She's been anxious about getting me and the other people under her to level up for some reason, so she'll be thrilled. I'm elated to take advantage of the spot reduction. I'm not sure how it works, but I've seen the results."

"Spot reduction doesn't work." As a longtime morbidly obese person, Becca had read extensively about diets, exercise, fad diets, and scams. She was becoming increasingly sure she was part of a scam. Leila's weight loss was because of her illness, not the Black Gill-Tea she ingested constantly. "Only liposuction and skin removal surgery work for spot reduction."

Leila laughed. "This is totally different. You're brand new at MyCo System. You've only attended one meeting. We left early, and you weren't paying attention. This stuff is miraculous. Do you not read the things you repost?"

"I don't have a lot of variety to repost."

"That's my fault. I'm not training you well enough. I would turn you over to Salome, but it's obvious you don't like her."

"She fired me." Becca's mouth twisted. "I'm in this mess because of her. I lost my flat because of her. That's why I don't like her."

"Okay, that's in the past now. I'm going to fix that." Leila waved long orange and red nails.

Becca shook her head. "I can't get my job back. My flat has gone to someone else. How are you going to fix it?"

"You live here now, and this is much nicer. I'll help you make more money than you made at that magazine. Then you'll lose weight and show your mum, and she'll pay you, too."

"I've lost four pounds. That's like one percent."

"I'm going to give you my advanced scripts. You copy them, and you'll get results."

"You have thousands and thousands of followers."

Leila waved her hand.

"And can you explain the Gill-Tea to me? If it's so good, why doesn't everyone sell it? I thought part of not being a pyramid scheme was that everything gets sold to customers, but the Black Gill-Tea is only sold to Rainbow Obsidians and above."

"It's a perk. A bonus."

Becca's eye squinted. "That seems convenient. You level up and stop using the thing you push on all the customers as being the best ever and only use something else? What about the supplements?"

Leila pursed her mouth. "Those are different with the Gill-Tea, too. You switch to the Red Fun Gi-Up drops."

Becca carefully placed her elderly laptop on the emerald couch and headed into Leila's kitchen. The fridge was full of pink, cream, and brown juice boxes, and glass bottles of water. No food. She opened a cabinet. Packs of black straws and a case of red glass bottles. Cases of the Cosmic Cleanse Caps liquid and powder capsules that Becca took. No food anywhere. Her stomach growled just knowing that.

"You don't have any food," she called.

"We don't need food."

"What if I want some food?"

"You don't need food, and you'll get over wanting it. It's head hunger. It's psychological."

"I want food. I want proper food all the time. These Shroomshee smoothies taste like dirt and shit. My stomach hurts from drinking them."

"Those shakes are delicious! Wait until you level up to the Black Gill-Tea; it's even better."

"It can't be worse." Becca closed the cabinet. "I want melted cheese. A burrito." She wandered into the living room. "Chips and salsa."

Leila sprawled in the big chair, sipping her black drink, eyes closed. She spit out her straw. "Ew. I don't crave that stuff at all anymore. I remember loving it, but now it's like a bad dream and I honestly don't want it. At all. Yuck. You need Black Gill-Tea Pleasure. I admit, when I started on the Shroomshee smoothie shakes, I wanted food. After a few days, I adapted. After a week, I had a few bites of food, which tasted bad. I returned to Shroomshee smoothie shakes gladly. I wonder what's wrong with you?"

"Nothing is 'wrong' with me," Becca snapped, using her finger quotes aggressively. "You sound like my mum and grand-mère. These shakes are gross, that's all. Why can't I mix in vanilla extract, cocoa powder, or strawberry flavoring? It would add a couple of calories but help the flavor so much."

"They are precision mixed. Most people think the flavors are perfect. Try mixing the vanilla and chocolate to make cookies and cream, the strawberry and vanilla to make strawberries and cream, or the strawberry and chocolate to make a chocolate-covered strawberry flavor."

"What about the green flavor?" Becca remembered the almost-mint awfulness.

"I never tried that; I saw it the other night on the table. Is it mint? I bet it's fantastic. Nyx would be crawling all over me every time I drank it. Nyx loves mint. Catnip is a kind of mint, you know."

"It was not good." Becca screwed up her face. "Shitty toothpaste."

"Well, that's one thing you can post, that you could taste-test an exclusive new flavor if you come to a meeting. Don't say what it is. Try to get people to join to find out it's green mint."

Becca stared at her friend. "People won't join just to find out what a flavor is."

"I thought you knew marketing. Tease them. Hint."

Everything about this seemed dishonest to Becca, even if Leila was right about the marketing idea. Others didn't really enjoy these shakes, did they? Did they really lose weight? Becca drank so many because she was so hungry. Maybe that's why she couldn't lose weight. Who knew how many calories were in them? They had barely any nutritional information. No allergens, not much in the way of ingredients, just a proprietary blend of rare mushrooms and minerals.

Becca didn't even like mushrooms on pizza.

Pizza. Thin, slightly burnt crust, melted cheese. Her eyes prickled with tears. She lived within walking distance, even for someone as fat as her, of the most wonderful pizza on earth, and she was drinking sludgy shakes from a square carton for all her meals with no weight loss to show for it.

My peeps! Last night, it was my privilege to attend an exclusive MyCo System meeting at the Newhaven pyramid. The energy was amazing! I will tell you in the coming days some of what I learned at this seminar, but the most important thing is: a NEW FLAVOR OF SCHROOMSHEE™ SMOOTHIE SHAKE. Yes, you heard that correctly. Soon you can purchase a fourth flavor of Shroomshee™ smoothie shake! I can't reveal what flavor it is, but I tried it, and I simply can't express how what it tasted like! Comment below what flavor you think this Shroomshee™ smoothie shake is! #MyCoSystem #shroomsheesmoothie #weightloss #bossbabe (Link to buy the original flavors in comments.)

CHAPTER EIGHT

"I'm going for a walk."

"Perfect, I'm about to have a video meeting with Salome about leveling up to Red Diamond."

Skinny bitch. Smoke-blowing dragon.

Becca pulled on a pair of hiking sandals, adjusting the Velcro across her wide, bare feet. She needed a pedicure. The rain had stopped, but it was still steamy outside.

She was going to quit MyCo System.

There was no point in being part of it anymore. She wasn't losing weight. She wasn't making money. It took up all her time, posting stupid appeals no one paid attention to. She would use that time to find a proper job that didn't care about her weight, where only her skills and experience mattered. She could always try consulting.

Becca felt fifty pounds lighter. No more being forced to drink the awful dirt shakes. She would never have to go inside that creepy pyramid again and gag on its wretched stench.

Dark clouds streaked the sky, as if the rain might return at any moment. The streets steamed with trash water. Becca ambled until the trash odors transitioned to garlic. She glanced around, as if someone might be spying on her, and ducked into Poppa's Apizza, a world-famous pizzeria.

It smelled like heaven inside.

These people knew their customers. They would never look down on Becca for being fat. She could order three large pies for herself, and they would fall over themselves to bring them to her. But for now, with only a few wrinkled bills in her pocket, a couple of slices would have to do.

"Two pepperoni slices, please, and a cola."

She wished she could sit at the counter, but the round bar stools would not hold her large ass. Becca crammed herself into a booth. The tables didn't move, but the benches did. No one was behind her, so she shoved the bench back.

The workers spoke a waterfall of Italian into the garlic air. Becca's stomach rumbled and gurgled. She patted it. Soon, soon, actual food. Instead of just salt and pepper on the table, a lazy Susan held grated cheese, oregano, flaked hot pepper, and a paper napkin dispenser.

Something Becca should have done a while ago: she opened the search engine on her phone and typed "MyCo System." Even though she was leaving, she wanted to know what had sucked in her friend.

Excerpt from *The Shadow Press* "The Mysterious Red Sarcophagus"

…Since the Red Sarcophagus was too large to be moved, the archeologists opened it *in situ*, inside a purpose-built, sealed shelter during a live-streamed event. The box's interior, also extensively carved with unknown glyphs, appeared full of foul-smelling reddish liquid, along with bone fragments and floating lumps of what may have been flesh.

The hashtags "#DrinkTheRedJuice" and "#DrinkTheMummyJuice" are trending across all social media. Archeologists sent samples of the contents to a laboratory for testing before resealing the sarcophagus.

Despite the popular hashtags, no one has ingested the red liquid, as far as anyone knows, although rumors continue to spread that someone smuggled most of the red liquid from the site…

Level 3: Red Diamond Body Management Partner

Your team: Rainbow Obsidian Body Management Partners & Quartz Body Management Partners

You sell: Shroomshee™ smoothie shakes, Cosmic Cleanse Caps™, MyCoLysis™ and SporeCode™ testing, ShroomSlim™ and FungiFuel™ custom supplements

Your nutraceutical program: Black Gill-Tea™ Pleasure drink and Black BubblyBoost™ drops

Your headscarf: Red

Your Meeting location: Red Diamond Balcony

Your perks:

- 40% discount/commission on Shroomshee™ smoothie shakes and Cosmic Cleanse Caps™
- 20% discount on Black Gill-Tea™ Pleasure drinks, Black Fun Gi-Up™ drops, and Black BubblyBoost™ drops
- 20% discount on ShroomSlim™ and FungiFuel™ custom supplements
- 20% of your downline's sales
- 7% of MyCoLysis™ and SporeCode™ testing fees
- Free LipoGest™ spot reduction treatments
- Free MyCoLysis™ and SporeCode™ testing

CHAPTER NINE

A woman in a tomato sauce-stained white apron brought two giant slices of pepperoni pizza laid across several paper plates. A minute later, she dropped off the soda in a thick red plastic glass, scratched and cloudy with age. No utensils.

Grease shimmered on the slices.

Heaven.

Becca hadn't known much about pyramid schemes or multilevel marketing companies—or what MLM even stood for—before her research at the pizza parlor. She wouldn't have joined MyCo System if she had. Frauds, all of them. Nothing about MyCo System appeared any different. The salespeople were the customers. MyCo System made a lot of dubious health claims, like so many others, but MyCo System was unique in that they made all the products from mushrooms and fungi.

Most of all, Becca didn't like the concept of leeching off the people in your downline.

After she finished her pizza, she would return to Leila's flat and talk to her about how she could get out of this stinking fungal mess.

Becca balled up napkins to blot the grease off the pizza. Even with the extra shine gone, the pizza was gorgeous, a meal to write home about. Gourmet magazines put this pizza, from this little old hole-in-the-wall Newhaven restaurant, on their covers. And she was about to eat it. Not for the first time, of course, but she had never been so hungry for it before. Her stomach heaved with excitement.

Becca flavored the slices with all the condiments and, using approved Newhaven pizza-eating tactics, she bent the crust, tilted her head, and aimed the slice's point into her mouth. A few drops of warm orange pepperoni oil hit her tongue. Becca shivered involuntarily. She inhaled meaty steam as she bit down into molten cheese; thin, slightly burnt crust; and crisp pepperoni. How many weeks had it been since actual food had been in her mouth?

A happy tear ran down her cheek. She put the slice down and chewed, savoring the…

The pizza tasted like hot grease. She couldn't distinguish the sauce from the cheese, the meat, or any of the spices. She might as well have been eating the balled-up napkin she had used to blot the pepperoni.

Becca kept chewing. Her saliva felt oily. Her stomach roiled.

The best pizza in the entire world, she told herself. People wait in line for hours to eat here. Half a dozen people were waiting for stacks of carry-out pizza boxes at that very moment.

She swallowed and licked her slippery teeth with her greasy tongue. Tears dripped from her chin.

She lifted the red cup. The dark soda fizzed toward her nose like tiny reverse comets. She wanted to drink deeply. Instead, she sipped and choked on the harsh acidic bubbles she had once loved.

Becca lifted her phone, glanced at the blank lock screen, and walked to the cash register, cutting in front of the people waiting for their carry-out pizza. "I'm sorry, I have an emergency," she lied. "May I pay?"

"Let me wrap your slices," the woman said. "And put your soda in a paper cup."

"I won't be able to take it with me, but thank you."

The woman studied her tearful face and nodded.

Becca tipped generously and fled.

Except from The Shadow Press "Black Pyramid, Redux"

…SeenIt users have posted more photographs of the small black step-pyramids. The first one photographed is now missing, perhaps stolen. Each pyramid that mysteriously appears is located farther away from the Red Sarcophagus, and each seems to be slightly larger than its predecessor. Since these pyramids appear on restricted government land, the Collective States Government considers the disappearance of these pyramids potential cases of theft.

The Bureau of Land Management, which owns the property, has no comment on whether its agents have investigated the pyramids in person.

Internet rumors claim that government agents themselves have confiscated the small step-pyramids.

Or that aliens placed the pyramids and have since removed them…

CHAPTER TEN

Halfway back to Leila's apartment, Becca vomited into a trash can. Although she barely ate a bite, the vomit kept coming, even out of her nose. It was raining again. She had left the heavenly garlic zone.

At least the rain kept people inside and from staring at her. It was as if her body was rejecting every pizza she had ever eaten, every slick piece of pepperoni, every stringy piece of cheese. She drooled out every red cup of soda she had ever consumed. It hurt. Her whole abdomen convulsed, her throat flexed, and her nose and mouth burned with acid. Hot tears of humiliation and pain poured down her face, mixed with rain.

Her chubby hands clutched the filthy sides of the trash barrel. That single bite of pizza expanded to splatter over fast-food wrappers, paper cups, and blue bags of dog poop. It kept coming.

It was disgusting and somehow cathartic.

Becca felt a rumbling in her backside.

She wiped her mouth and hobbled toward Leila's building, holding her butt cheeks together, her whole middle aching, adding to the usual pain in her knees. One juicy fart let loose as she arrived at the building. She might have lost a pair of panties.

Worrying she stank, Becca walked, cheeks clenched, toward the elevator. *Please, please be in the lobby. Please have no one else in there.* She wiped her mouth and chin on the shoulder of her black t-shirt. Somehow, she was hungry again, even as her guts rumbled to evacuate.

Leila was on a video call when Becca stumbled in and headed straight to the bathroom. Leila's bathroom was a dream, with an oversized shower with several heads, a handheld shower nozzle, a big separate tub with jets, and even a bidet attachment on the toilet. Becca only cared about the toilet. She yanked at her pants. They weren't tight, but she was frantic to get the poison out of her body.

The underpants weren't ruined. She couldn't be grateful, barely reaching the toilet seat before purging violently, hotly. She sat in her garbage stench and cried.

Her bottom trumpeted. It echoed. The stink cloud seemed visible. Liquid fire spurted.

She hadn't fully closed the bathroom door. The stink tendrils had to be questing down the hallway toward Leila in the living room, where she was on the call with Salome.

Becca wished Salome could smell it. Everything she ever had eaten had just fallen out of her ass. She was probably clean enough to get a colonoscopy.

She triggered the bidet attachment and wiggled until she was sure she was as clean as the blast of warm water could get her. She stood, studiously not glancing into the toilet. Extra stench from the bowl, released from under her ass when she stood, found her nose and made her gag. No. She would not puke into that mess. Becca wiped and wiped between her wet cheeks, throwing the paper wads on the chunky brown and black liquid that she would not acknowledge as coming out of her, and flushed and had to flush again. She didn't want to pull up her fart-damp panties. But she also would not run down the hall bare-assed to her new room to get fresh ones.

She pulled up the underwear and shivered, feeling unclean. She washed her hands twice.

Leila knocked. The door swung open.

"Are you—" she gagged. "Oh my gods. Beck."

Becca finished adjusting her clothes and used the deodorizing spray. "I'm sorry. I'm a little sick."

"A little?" Leila waved a hand and then pinched her nose. "Did you try to eat?"

"Yes." Becca studied her feet, still in her black sandals. They were puke splattered.

"What did you eat, silly girl? I told you once you started the Shroomshee smoothies, food could make you sick."

"I want to quit MyCo System." Becca's voice was tiny.

"Quit? Why?" Leila sounded genuinely confused. She let go of her nose. "Why would you want to quit?"

"Why? The shakes don't work—I'm not losing weight. No one wants to buy them from me. I'm a failure. I won't get any money from my mum as long as I'm fat, and I won't get a job as long as I'm fat. The shakes were supposed to fix both the fat and the money, and they aren't doing either."

The pizza puke stain on the left sandal looked like a mushroom.

"You need to work the system harder to sell, that's all. I'll have to help you even more, that's all. Now that I'm leveling up, I can access advanced materials. As for the weight loss, maybe you just need a different set of supplements. There's a gadget that tests for that. I'll have access to it soon, I hope. I can use it on you. It tailors everything to your needs."

Becca rinsed her mouth in the sink. "I feel done."

"But you can't eat, can you?"

She found some mouthwash and used it even though it was mint.

"I tried to eat too, and I also exploded from both ends."

Becca sighed. "I walked to Poppa's Pizza."

"How much did you eat?"

"A bite of pepperoni pizza and a sip of soda."

"That much?" One elaborate eyebrow raised.

"What did you eat?"

"Two bites of a gorgeous lobster roll dipped in butter." Leila closed her eyes in memory.

"Did you miss eating fat?"

"I miss fat, still." Leila opened her eyes and gave Becca a tiny smile.

"I'm hungry all the time. Starving. I thought some pepperoni might fill me up. And the bubbles of soda and the bite of the citric acid."

"Soda," sighed Leila. "I'm not hungry anymore, though. Black Gill-Tea and the Red Fun Gi-Up drops are super filling."

"I should try the black drink. The pink, brown, and cream shakes do nothing. And neither does the green one." Becca pushed past Leila and left the foul bathroom.

Leila wheeled around and followed. "I know you're frustrated, but your body has to adapt to the drinks. And there are rules about switching to Gill-Tea and the Fun Gi-Up drops."

"Who made these rules?" Becca kicked off the sandal with the mushroom-shaped puke stain and then the other, which just had a small splash. She would have to throw them into the washing machine. Which, handily, Leila had right in her flat.

"The rules come down from high above. From the top. Above Salome."

Leila followed her. Becca's damp underwear was riding up. She plopped onto the emerald couch. "I thought Salome was the top."

"They brought her in toward the top, but she's not at the tippy top."

"Who is?"

"Well, Milo Cobalt started the company. He's the ultimate authority; I believe he's level Hematite. Milo's wife is very involved. The whole thing was her idea." Leila settled into the red chair.

"Is she fat? His wife."

"I doubt it. I don't know if she ever was. She just came up with the idea."

"This random skinny lady came up with the idea to have all these different color drinks to lose weight?"

"It was the red sarcophagus." Leila put her head back and stared at the ceiling. Nyx wandered over and curled up on her lap, staring at Becca like a gargoyle.

"The what?"

"You don't remember that?"

Becca shook her head.

"You know there is a massive drought in the Compass States, right?" The center states all had directions in their names—West and East Dakota, North and South Colorado. "With the rivers drying up and the reservoir levels dropping and all that?"

Becca waved a hand. "Climate change, we're all gonna die. Our parents and grandparents killed the Earth."

"Yeah. You remember a while ago when Hall Lake got really low, and they started finding bodies and cars, all sorts of stuff? We were still at school."

Becca did not remember. She shrugged.

"They found an old Native settlement at the very bottom. Part of it was this big rock box, red rock that didn't match the kind in the area. The archeologists who investigated it called it the Red Sarcophagus." Leila leaned forward and scratched the sore on her neck. Nyx squirmed, squished.

"Was it Egyptian?" Becca shifted. Her butt ached. Her stomach growled. She thought of the gorgeous pizza she had left behind on the table, the sparking glass of soda, and wanted to sob.

"No, but there were human bone fragments in this weird red juice inside. The stone box was about seven feet long, the right size to hold a body. I guess it started as a joke. But someone posted on social media about it, that it had these bones in this juice, and there was this big trend with everyone posting with the hashtag #DrinkTheRedJuice. How did you miss that?"

"I kind of remember; it was gross. I thought it was mummy juice, something from Egypt, though, not out West."

"It was supposed to be gross!" Leila laughed and scratched Nyx's head. "One archeologist working the site was Milo Cobalt's brother-in-law. The archeologists were sneaking in people they knew, even though they had blocked the site from the public. When Milo and his wife, the archeologist's sister, saw the big red sarcophagus, which of course was just a rock box that they gave a fancy name to, somehow, she got this idea to make this weight loss MLM."

"From seeing a red box full of bones and mummy juice." Becca screwed up her face. "How did that work, exactly?"

"I don't know. But she was one of those professional boss babes, like Salome, and she had the ears of the right people, and her husband Milo had some startup money. I'm not sure why he is the face of the company and not her. Her name is Missy." Leila fake-gagged at the girly name.

"Is Milo fat?"

Leila shook her head. "He's strange. I've seen him on a video call, maybe prerecorded. He is really stiff and emotionless, like a robot, or a cartoon character, like something programmed. I would have said he wasn't real except that in the past I've seen other videos and photos of him and those seemed more real. He's just a weird one. Maybe he's neurodivergent."

"Hmm. What was in the red juice that the hashtag was about?"

"I don't know; that got hushed up, I guess. Or nothing."

"Hushed up? Archeology? Was it alien?"

Leila's laugh sounded off. Nyx jumped off her lap and returned to the cat tree. "Alien? No, it was Native. Some plant juices or something, and mummy juice, like you said, I think. But don't you remember the little pyramids that started appearing all over the place? People would post photos of them on social media, saying 'this wasn't here last week'? And then the pyramids would disappear? If you can find any of those old photos, guess what? The MyCo System pyramids they build, like the one we go to, all look like big versions of those tiny ones!"

Becca stared at her friend. "This is insane. Why did you want me to join this company? Founded on disappearing pyramids and mummy juice? Am I drinking mummy juice?" She gagged, even though there was no way that anything was in her digestive tract after the massive purge.

"No, Beck; no, you aren't drinking mummy juice!" Leila frowned and scratched her cheekbone.

"What have you gotten me into? You said you were helping me!"

"I am trying to help you! I will die of kidney failure unless I lose weight, and this is how I'm choosing to do it! Why would I do that if I didn't think this was worthwhile?"

Becca froze. "You aren't dying."

"Yeah, Beck, I could die. I'm still too fat to get a kidney transplant or even get on the list."

Becca's face twisted. "Yeah, because of the old refrain: being fat is considered a choice, a disgusting one worthy of scorn and death. So, you're choosing to die, in most people's eyes, by being fat."

"There is that, but also because the surgery is too risky at my weight. I'm having to give up a lot. My work, my existence, is bound up in my weight. Mukbanging, modeling, being on BBW dating sites, fostering body positivity, making clothes that look good on big people of all genders."

Becca drew up her knees as far as she could, wishing she could pull them up enough to put her arms around them. Thin people didn't understand how much room being fat took up. Not just the stomach fat, but the thighs, the butt. The arms. Her arms were massive. She didn't fit anywhere. She appreciated Leila's oversized furniture.

Leila continued, “You, you have nothing to lose but the weight. It’s not who you are. You aren’t known for being fat. Being thin wouldn’t ruin your life; it would enrich it. Your mother would talk to you again. Although why you want to talk to that pretentious bitch, I don’t know. You’re still healthy, and it doesn’t matter to you right now if you’re thin or fat.”

“I wouldn’t mind being thin. Fitting in.” Becca stared at Nyx, who was gazing out the window. “I don’t know if I miss my mum exactly. My whole life, her and my grand-mère badgered me about being fat. I don’t know how she would relate to me if I wasn’t some kind of punching bag to her. She wanted a perfect, adorable living doll she could dress up. Getting a fat, horrible thing like me angered her. She would have sent me back if she could have. Like a dog or cat back to the pyramid shelter. ‘This one’s no good; please give me another.’ Or, ‘This one bit the neighbor’s child.’” Becca used bitter finger quotes. “That was me. I was no good, but when you adopt a child, you’re stuck with that child. That shouldn’t be the rule, but it is. We were not at all compatible as mother and daughter. And my grand-mère might have eased it, made it better, but she was just a clone of my mum, and she made everything much worse. She was an amplifier, not a pacifier.”

Leila snorted. “You want to lose weight and can’t. I don’t want to lose weight, and I can. It doesn’t seem fair.”

“Too bad we weren’t in a movie so we could switch bodies.”

Leila appraised her friend. “I guess I could be all female if I had to live in your body. You aren’t the slightest bit androgynous. You dress awful, you wear no makeup and don’t know how to walk sexy. And you’re a pasty red-haired white girl. I would have to take a year in hiding to make that body into something I’d be willing to go out into public in.”

“Seriously? You would body-snatch me? And what would I do as a six-foot-tall androgynous Black woman with kidney disease?”

"Lose weight, for one thing. Nothing you can do about the height, sorry. But you know I'm sexy. I think my body would remember how to be sexy even if I wasn't in it anymore."

To be tall and thin, even androgynous. Leila wasn't that masculine unless she wanted to play it up, which she often did.

"Well, we aren't in a movie. This is real life, and what I have are Gill-Tea Pleasure drinks, and what you have are these Shroomshee smoothies." Leila shifted in the oversized chair, crossing her long legs.

"I don't know how to make it work," Becca confessed. The fitness tracker on her wrist buzzed, telling her she hadn't taken enough steps that hour. She wondered if her mum got those alerts, too. Another hour of her fat daughter being a lazy failure. And here's her morning weigh-in, look how fat she still is. "I thought the shakes were only a few hundred calories each. I drink three or four a day. That's not even a thousand calories. The few pills I take: How many calories can they add? How can I not be losing weight?" Her wrist buzzed again. She got up and paced obediently.

"Look, when I officially level up at our next meeting, I'm going to ask about the new device. I'll test you. We'll figure it out. There's a way I can level you up with me. If that's what you need, I'll find more people to sign up under you somehow, move you to the Black Gill-Tea."

"What if I need the black drinks and there is no one to sign up under me? I mean, do the math. Everyone can't sign up three or five people underneath them. We'll run out of people in Newhaven."

"That's why they'll open a new MyCo System pyramid in another city. Everyone in Newhaven who needs to lose weight will be on the drinks and supplements."

"But the last people to sign up, no one will be under them. They won't be able to level up. They will never get the black drink or access to the testing machine."

"No, you're wrong. They are the ones who will pick the next city. They will recruit in a new place."

"Won't the world run out of fresh places, though?"

Leila shook her head. "There will always be fresh places and new people to recruit. We'll find them. Everyone needs these drinks and supplements. They are life changing."

"Not for me." Becca stared at her dirty bare feet.

The fungi used in MyCo System Shroomshee™ smoothie shakes have mutagenic properties, which can help support healthy weight loss. Our proprietary blend of nutraceuticals contains bioactive compounds that can provide numerous health benefits. Not only can MyCo System Shroomshee™ smoothie shakes help you lose weight, but they can also support your overall health and well-being.

These statements have not been evaluated by the Pharmaceutical Industry Oversight Administration (PIOA) or the Department of Agriculture and Food (DAF). MyCo System products are not meant to diagnose, treat, cure, or prevent any disease.

CHAPTER ELEVEN

Becca was not happy sitting without Leila in the pyramid's Quartz Auditorium. She took advantage of the free drinks, although she had not yet paid for any shakes—Leila used her profit credits for Becca's shakes and nutraceutical supplements. Becca craned her neck, searching the first balcony. Leila had promised to spill everything that happened up there, even if she had signed NDAs. She had absolute faith that Becca would be up there soon.

Becca had sold a few Shroomshee starter packs to random followers, but no one was interested in selling. She had mixed feelings about bringing people in as her competitors. It made no sense. It would be one thing if she was selling to people in North Mexico. Let them start their own Mexican MyCo pyramid. She would be shocked if there wasn't one down there already. The architecture would fit in. If Becca spoke Spanish, that would be a market for her to exploit. But she spoke only French, which she'd picked up from her grand-mère.

Dr. Opal Knox, wearing a different Leila Duncan-original corset belt over her black bodysuit, danced around on the video screen, shaking her massive, round ass. She shouted platitudes, telling them to push themselves to sell the fabulous MyCo System bioceutical products even more. "You are losing weight! Shout it to the rooftops! Shout it from the top of the pyramid!" Opal yelled into the camera. She patted her waist, accented by the gorgeous belt. Her giant ass only made her waist look smaller. That ass had to be surgically enhanced. Opal's shoulders were bony, and skin flaps hung from her chin. Her upper arms were barely larger than her elbows. Come to think of it, those tits had to be fake too. They were not huge, but they were too round and perfect.

I'm not losing weight, though, Opal, Becca thought at the screen. She sipped a green shake. So far, the green drink was only available here at the pyramid. She could theoretically walk into the pyramid anytime, show her ID as a MyCo System Body Management Partner, and get one for free. She wasn't sure how often they would let her do this, but she took a long walk every couple of days. Her knees screamed, her calves ached, and the bottoms of her feet felt flattened. Only her fitness tracker was happy. The scale didn't budge. Her mum continued to ignore her messages. No money appeared in her account.

The green shake was the least offensive, but that wasn't saying much.

Becca had read an article where cruise ship passengers complained about being fed lemon gelatin desserts every day; that's all the chef had. The beleaguered chef dyed the yellow gelatin orange one day, red the next, green another day, and everyone was happy to have assorted flavors. All from the same yellow box and a few drops of dye. Becca felt confident that was the case with the shakes. She didn't think she could tell the four shake flavors apart if she was blindfolded. They didn't smell different. They were equally awful.

The Black Gill-Tea drink had an odor like dirty anise or moldy fall leaves. Leila couldn't tell her what was different about it. If Becca ever had any kind of party, she could mention the Gill-Tea. Like it was a Holy Grail her customers could obtain if they joined MyCo System as her sales reps. Then maybe Leila wouldn't have to recruit anyone for her.

But she couldn't have a party because she was still fat. How could Becca shill weight loss smoothies in person when she weighed almost four hundred pounds? By showcasing Leila as proof of concept? *Well, it works for my friend. Ignore that she has a terminal illness she's trying to reverse, one that could cause weight loss. Or how about Opal Knox*? Yeah. Not that she's rich and could lose weight in other ways. Liposuction or weight loss surgery or whatever.

Spot reduction. That was the other thing that Leila was going to learn about today.

Becca should have been trying to socialize, especially since Body Management Partners of all levels were down on the auditorium floor. These people could help her, she supposed. But they were also her competition. Why should they help her succeed? If they told her how to get customers and sign people under her, local people, those were all people they couldn't recruit. This seemed like a dumb idea. How had Leila gotten sucked into something so illogical? But now they were both physically stuck drinking these dumb drinks. How could Becca get off of them? Were they addictive, like a drug? Was she supposed to return to her mum and beg into the void? *Mum, I'm addicted to diet shakes that don't work, and if I eat regular food, I vomit and shit myself. I need medical intervention I can't afford because I have no job and no insurance.*

She wondered if this had happened to anyone else. She only had Leila's word that she had tried to quit and been unable to. Had Leila ever lied to her? She had been evasive, sure, but who hadn't been evasive at some point? It couldn't be right that these drinks messed up your insides so severely that you could never go back to regular food. The government wouldn't let MyCo System sell something that did that. There were regulations, right?

The lights inside the auditorium dimmed. Since the walls were black and the lights reddish, it only got creepier inside. With the increased darkness, the sour smell of plant rot increased. The walls seem to slither in the shadows as people found their seats.

When the lights came back up, someone in a red and black robe occupied the podium, a large red headscarf, almost a hood, draped over their head and around their neck. Becca couldn't tell the gender, but they weren't tall enough to be Leila. And Leila would never wear that boring outfit.

When the person spoke, Becca realized it was Salome, for once without the vape pen in her mouth. In a hoarse voice, she announced who had leveled up since the last meeting. "These are our new Red Diamonds." She recited names, and people came forward, wearing similar robe-like outfits that hid the contours of their bodies. Salome draped a red headscarf over their heads. All were women. Leila was last, the tallest, and her robe was too short. Her high-heeled boots, black with red accents, stuck out underneath. She towered over everyone on the stage. Salome stared up at Leila helplessly, lifting the red scarf. Leila clutched the lectern and crouched until Salome could reach over her head to arrange the scarf. It seemed strangely religious. She covered the new Red Diamonds' heads from the front with a drape similar to the one used by several religions.

Leila's black and red braids spilled down her back. The black braids had red rings around them and the red braids had black rings. Most of the braids were extensions, but they looked fantastic. Leila appeared frail with her body hidden; somehow, the oversized robe only accented where she had lost weight. The bright red fabric around her face made her dark skin seem pale and sallow. It wasn't attractive, but Becca's friend beamed with happiness. She sought Becca out and grinned directly at her, flashing a thumbs up from under the flowing sleeves of the red robe.

Becca sipped a green drink and let her mind go. What other color drink could they come up with? She could invent some, send them up the chain, and maybe receive some credits. A lovely citrus orange for this end-of-summer heat. Poured over ice. Yes. Orange drink. She made a mental note. Orange flavor.

A purple one? Grape. There was no way they hadn't thought of these things. So obvious.

She obsessed about work. Her time in the business world had taught Becca that generating ideas showed she was a team player. Even if her job didn't implement the ideas, even if they were laughed at, at least she had put effort into trying to make *Fast Fashion* better.

MyCo System could mix the orange shake flavor with the vanilla to make creamsicle, but Becca wasn't sure what could be done with grape. Could it be a wine flavor, an adult shake flavor? Her mind stashed away more notes in the work vault. Wine had been the only indulgence of her mum and grand-mère, which was why Becca had never acquired a taste for it. She liked flavored vodkas and liquors. She wondered if alcohol would make her as sick as the pizza had.

The Quartz-level gathering had broken up into little groups while Becca made mental lists. The Body Management Partners were supposed to mingle, share their successes, and give each other tips.

Becca sipped dirty toothpaste and searched for a likely group to infiltrate. Some were too high energy. Any group where everyone was thin, high-pitched, and moving around a lot wasn't for her. They were probably the most successful, but Becca couldn't bear it, being the size of any three of them, her thighs like their waists. She felt like a fat monster lurking nearby, a hungry thing that wanted to eat them, to ingest their knowledge and endless energy almost as much as she craved proper food. She had as much chance of devouring their energy as she did eating pizza.

Wandering, she eavesdropped. "Within an hour of my first post, I had made a dozen sales! My friends can't get enough of this!" one woman gushed, sipping from a green shake, licking her lips with joy. "And wait until this amazing mint flavor goes public!"

Becca glanced at her own green container. She was being pranked, right? The only thing "amazing" about the mint flavor was its awful taste. Toothpaste was nice to brush your teeth with but not to drink. Especially not mixed with shitty dirt.

The darkness under the balconies writhed. Becca figured there were ventilation fans behind the wall vents. What else could it be?

The Body Management Partners kept chatting about how great their sales were, with no information about how they had done it. Becca moved on to the next group, a pair of chubby ladies with one man, lost and peckish, his protruding eyes shadowed. He had a blue kerchief around his neck. He and the two women were staring at each other.

Becca stepped in, clutching the green container. "Hi. I'm Becca."

Nods all around. These people were worse than her.

"My sales are awful, and so is my weight loss. Got any tips for me?" She tried to appear as helpless as she felt.

The man lifted a cream shake. "I just drank the Shroomshee smoothie shakes. Three or four a day. I'm not hungry anymore. I went down twenty-five pounds in six weeks."

The two blond women made encouraging noises and widened their eyes.

Becca widened her eyes like a proper mimic and aimed her green carton at him to continue. This was not magic he was telling her; it was following directions. Which she had already tried. "I took the two kinds of pills also?" he concluded, confused about what Becca wanted from him.

"Yes, I do all that." She studied her round abdomen. "I lost only three or four pounds."

"It's only been a day or two, right? That's normal," the blonder woman said.

"It's been two months." Becca lowered her chin and raised her shoulders. The flesh around her throat choked her. "I feel like a failure. I want to quit this entire program, but my mentor won't let me." The shit smell in the room intensified. Why did no one else seem bothered?

"You can't quit!" Blondie said.

Her friend nodded vigorously. "Did you try going up to five shakes a day?"

"Or down to three?" suggested the man.

Becca blinked rapidly. "That's a big difference. I do four most days, with four of each pill. My mentor is on the black drink."

"Your mentor should not be letting you have these thoughts. How many people have you signed up?" Blondie eyed her friend, then Becca.

Becca shook her head. "None. And hardly any sales. It seems like this just isn't for me."

"No, no, you need this," the man said, leaning forward.

Becca eyed him sideways. It was an obvious reference to her rotund body and excessive size.

"It's such a confidence builder to make sales, to build a team. Weight loss is a bonus. It means you gain the health and lifespan to enjoy the sales and lead your team."

She narrowed her eyes. Nice save. "No team. I'm not a team leader, I'm a failure. I'm trying to learn how others are doing it. Following the scripts, posting the memes, drinking the shakes." She held out her arms, displaying her round body. "Nothing."

"That's all we're doing, hun," Blondie said. "We don't know any secrets. My friend and I signed up to get the discount. I posted a few times so it wouldn't look like I wasn't trying. It surprised me as much as anyone when people bought from my links. I thought Newhaven was saturated with MyCo System Body Management Partners, but apparently not. These Shroomshee smoothie shakes are the real deal for miracle weight loss. They really are out of this world." Her eyes went vague and unfocused.

"My team is small, and all of them are out of state," the man said. "I'm waiting for them to build their own teams, and then I'll level up. I'm eager for that specialty spot reduction to eliminate this." He patted his tiny beer belly. "It's smaller, but now I look pregnant."

"My mentor moved to Red Diamond this meeting. She was the very tall one."

"Oh, her?" Blondie gulped from her green carton.

The man sipped his cream drink. "You don't seem worried enough about your own sales and weight loss."

Becca cocked her head. "I'm trying to learn. That's why I came over to you."

He raised his eyebrows. "There is no secret. The shakes work. They sell themselves. Opal is on daytime TV, shilling them and showing everyone her hot ass. People see her, look the shakes up on social media, and get guided to posts of people they already know, and bam! Sales. I can only suggest that the people you know aren't looking for the shakes." He shrugged, finished the shake, and crushed the carton in his fist.

Becca felt afraid of him. "I have social media accounts about fashion, makeup, and similar subjects."

The other, less blond woman, snorted. She was even chubbier than Blondie, so she had no business being rude about someone else's weight.

"I grew up in the fashion business, so I know a lot, and I live with someone who is also an expert. Leila designs plus-size clothing for all genders and body shapes and makes amazing corset belts. Opal wears them."

Dark Blonde inspected Becca up, down, and around. "You grew up in the fashion business?"

Becca closed her eyes for a long instant. This was where she longed to throw her mum's name in people's faces. Willow LeNoir wasn't exactly a household name anymore, but she had been, and most people would recognize her name or her face, if not both. But Becca had vowed that as long as her mum was a narcissistic, fat-phobic bitch, she would not trade on her fame. "Yes, I did." She raised her chins. "We lived near Londinium, hence the accent, but I traveled the world as a child because of the fashion business."

Dark Blonde muttered, "Ate your way through the world, more likely."

Becca's stomach growled, even though she had guzzled most of the green shake. "I shall not explain myself or my childhood to you. I came to this small group looking for help since you are all in the same business, and I thought we could share ideas and support each other."

She pivoted on her heel. This was a nightmare without Leila. She wished she could go upstairs and wait. She wouldn't listen in. Well, yes, she totally would listen in. Still, this Quartz Auditorium was cutthroat. There was no help here. Her thought process had been accurate. These people were her competitors. They did not want her to succeed. It was a zero-sum game. If she won customers and sales in Newhaven, they did not. Why should they assist her? She was not part of their downline or upline or sideline or any shape of how she understood these lines to work.

Becca strode over to the table and tossed her partially consumed green shake into the trash. The smell was overpowering. The shadows by the wall shifted. She studied the posters and their slogans. Some of them looked old. She tried to remember how long ago archeologists had discovered the red sarcophagus—Leila said while they were still at uni. How old was MyCo System? She thought it was pretty new, a couple of years at most.

Their marketing slogans, to her eyes, seemed lame. She also hated that the scripts included deliberate misspellings.

"I don't send out misspelled posts," she had argued with Leila. "It's unprofessional. If this is my business, I will check and double-check everything."

But the point was that if someone didn't react, Becca was supposed to respond to *herself* in a self-deprecating way. "Stupid autocorrect" or "oops forgot to proofread" or something like that, which would push the post toward the top and give it a boost in engagement. And also, the company probably thought fat people were dumb and would respond better to poorly written, misspelled crap full of emoticons. A picture of a drink instead of the word "shake." It made Becca feel insane. To her, a post full of pictures was impossible to read. "We aren't Egyptians writing in hieroglyphics! I want to use words!"

Oh, but certain words trigger spam filters. Pictures don't. We don't want our posts being marked as spam.

If she hadn't gotten that stupid eviction notice, she never would have said yes to this mess. It was all her mum's fault. Obviously, somehow, Willow LeNoir had sent Salome to fire her. Even though it was likely her mum did not know or care where Becca worked. Becca's mum didn't care enough to track her down. If Becca changed her phone number and didn't give her mum the new one, oh well. If she moved with no forwarding address, again, oh well. Maybe, if her grand-mère was alive, but no. In her own way, Grand-Mère had been even worse.

Becca's phone beeped just as she raised it to take photos of the posters. Leila messaged she was getting her first LipoGest spot-reduction treatment *tonite!!!!* and that Becca would need to drive her home if she felt woozy afterward.

How does it work? Does it hurt? She messaged back.

No answer.

Becca snapped photos of the posters. No one stopped her. She tucked some green shakes into her messenger bag, and no one said anything about that, either.

How long does LipoGest take?

No answer.

Becca dropped heavily into one of the padded folding chairs and managed to log in to her social media manager, although the internet was spotty. She posted some slogans from the wall, minus the stupid cartoons. She used all the hashtags because hashtags were good. The more hashtags, the better. She clicked through some of her tags to see what other people were using them for, making some screenshots. If she was hooking her wagon to these people, she might as well try to do her best.

Her stomach growled loudly.

She stood and took photos of the depleted table with the free shakes, which had been piled in, predictably, a pyramid. The three original flavors, pink, cream, and brown, were still stacked high. The green pyramid was demolished. She took a photo of her hand holding a green shake and then tucked the nasty thing into her bag. Sitting, she edited the picture by placing a cutesy cartoon face over the flavor name to obscure it. The face looked amazed and had hearts for eyes.

"Mystery flavor!" she posted, with a sickening string of more vapid cartoons. "Only available to Body Management Partners. The taste is unbelievable!" That wasn't a lie. "Join my team to learn more!" She changed her profile picture to her plump hand holding the obscured drink. She added her enrollment link and pushed the post out to every one of her social media accounts, hoping she would keep the internet connection long enough for it to work.

Her phone buzzed.

Becca's heart galloped. Had someone signed up already? She wrapped her hand around her throat and squeezed, feeling her heartbeat under her thumb. The groups were breaking up around her; many people had already left. Shouldn't Leila be done with her spot treatment soon?

The phone buzzed again.

Im comin out now pleas get the car

It hurt

Fine, except that Becca didn't have the keys. Leila did. Becca couldn't get the car. She didn't even know which of the four staircases Leila would come from to meet her. Becca swore and searched for someone in a headscarf of any color. Someone in authority. No one.

U have the keys Lee

Becca positioned herself in the middle of the aisle. Was there an elevator? Could there even be an elevator when the walls slanted inward? She thought Leila might have gone upstairs from a staircase behind the stage.

Where r u lee?

Plump women with red headscarves emerged from behind the stage area, plodding. None of them were anywhere near tall enough to be Leila. Becca moved in that direction. Her right knee locked; pain wrapped around it, and she almost fell.

"Not now," she admonished her knee. She took a step and her right leg buckled.

Her phone beeped. *Were u r?*

Fuck. Becca hobbled to a chair, half dragging her leg. *Sitting. My knee.*

She kneaded her knee furiously. Probably the bones shouldn't move under the skin like that or make those broken glass noises when she walked. Doctors said, "You are morbidly obese," when she complained about the pain. She had never gotten an X-ray or an MRI, even after a nasty fall on some ice. "If you weren't so fat, you wouldn't have fallen on the ice," the doctor had told her, or at least that was the upshot of it. He had grudgingly given her a disabled tag, but that had gone away with the car.

Hurts

Becca searched the areas on either side of the stage where darkness writhed. She was sitting directly under the point of the pyramid. Leila might have been behind her, already at the front door.

Leila emerged from the dark. Her belt was off—since Leila wore a corset belt even when dressed as a man, this was a big deal—dangling from her hand. Her other arm was wrapped around her middle. She inched along, hunched over, with small steps, alone. The brand-new red headscarf was in disarray, as was her clothing.

Becca forced herself to her feet. Her knees popped. The right one was a painful white ball. She sucked in a big breath of damp, shit-scented air that made her choke and gag instead of perking her up. Holding onto the backs of chairs, she moved forward.

Leila stopped, leaning on the front corner of the stage. "Beck?"

"I'm coming."

"I don't feel so good."

"I'm not at my best either."

Becca took the elaborate belt and tucked it under her right arm. She hoisted Leila to her wobbling feet and wrapped her left arm around her friend's waist, feeling a bulky bandage under her clothes.

"It hurts." Leila moaned and tried to move away.

"We have to get to the car."

"Don't touch me."

Becca dropped her grip and stepped away. Leila swayed. Becca held up her hand as if she could stop her friend from falling over from a distance. "I have to go into your bag to find the car keys, okay?"

An inarticulate noise boiled from Leila. Since there was no way Leila was driving home, Becca took it as assent and dug for the keys in Leila's stylish bag.

Groaning, Leila dropped into a folding chair. The folding chair also groaned.

"How am I going to get you home?"

CHAPTER TWELVE

Leila lay on the emerald couch. "I don't remember," she fussed. "And I signed an NDA."

"For spot reduction?"

"The technique." She groaned as she adjusted her position. Her hands cradled her abdomen. "How much smaller am I?"

Becca inspected the area. An elastic bandage wound around Leila's belly with gauze under that. An unpleasant odor lingered near the dressing. "You always have a belt on, so I don't know. You look swollen."

"It hurts so bad." Leila's head fell back.

"Was it like liposuction?"

"I can't talk about it." Even with her eyes closed, her face looked crafty. "It wasn't like surgery. I don't think."

"What was it then? I mean, there are bandages and everything."

"I can't, Beck; stop asking! Just bring me a Black Gill-Tea and the new black drops I need."

"What black drops?"

Leila's grip tightened on her swollen belly. "Black BubblyBoost drops. In my bag."

Becca retrieved the bag from the side table by the door and found the black bottle. It was the same size and shape as the red bottle, except the red bottle was translucent; this bottle was opaque. It lacked any markings except the raised embossing. She shook it next to her ear but could not hear any liquid inside.

"How many drops, Lee?"

Leila's head rolled on the couch's arm. "Oh, I don't know. Two? Three? I don't remember. Message Salome."

Dragon bitch. "I don't know her number." Becca carried the bottle into the kitchen, limping on her fiery, crunchy knee. The glass bottle felt cold. She had never prepared a black drink, but had watched Leila do it.

Becca removed a large glass from the cabinet and filled it halfway with icy cold water. She popped a black straw, added the powdered contents, opened the other end, and used the straw as a stirring stick. Becca located a knife to remove the clear plastic seal from the black bottle.

She sliced her finger and went hunting for a bandage in the bathroom.

"Beck? My drink?" Leila sounded weak and sad.

"I'm bleeding. I'm sorry. It's almost ready." Abandoning the search for a bandage, she returned to the drink.

In the kitchen, Becca had spilled more blood than she had realized. It seemed more important to get Leila's black drink to her than to clean the mess. Holding the wounded, dripping finger away, she shook the bottle and unscrewed the eyedropper cap. She didn't expect the drops to be reactive, and some fizzed onto the counter. She sucked more into the dropper and carefully added three to the glass. The nebulae already in place whirled, contracted, and expanded; it was like watching the birth of a universe in the hand-blown drinking vessel. Becca wrapped a damp paper towel around her injured hand and held the glass under the refrigerator dispenser, filling it with crushed ice.

Leila struggled to sit up, but did not want to be touched. She groaned, holding her abdomen. All Becca could do was pile pillows behind her. Leila took the glass with both hands like a toddler and had trouble getting her generous lips over the thick, black straw.

The contents of the vessel fizzed much like the cola at Poppa's Apizza had. Leila moaned, her eyes closed, and lowered the glass. Becca stood ready to take the heavy tumbler as Leila's entire body shook.

"Are you okay, Lee?"

"I'm better now, yes. Salome said as soon as I started on the Black BubblyBoost, I would feel better." Leila sucked on the straw, eyes closed, consuming almost half of the fizzing, popping black-on-black nebulae drink. "Can you hand me my phone?"

Becca had seen the phone in Leila's purse, so she retrieved it. "Should I take the glass?"

"Um. No. Let me finish." And she did, slurping the beautiful nebula through the straw and exchanging the empty glass for the phone.

Becca returned the glass to the kitchen. She wasn't Leila's servant, but she was living on Leila's money, and Leila needed help. She washed the glass and put it in the drainer, put the black bottle in the cabinet next to the red bottles and grabbed a sponge to clean the counter where she had spilled blood and black drops.

Except that the counter was already clean.

It was nearly midnight. Becca was drooping with exhaustion and pain. She must have wiped up the spill and forgotten. That was it.

CHAPTER THIRTEEN

Becca received a few orders from her "mystery flavor!" postings, but no one wanted to sign up as a Body Management Partner. Which made no sense to her. Ordering the three standard flavors didn't get customers any closer to "Mystery Mint."

Salome constantly messaged and video-called Leila, trying to get her to come in for her next spot-reduction treatment.

"What about your roommate protégée? When will she be leveling up in the organization? She hasn't on-boarded a single Body Management Partner." From across the room, Becca heard Salome's exhale of vapor through Leila's speaker. Leila looked pained, eyebrows clenched, lips thin.

"She is fine with where she is. She doesn't see this experience the way we see it."

"Part of the MyCo System experience is to evolve, constantly leveling up. If she is content to stay at the Quartz level, she's not really the kind of person we should have brought in."

Becca watched Apep circle his tank, listening to herself be insulted. Which was it? Bring in as many people as possible, or only bring in those of the highest quality who wanted to rise like the dragon smoke from Salome's nose?

Leila stared over the top of the tablet at Becca, who avoided her gaze. The fish flared his gills at his reflection in the floating mirror toy. *Fight yourself, fishy.*

"I will try to talk to her." Leila scratched the weird, unhealing sore on her neck.

Becca hoped that was a lie. Her stomach growled. That was its constant state, gnawing hunger. It seemed stupid to drink more calories to lose weight. Becca didn't exceed four shakes per day and tried to stick with three. She had killed her metabolism. Certainly, she had killed her digestive system if a bite of pizza and a single sip of soda could provoke a massive outpouring of vomit and diarrhea. Becca had not attempted proper food again, although she felt tempted to take a sip of Leila's black drink. It had to be all hype, like the green shake. Just to make you want to level up, to make you want to join. Fear of missing out. And Becca couldn't quit now because she was in it too far in a terrible sunken cost fallacy. She was afraid to find out whether she had made herself permanently ill.

She sent a message. *Hey mum. Selling these diet shakes and taking them isn't working out great for me. I'm hardly selling any and, as you well know, I'm not losing weight drinking them. But I can't eat proper food anymore, so I need a doctor, and I have no insurance …*

She stared at her phone for a long time. Her mum didn't have read receipts activated. No dots danced to indicate Willow LeNoir was answering. The outgoing message sat there under a long line of unacknowledged messages.

Becca hated Willow LeNoir.

Across the living room, Leila ended the video call. She dragged herself from the oversized chair. Under the now-loose corset belt, a swath of stained bandage padded her belly. With one hand, Leila held her stomach as she walked into the kitchen. Nyx trailed her, naked skinny tail in the air.

"I would have made your drink," Becca called.

"Moving will help me heal faster," Leila said from the kitchen, "So I can get my next LipoGest spot-reduction treatment."

Becca shook her head. "Why do you want another? This one seems to have hurt you badly."

"It's going to help with my kidneys. In fact, I'm taking you to the pyramid later. A whole new program is starting, and I'm volunteering you alongside myself."

Becca raised her brows at Apep. The fish continued to battle himself in the floating mirror.

Leila tossed a pink shake to Becca, who missed. The carton dropped to the floor. Nyx stalked it.

"I can't bend over," Leila said.

"I can barely bend over. My stomach is still massive." But Becca had no choice. She pulled her body off the chair, holding onto the arm, and got the shake without falling over. Nyx contributed by smacking her hand for taking her toy. "What are you volunteering me for?"

"It's a DNA study."

Becca popped the top of the carton. A dank smell rushed out, and the slightly bulging sides of the carton deflated. This drink smelled like the morning breath of someone who fell asleep chewing gum. "Why do you think I need a DNA study? I don't know where I come from. I'm useless."

"No, you are perfect for exactly that reason."

"I have no family tree, nothing to trace, no family to link to. I never signed up for any of those silly ancestry-tracing sites. Why should I care who Willow LeNoir is related to? They aren't part of me."

"Don't you want to find out who you *are* part of?"

Becca shrugged one shoulder and sipped rotten strawberries, grimacing. "My grand-mère said the adoption records were all sealed. Or destroyed. It's useless. And if they gave me up, obviously they didn't want me, so why would I search for them now?"

"But." Leila raised the hand holding the glass full of galaxy. "If anyone related to you genetically is on one of those sites, testing would find them, even if the records were sealed. They can't erase your DNA."

"What, like a cousin or something?"

Leila sipped black drink; her eyes closed. "Even a sibling. Who knows? Sometimes teenagers give up babies for adoption and end up getting married and having more kids together."

"You have lots of siblings. Do you recommend it?"

"Well, I'm the baby. It has its perks and its downfalls. You would be the oldest, most likely."

"I guess." Foul berries flooded her mouth. Awful, just gross. Becca choked. Maybe everyone but her vomited everything up and that was the weight-loss secret they didn't want anyone to know. She was the only non-bulimic in the MyCo organization.

"Did these shakes ever make you vomit?"

"What? No, where did that come from?"

"I thought everyone but me loses weight because the shakes make them vomit."

"I don't think that's how it works. But that's another reason to do your tests. To find out why it doesn't work on you. Pharmaceutical companies do this with drug testing during initial trials. Everyone who gets the drug also gets DNA tests. Because if the drug works or doesn't work, there may be underlying genetic reasons."

Becca screwed up her face. "Lee, this is a fucking diet shake that tastes awful. Not worthy of a clinical trial."

"It's an amazing diet smoothie that tastes delicious; you're just a baby. Don't you even read what you post about it? It's a nutraceutical adaptogen. Nothing else like this shake is on the market."

Becca threw up her empty hand. "Lee, think about this. If this shake is so great, why doesn't MyCo System sell it everywhere instead of relying on idiots like me with no sales training to randomly post shit on the internet trying to sell it for them? They could have TV ads and giant billboards and make billions of dollars. This 'sell by random people'," she used her finger quotes, "is the least effective way to get the word out there. Via unproven testimonials, stupid hashtags, dumb little cartoons of everything instead of words, and deliberately misspelled posts that make me want to scream every time I copy and paste them!"

"Okay, Beck, calm down. Why are you so upset?"

To her horror, Becca started to cry. "It's all so stupid. And if this shake is so good, why doesn't it work on me? Why can't I sell it?" She lifted the carton and drank deeply of putrid pink liquid. "I'm a fat failure. My mum won't talk to me. No one thinks my British accent is cute anymore. I'm not even thirty years old and don't even think I will live that long. I have no job, no income, no insurance, no prospects. These shakes smell and taste like shit and don't work on me, and I wonder why no one will buy them. Who buys weight-loss products from a woman who weighs almost four hundred pounds and whose BMI is twice what it takes to be fat?"

Leila finished the black drink and set down the heavy, hand-blown drinking vessel. She approached Becca and stroked her hair with one hand while holding her bandaged belly with the other. "I wish you got along with Salome. She is so wise. I don't pretend to know what happened between you two at your old job, but I think she regrets that, except it brought you to MyCo System. Can you agree to put that aside and listen to her? She is one of the leading experts in direct sales. MyCo System recruited her to bring the Body Management Partners up to speed and perfect their sales materials. She sees any failure as a personal reflection of her performance."

Becca glared at her friend. "She is a skinny dragon-bitch. If I found out my mum sent her to Newhaven specifically to torment me, it would not surprise me."

Leila set her lips. "I don't want to be mean, Beck, but honestly, I don't think your mum cares enough about you to plan something like that."

"I know." Becca sighed. "My birth mother threw me away, and my adoptive mother hates me. I might as well do my DNA and find out what other coconuts I have in my family tree."

Epigenetic changes noted in populations served by Hall Lake Reservoir (excerpt) from *Epidemiology Digest.*

...The damming of the Kimi River valley provided irrigation and drinking water for a vast population. Within a generation, geographic areas served by Hall Lake drinking water reported a noticeable increase in rates of obesity among the general population, which has continued to grow with each generation. (See table 1.2) A BMI heat map of the area demonstrates the closer a population is to the dam, the higher the average BMI. (See illustration 1.3)

As agriculture in the area grew, farmers shipped crops irrigated by the water farther away, and this BMI effect became somewhat diluted. (See table 1.2) With today's varied food sourcing and distribution landscape, it is difficult to isolate and track populations consuming crops irrigated with Hall Lake water. The effect appears to be anthropospecific, as animals who drink the water do not display signs of increased obesity, just as crops do not seem adversely affected in viability, growth, yield, or propagation. However, humans in the Hall Lake region who feed almost exclusively on these animals and crops still show a tendency toward high BMI.

Initially, epidemiologists (Brandt, Stuckman, et al.) posited this diffused BMI effect across the Collective States as a result of an obesogenic environment, which may be the case (see also Thomson and Levy), but only when applied to this particular water source. Extensive testing of this water shows nothing out of the ordinary chemically.

Though likely unrelated, public mental health agencies have also reported an increased incidence of auditory hallucinations in that same watershed area (see table 1.4) …

CHAPTER FOURTEEN

Becca expected a normal-sized meeting in the Quartz Auditorium. Instead, it was her, Leila, Salome, and a male doctor. Salome led them to one of the front staircases, and Becca got her first glimpse of a balcony level. Except for the open balcony over the auditorium, it was like any other office hallway, with the slanted walls painted black.

The smell was terrible.

The four sat inside a small conference room at the front of the pyramid. Leila held her stomach when walking and moving, and she had taken in all her corset belts by several inches.

Salome exhaled twin smoke plumes through her nose. Her scent today wasn't chocolate; it was cinnamon, or maybe apple pie. "Out of the thousands of Newhaven recruits, I chose you two to begin this process here. This is Dr. Lee."

Dr. Lee appeared to have an interesting mix of ancestry; the older man was tall, thin, with the beginning of a beard; he had folded eyes and streaky black and gray hair. He nodded at Leila and Becca, blinking furiously behind his glasses.

"Our newest campaign will be SporeCode blood testing," Salome continued. "Dr. Lee will be available via telemedicine to order these tests and interpret the results. Eventually, we will have more medical personnel. The test kits are only available to Red Diamond or higher. Those tests will be available to anyone, even non-Body Management Partners, who will be charged a nice fee, with a generous commission structure for Red Diamonds and above, who administer the tests."

Leila was a Red Diamond. Because she was in the pyramid, she had wrapped her head in the requisite red scarf.

Becca wasn't following any of this. She wasn't a Red Diamond. Leila had honored the NDA and refused to give up any secrets. But Leila wanted Becca here for this meeting, and supposedly Salome, for whatever reason, did too.

"Red Diamonds and above get free testing. Body Management Partners at lower levels get a reduced price on SporeCode unique bloodwork to discover your unique MyCoType and the non-invasive MyCoLysis biometric testing."

"I'm excited about those MyCoLysis tests," Leila ventured, smiling at Salome.

The doctor had been busy at the sideboard. He returned with a heavy-duty tablet computer in a rubber sleeve and a phlebotomist's kit. He had a broad face with stark cheekbones and remained handsome in late middle age.

"Well, we'll learn how the MyCoLysis works first," Doctor Lee said. "I initially wanted a program anyone could install on their personal tablet, but there were too many security concerns and parameters. It was easier and less expensive to purchase special tablets that only run the software and nothing else. We'd like you two to be the first to test out our training program. Leila will help to train others in the future."

"You will have the choice," Salome exhaled an apple pie cloud at Leila, who flinched, "of purchasing the tablets outright for an up-front fee or having a percentage deducted from each completed test fee until it's paid for. Either way, Red Diamond Body Management Partners are financially responsible for their tablets. Dr. Lee will biometrically key the tablet to you, which is your security access. You can't add any unauthorized software."

Dr. Lee held up the display tablet to Leila. "I will key this one to you at the end of the session, and you can let Salome know how you want to pay."

"Up front." Leila leaned across the table toward the small screen and winced as her sore stomach pressed into the edge.

"The MyCoLysis biometric test and the SporeCode blood test work independently. Your commission is seven percent."

Becca stared at the tablet. She would be happy to administer a probably fake test on a tablet and make a few dollars.

"The introductory rate of the skin-fold test on the tablet test is fifty dollars, and it will go up to seventy-five dollars." Salome said.

Leila leaned further, wincing. "How long does the test take? If I had an in-person party and offered the tests, would that make sense?"

"In reality, a few minutes, but you dress it up with an explanation."

Leila nodded.

That made perfect sense. People had to believe they were getting their money's worth. But for a party, one explanation would do for everyone. What a profitable evening that would be. Especially if they could coax some people into blood work.

"The SporeCode lab work on the blood starts at two hundred dollars and is going up to three hundred dollars, with the same commission, seven percent."

Becca lusted violently after the Red Diamond title.

Then again, most people would only get one test, while the shakes needed to be reordered. Becca added to her mental list there should be some kind of auto-ship program. One hard to cancel, although if everyone got as sick as her, no one ever would want to.

From SeenIt s/anti-MLM

… I infiltrated a consultant-only group (they call themselves "body management partners" — gag) for MyCo System for a short time before being kicked out. Most of what I read was quite boring, run-of-the-mill MLM crap. But I saw one thread on their message board about people not being able to eat food anymore after switching exclusively to their shake diet. I wasn't able to get a screen print (they caught me quickly), but the gist of the thread seemed to be that people who were drinking 3-4 or more (can you imagine) of those shakes a day and tried to go back to eating real food basically started puking and shitting their guts out after only a few bites. And it didn't seem like it was shocking or unusual. The higher-ups were jumping in and taking the discussions quickly offline, saying there was a way to circumvent that.

This deeply troubles me. No MLM should sell diet shakes that make you unable to eat food. There were hints in some posts about addiction, that people craved the shakes like drugs. They drink them morning, noon and night, and nothing else. Did you know MyCo System doesn't allow their consultants to drink water? How are these people hydrated? We need to see if there's anyone on the inside who can give us more information. A whistleblower. This company needs to be taken down…

CHAPTER FIFTEEN

Dr. Lee explained, “We ultimately went with a special glass with a unique bio-reactive coating for the MyCoLysis testing tablets. These measure blood flow and blood composition and read the lines on the palms.”

Becca’s eyebrows raised. Palm reading? Really?

“Well, which of you three ladies wants to go first?”

He hadn’t tested Salome yet? Interesting.

“I’ll go.” Becca offered her plump hand.

Dr. Lee moved around the table. “Well, usually, the Red Diamond will take all your information, but I knew the three of you were coming, and I mined what I could out of the info we have on file for you.” He handed Becca the rubberized tablet and a stylus. “Fill out as much as you're comfortable with. If you choose not to, no judgment, but the more you fill in, the more accurate your reading will be.”

Becca stared at the on-screen health questionnaire. They wanted her height and weight, of course. But Dr. Lee wasn’t her personal doctor. She didn’t know what kind of doctor he was. He could be a psychologist like Opal. HIPAA might not cover this. She couldn’t refuse, though, so she added her height, weight, and details about daily exercise, thanks to her mum. She glanced at the extensive section on family health.

“I’m adopted,” she told Dr. Lee.

He tilted his head. “Well, I didn’t know that. Perhaps we will pick something up with the other tests. Just do your best.”

The air vent grating on the slanted wall rattled.

Because of her lack of family history, she could fly through those questions. Her personal medical record took longer, despite her young age. Her painful knees, the aches in her lower back, the jagged areas in her shoulders where her bra cut to the bone from holding up her pendulous breasts. The flattened arches on her feet. The comorbidities of obesity. She had to admit how long it had been since she had blood drawn for routine lab work or a physical.

As Becca made her way through the form, Salome explained party guests could do this on paper with scannable fill-in-the-bubbles sheets if Leila did a party where many wanted the tests.

"I'm done." Becca pushed the tablet away.

Dr. Lee opened a small cardboard box and removed a package the size of a condom. He unfolded it to reveal it was actually two packets. "The 'A' packet, you clean the screen with; the 'B' packet, the person must thoroughly wipe their dominant palm with."

He handed the B packet to Becca. She tore it open and scrubbed her right palm.

He showed Salome and Leila how to start the program to read Becca's hand. "Now wipe the screen with the 'A' packet." He demonstrated. "Use the stylus to trigger the clean screen to read Becca's palm. Now, Becca, place your clean palm in the outline and press it flat."

The tablet laid screen-up on the table. Becca stood, lined up her slightly damp hand, and mushed it against the glass. It tingled. The screen flooded with white light. She could see her bones as if in a dark room with an LED flashlight. The whole tablet vibrated. Becca glanced up. "When is it done?"

"Well, hold your hand there. It will say." Dr. Lee pointed at her fingers, outlined by the glow.

The intense light moved around like a living thing under Becca's hand. She had to squeeze her eyes shut for fear of being blinded. The hard glass screen seemed to soften under her palm, molding to the shape of her fingers, letting her hand sink in. She couldn't tell if she was leaning with all her weight on the tablet or if it was sucking her in. She felt dizzy. Wasn't this only supposed to take a minute?

Now it felt like liquified glass fingers were stroking her skin, ticklish but also disturbing. Just when Becca couldn't take the sensation anymore, the glass hardened and pushed her hand away. She swayed backward and grabbed the arms of the office chair. "Is it done?"

The doctor chuckled. "Oh, yes."

"When do the results come back?"

"Almost right away, for this." The doctor retrieved the tablet and tapped it with the stylus, showing Leila and Salome what to do. "That's why it's best to do several tests at once at a party. The results of the first one can process in the background as you do the next. You need high-speed internet access; the tablet doesn't have enough processing power beyond the initial scan. Plus, the excitement of seeing the test results come back might encourage those who initially said no to change their mind about having the test done."

Becca studied her reddened, stinging right palm. "My hand feels weird. It's tingling."

The three stared as if they had forgotten she was there. Well, she was only in place as a guinea pig.

The doctor pointed the stylus at her. "Nothing happened to your hand. The tablet took a photo. It's as if you put your hand on a photocopy machine. Or maybe your skin is a little sensitive to the bio-reactive coating."

The air duct rattled. The stench intensified, even over the smell of Salome's sickeningly sweet apple-pie vapor.

The other three bent over the tablet. Becca sat back, feeling left out. She might not be a headscarf-wearing Red Diamond, but there was no reason she couldn't learn how to use the program. She glanced at the sideboard. At an ordinary business meeting, there would be a carafe of ice water and a pot of coffee. Here, Becca scanned for cartons of shakes.

The water was there, along with black straws, but no shakes for her.

Her body could no longer tolerate plain water. She had tried. No wonder MyCo System advised so strongly against it.

The doctor's voice drifted across the table. "…formulations of FungiFuel and ShroomSlim not available to everyone."

"More effective than the generic Cosmic Cleanse Caps," Salome said. "We can custom tailor them according to the results."

Not available to everyone, only to those with a tablet. Becca understood what was happening. Body Management Partners would want to rush up levels to purchase the tablet and sell the expensive and profitable tests and have access to the specialized supplements. Customers would clamor to become Body Management Partners to get discounts on everything.

"Will all Body Management Partners get the discount on the new supplements or just Red Diamonds and above?" Becca wondered aloud. "Once a customer takes the new supplements and then signs up as a Body Management Partner, won't they expect a discount on everything right from the start?"

They stopped their discussion to stare at her. Salome huffed an apple-pie cloud to express her displeasure at being interrupted.

"I'm guessing I can't buy the new supplements at a discount because I'm not a Red Diamond."

Salome exhaled cinnamon steam from both nostrils. "Well, darling Becca, *you* also won't be selling those supplements to anyone, so why would they expect to purchase them at a discount from you if you are the one to onboard them as Body Management Partners?"

"Maybe they heard about them from someone else or even bought them from someone else."

"They would sign up under that Body Management Consultant. Don't make trouble, Becca."

Salome was ducking this valid concern.

Of course, if someone wanted advanced supplements, they would be steered to begin their journey under a more advanced Body Management Consultant. Becca stared at Salome, wanting her to admit that out loud.

Salome blew vapor at her.

The tablet made a tiny noise.

The air duct rattled.

Dr. Lee chuckled and scratched his ratty beard. "Well, let's see what Becca's hand analysis says. We already know she is morbidly obese. Hmm. The report calculates she needs to lose about two hundred and fifty pounds. Wow, Becca."

Becca's face heated.

"The program fills in a matrix of formulas showing which supplements Becca needs to be the healthiest she can be. Like ticking boxes. It looks at both the surface lines on the palms and what it can see through the skin. Then the Body Management Partner has to…" Dr. Lee's voice trailed off as he flicked to the next page on the screen.

"Her supplements look wrong?" Leila asked.

Becca stared at her hands, the plumpness around the fitness tracker's pink strap. "Let me guess, every box ticked?"

"It filled in zero boxes." Dr. Lee pointed at her with the stylus. "It believes you don't need any of these supplements."

Level 4: Black Sapphire Body Management Partner

Your team: Red Diamond Body Management Partners, Rainbow Obsidian Body Management Partners, & Quartz Body Management Partners

You sell: Shroomshee™ smoothie shakes, Cosmic Cleanse Caps™, MyCoLysis™ and SporeCode™ testing, ShroomSlim™ and FungiFuel™ custom supplements

Your nutraceutical program: Black Gill-Tea™ Pleasure drink, Red BubblyBoost™ drops

Your headscarf: Black

Your Meeting Location: Black Sapphire Balcony

Your perks:

- 50% discount/commission on Shroomshee™ smoothie shakes and Cosmic Cleanse Caps™
- 30% discount on Black Gill-Tea™ Pleasure drinks, Red Fun Gi-up™ drops, and Black Fun Gi-Up™ drops
- 30% discount on ShroomSlim™ and FungiFuel™ custom supplements
- 25% of your downline's sales
- 10% commission on MyCoLysis™ and SporeCode™ testing fees and 25% commission on ShroomSlim™ and FungiFuel™ custom supplements.

CHAPTER SIXTEEN

Becca sipped a rotten green toothpaste shake Leila had convinced Salome to find after Becca's growling stomach noises had filled the conference room.

Becca's left hand showed no need for supplements either, and now both palms were red and tingling. If they had programmed the tablet for feet, she was sure Dr. Lee would have had her shoes and socks off, too.

Dr. Lee became convinced the tablet was broken, except scanning everyone else's left and right palms showed consistent results.

He showed Salome and Leila how to order custom supplements and created the blends for them.

Salome explained the supplement's insane markup and pricing structure. "Anything custom, people go wild for it. And, of course, there's a higher price involved. Each custom label will have the person's name and blend information. It's like print-on-demand books, but with supplements. It's the future of nutraceuticals. Everyone is going to go nuts for this idea. Big corporations and fly-by-night places will copy it poorly and give it a bad name. But we will be first with our custom adaptogenic nutraceuticals."

Did she really need to sell them that hard? They were already part of MyCo System.

"Now for the SporeCode blood tests." Dr. Lee picked up the rubber tubing and walked toward Becca.

Leila recoiled. "I'm not doing blood tests on people!" she almost yelled, holding up both arms in front of her face. "I'm not qualified."

“No, no,” Dr. Lee soothed, tying Becca’s arm roughly. “We will send people to a regular lab to have blood drawn. We don’t expect you to be a phlebotomist. Just for today, I’m drawing the blood.”

He poked and squeezed at Becca’s inner elbow. Her vision darkened. She leaned her head back. “I’m not very good at this,” she whispered. “I have hard-to-find veins.”

“It’s because you have so much adipose on your arms. I must shove through all this extra tissue to find your veins.” He wasn’t gentle. “Ah, here’s one.”

She squawked and convulsed, knees drawing in at the sharp pain.

“Stop moving and it won’t hurt so much!”

She kept her head back and tried not to moan audibly as the doctor milked her arm for blood. Leila hadn’t warned her this was going to happen. Oh gods, it hurt. How did all those who worshipped the Mesoamerican gods deal with the bloodletting parts of their religion? Perhaps they got numb to it.

Finally, Dr. Lee disengaged the blood tube and unsnapped the rubber hose. He bent her arm and told her to hold the cotton ball in place.

That had been awful. He had zero training in how to do that with sensitivity. Becca let a groan escape.

“The customer will pay the Red Diamond for the SporeCode blood test and receive a code generated by the tablet.” Dr. Lee snapped off his gloves. “They bring that code to any authorized lab, get their blood drawn. Their code will act as both proof of payment and the order specifying what tests to run on the sample. We pay the lab a very reduced rate from the patient’s prepayment and receive the results. From that, we work up an obesity DNA profile, called a MyCoType, and the advantage of this is we can offer even more targeted custom supplements than the MyCoLysis test. If several people in the same family have their bloodwork done, the tests and supplements are even more precise."

"You are basically running Fat Ancestors Tree?" Becca could barely speak without moaning. Her vision was still gray around the edges. Her arm ached where she pressed the cotton ball.

"Kind of." She got a glare and a cinnamon smoke cloud from the skinny dragon bitch.

"Are you going to integrate the information with commercial DNA sites?" Leila wondered.

"We haven't decided yet." Dr. Lee opened a new disposable phlebotomy kit and advanced on the dragon bitch.

"Because if you did, Becca could find her blood relatives," Leila continued.

"Becca could purchase herself a DNA test kit from any or all of the commercial sites to see if any of her relatives are there," Salome suggested, baring her slim arm. She didn't flinch as the doctor took her blood, although she might have exhaled more forcefully. The apple-pie cloud over her head expanded.

"You should stop vaping. Those extra chemicals aren't part of the program." Dr. Lee removed the tubing and pressed the cotton into place.

Salome took the pen from her mouth and looked at it. Then she studied her slim body. "I don't need to lose weight. I'm here to lead the company. And the gods know I enjoy the extra flavors."

Leila watched Becca eying the pen and shook her head, widening her eyes. *Don't start vaping,* she was clearly signaling.

It still tempted Becca. Flavors that weren't gross dirt.

The doctor labeled Salome's blood vials and moved on to Leila. "I am sorry to ask, but genetically…?"

Leila huffed out her nose. "Female."

"Ah, okay. I mean no offense at all and no judgment. I have to label the sample, just so."

Leila set her jaw as the doctor extended her arm and set the fresh tubing. Her blood took a bit more poking around to get than Salome's. Leila stared out the window toward the harbor, looking across Thin Island Sound, face clenched.

The doctor swept the used medical supplies into a red plastic biohazard bag and handed out adhesive bandages. "The results will be back tomorrow, and we will meet here again." He stared at Leila. "You can come with me now for your next spot reduction session."

Re: Chemical Analysis

To: Kelvin Pilz, Compass University North

From: Unieda Testing Laboratory, Biochem Division

Dr. Pilz, we regret to inform you we are unable to analyze your samples. An accidental explosion occurred in our labs, causing a fire and the escape of many dangerous bio-engineered species[1], and the samples were inadvertently destroyed before we could analyze them.

We hope you have retained additional samples of the fluid, which we would be happy to test once we have located our specimens and rebuilt our facility with better security. We apologize for the inconvenience. Please advise.

---

[1]*To learn more about Unieda Corporation and the escaped specimens, please consult* The Maw and Other Time-Traveling Lizard Tales, *available in paperback and Kindle Unlimited from Amazon.*

CHAPTER SEVENTEEN

Leila appeared visibly smaller after the second session. "I'm going to call my nephrologist and get tests done," she gasped, barely able to walk to the car. "I'm hoping they took enough bulk from around my middle to help with the kidney disease. Plus, I'll be getting the new supplement formulas."

Although Leila weighed less than Becca, she was much taller, and guiding her across the parking lot was difficult. Becca steered her groaning friend into the car.

As they drove the short way home, Becca remarked, "The supplements are for weight loss, not kidney damage."

"Really, don't you read anything you post? Adaptogenic. They do whatever you need them to do."

Becca bit her cheek as they sat at a red light. Finally, she burst out, "That is such total bullshit, and you know it. If supplements did that, doctors would prescribe them, and giant pharmaceutical companies would make them. Stay-at-home mums in floral leggings who meet in weird pyramids while wearing color-coded headscarves wouldn't be selling the supplements! Listen to yourself, Leila!"

Leila kept both hands wrapped around her middle. Becca shouldn't be yelling at someone in such pain. "No, you listen to yourself, Beck. It's like you want all this to be fake. It's like you want MyCo System to fail and you to fail along with it. That means I fail too, and I'm supporting you. That means you want me to be a sucker who was taken in by this. What does that say about our friendship, that you want me to fail?"

"I don't want you to fail." She guided the car into Leila's reserved spot.

"But if you believe everything having to do with MyCo System is bullshit, then you think it's going to fail. And I think it's not bullshit. So that's a fundamental disconnect right there."

The argument had to pause while Becca helped Leila out of the car. Although it hurt Leila to be touched, she had no choice but to lean on Becca to get into the building.

"It's unrealistic," Becca tried to backtrack. "I find it hard to believe."

"Because you can't lose weight, it's unrealistic, even though everyone else loses weight. So, it's only you." Leila groaned, leaning on the wall as Becca called the elevator.

"Okay, fine, it's only me. But the MyCoLysis test didn't work on me, either. Explain that." She loaded Leila into the elevator. Leila's eyes were crossing as whatever sedative they had given her wore off and the pain was hitting hard. Leila groaned and bent over.

"No, no, we're almost home. Stand up."

Becca dragged her friend down the hall and propped her next to the door. Leila slid. "No, no, no." There was no way to grab her without causing pain. Leila was so much taller; it was just awkward. She pulled Leila inside and onto the emerald couch, where Nyx took over guard duty.

As Becca hurried into the kitchen, knees aching, Leila was sobbing with pain.

Black drink, bubbly black drops. Becca mixed the drink and watched the galaxy bloom. She added crushed ice, a little too much, and it overflowed.

Without thinking, she lifted the glass to her mouth and sipped.

It didn't taste like gross dirt. It tasted like dirt someone had washed and bleached. Sun-warmed dirt. She took another tiny sip. Her stomach stopped growling for the first time in weeks.

Leila called out incoherently. Becca moved back into the living room, dragging her aching right leg, and held the thick straw to Leila's painted lips. She watched with jealousy as Leila sucked down all of it, leaving only the dregs among the thin shards of ice.

Becca needed to level up to Rainbow Obsidian. She needed that Black Gill-Tea.

Becca returned to the kitchen, took a brown shake from the fridge, shook it, and sipped. Dirty sludge. She shook her head. No more.

CHAPTER EIGHTEEN

Three glasses of black drink. One green shake. One cloud of orange-scented vapor.

Dr. Lee sat across from them, blinking behind his glasses. "Well, I'm sorry about having to reschedule. But the extra wait, I think, you'll find is worthwhile." He pointed vaguely with his pen at the three women. "I have your SporeCode test results and your FungiFuel and ShroomSlim supplements."

He pushed four glass bottles across the table. "Obviously, Becca, we could formulate nothing for you since you failed the test."

"I didn't fail the test. The program didn't work on me."

"Well, I'm trying to figure that out. Perhaps your BMI is simply too high. I'll need to find more morbidly obese people to test. I may need to test you again. It's possible the light couldn't penetrate deep enough."

Becca remembered seeing her bones, the light had penetrated so deeply. "What about the blood test? How come you don't have any supplements for me from that?"

The rubber-sleeved testing tablet waited on the table while the doctor poked at a different tablet. "Well, normally, the Red Diamond Body Management Partner wouldn't see those results, as they are medical tests and private by law. They would simply receive a completed test notification and codes for ordering the two formulas."

Becca sat with her arms on her breasts. "I have an idea."

Leila raised her brows.

The doctor's face stayed composed and neutral; what could Becca know?

Skinny dragon bitch snorted out a cloud of orange steam. Her plumped, painted lips turned down.

"There should be subscription plans," Becca ventured in a small voice.

Salome blinked at her.

"For everything. Twenty-eight shakes a week, mixed flavors, plus Cosmic Cleanse Caps, auto billed. Maybe even thirty shakes a week?" Becca hated how she couldn't make a firm statement.

Salome leaned forward and blew vapor from the corner of her mouth and over her shoulder instead of into Becca's face. From Salome, that was almost a kiss. "Cancellation fees?"

"Of course. But lock them in for…" Becca thought. "At least three months of auto-deliveries before they could cancel. And anyway, we all know once they drink the shakes, they can't stop."

Leila nodded and started to say something. Salome held up a hand to stop her.

"They won't want to cancel," Becca continued. "Plus, we can offer a small discount, the thirty shakes versus twenty-eight. Pay for twenty-eight shakes a week, get thirty?"

Salome glanced at Leila. Leila scratched her neck and frowned.

"I have lots of ideas," Becca explained. "That's part of what I did at my old job before you fired me. I was an idea generator."

"I didn't fire you." Salome blew a cloud of orange-scented vapor as she shifted in her seat.

Becca wondered if Salome was feeling guilty for having her fired.

Dr. Lee glanced between them. "Can we get on with this?"

Becca, having drawn Salome's full attention, added, "Add two more flavors. An orange one and a grape one."

Although she had expected Salome to dismiss that completely, Salome replied, "Why do you think we need more flavors? We're about to roll out the mint." She nodded toward the carton next to Becca's hand.

"The more flavors you offer, the more people will buy. They want a variety. With six flavors, they get five each in the weekly thirty-pack. They think, 'I might want more than five chocolate in a week,' or 'more than five orange.'" Finger quotes. "Or they will want to mix flavors. Orange creamsicle. Fruit medley. They might buy extras. Add-ons."

Vapor leaked from Salome's lips. She appeared thoughtful, her dark eyes slitted.

"How difficult can it be to dye the smoothie base a different color, add flavoring drops, and design a slightly new box? I could create more boxes in a day if I had the software and access to the old designs."

Leila stared at Becca with wide eyes. "Really? I didn't know how talented you are."

"I'm just a fatty; what do I know?" Becca said resentfully. "I just know how to eat and be lazy." She turned to Dr. Lee. "Get on with telling me everything the bloodwork said is wrong with me."

"I thought we would begin with Salome." Dr. Lee read out her genetic ancestry results, which included Spanish, Mexican, and some First Native, and mentioned she had a dozen relatives on various commercial DNA ancestry sites she could connect to for a small fee.

Salome aimed vapor at him.

"Well, you wouldn't have to pay. I'm mirroring what you would tell a customer. I'll link your account to the other databases for free."

Salome sucked vapor up her nose.

"As far as standard blood testing goes, you are healthy. We already know your weight is normal, tending toward underweight—"

Skinny dragon bitch, Becca thought.

"—your lungs are a problem, not processing oxygen and carbon dioxide efficiently, probably from vaping, and you have genetic tendencies toward asthma and liver problems."

Salome narrowed her dark eyes, took an extra-big hit off the vape, and coughed. Becca covered her smile with her hand.

"Your custom adaptogenic capsules have been formulated to strengthen your lungs and liver."

Salome took her bottles and put them in the pocket of her tailored jacket.

The doctor turned to Leila. "Your ancestry is from North and Central Africa, with some Western European and First Native, from the Carib Islands, I'm guessing. Your blood sugar and lipid levels are elevated. This is typical of obesity, although you have made substantial progress on your weight loss. Your kidney function is terrible. Are you aware you're approaching kidney failure?"

Salome's face snapped to Leila, leaving a horizontal cloud of vapor. Obviously, she didn't know how sick Leila was.

Leila's darkly painted lips compressed, and she barely nodded.

"Your markers show a consistently poor diet for an extended period." That would be the mukbanging, Becca realized. "They would likely be worse, if it weren't for the Shroomshee smoothie shakes and the Black Gill-Tea Pleasure drink, which is more refined. If you enjoy the Shroomshee smoothie shakes, you can have one occasionally for variety, but try to stick with the Black Gill-Tea Pleasure drink. The program geared your custom supplements toward supporting and repairing your kidneys, along with metabolism boosters and some extra hormone balancers."

Dr. Lee, blinking, gazed at Becca, and left the conference room.

Leila examined her bottles and offered them to Becca. Neither had an ingredient list, just Leila's name. The labels were white on the red plastic bottles, with red and black print. Leila retrieved the bottles and broke the seals, sniffing the contents. She gave one to Becca. The earthy shit smell clogged her nose. It was the same one that permeated all MyCo System's products. She supposed it was their special mushrooms and whatever substrate they grew them in, but couldn't they wash the mushrooms before using them?

The doctor returned. Two people wearing dark-gray headscarves were with him.

The third person was Opal Knox.

Becca froze. She hadn't known Opal was in Newhaven. Usually, she did the talk show circuit in New Amsterdam.

Even Salome appeared surprised. Leila was sitting close enough that Becca could feel her twitching. Opal wore one of Leila's designs around her small waist, but Becca didn't think the two had ever met.

The four sat on the other side of the table.

"I know I said the results would be back quickly from the bloodwork." Dr. Lee twirled the tiny point of his beard. "Well, I didn't lie. But when I saw Becca's results, I postponed the meeting until I could get these special people here."

He pushed a folder and three pens across the desk. "You need to sign these non-disclosure agreements first. Salome and Leila, you can leave the room and not sign if you wish."

What? An NDA? For test results? For Becca's test results, to be precise. Becca's cheeks heated and she gnawed her lower lip. Why? What now?

Leila stared wide-eyed at Becca. Her lashes looked like bug legs hugging her eyes.

Becca shook her head. *Don't leave me*, she mouthed.

Salome sucked deeply on her vape pen and scrawled on one document without reading it, shoving the paper across the table.

Leila skimmed hers, running a finger down the dense text, and signed it carefully.

Becca tried to read, but her eyes kept blurring. Non-disclosure meant she couldn't talk about it. She would only talk about it with Leila, who also signed it, so whatever.

She signed.

The shadows by the air vent shifted.

A gray-scarved person, who had the wiry, veiny hands of someone who did yoga and disdained animal products, collected the signed NDAs into the folder. Their scarf was hooded so far over their face Becca couldn't tell their gender. They appeared to be female, but she had learned not to assume after years of being besties with Leila and meeting Leila's many non-binary friends.

Opal stared at Becca as if Becca were a huge chocolate bar, and Opal was starving.

Becca's stomach growled loudly. She had snuck a small sip of Leila's black drink that morning, but it only satisfied her for a moment. She chugged a horrid green shake, gagging on minty shit. Opal watched this as if Becca were an exhibit at the zoo. Was Opal a weirdo? Maybe she knew Willow LeNoir and marveled that Willow's daughter (adopted! adopted daughter!) could be so vastly obese?

Of course, Leila stared at Opal the same hungry way.

The mysterious people beneath their gray headscarves were also watching Becca. At least, that's what their body language seemed to suggest.

Becca put down the green carton and turned to Dr. Lee. "How come Leila and Salome could have left and opted out, but I can't?" But she already knew. This was about her extra-special fatness and how her hands didn't register on the scanner.

"Well, my dear Becca, your bloodwork was extraordinary." Dr. Lee blinked at her.

Becca cocked her head.

"You have disease markers and disease progressions. Your blood sugar is high, your liver and heart are stressed, and your endocrine system is out of whack."

Was "out of whack" a legitimate medical diagnosis? What kind of doctor was Dr. Lee?

He waved his hand, holding a pen like a magic wand. "All that is easily reversible and not of concern."

Easy for him to say. He didn't have a stressed, out-of-whack body with no medical insurance. Becca should message her mum with this insane diagnosis.

"We can create a formula to counter all that with no problem. It doesn't concern us."

The two people in gray headscarves nodded slightly. Otherwise, they sat still, hands crossed, just observing.

Opal kept staring as if Becca were something rare and precious.

"It concerns me a lot. I don't have medical insurance, and I'm not making sales. I can't afford to buy more supplements." She couldn't admit Leila paid for everything; that would get Leila in trouble. "If I'm sick, I need to see a doctor. I lost my job and haven't been able to get a new one." She glared at Salome, who widened her eyes innocently behind a cloud of citrus vapor. "MyCo System was supposed to be a moneymaker for me and help me lose weight so I would look better when I apply for jobs. It does neither. Now you're making me feel worse."

"Let me explain. You don't understand the true importance of these findings."

Becca swallowed. Her mouth filled with dirty toothpaste flavor.

"Your genetics are extraordinary. It's as if someone designed you to be the perfect person to work for MyCo System. We could have searched for you a hundred years and not found you."

Becca blinked. "My genetics? I'm adopted. My mum hates me for being so fat."

"Well, that's her loss. We'll look for your birth parents to see if you have any siblings who exhibit the same characteristics."

"I don't understand what characteristics I have."

"These genes that have fully expressed in you must have taken generations to come to fruition. You could almost say your DNA was specially engineered for this. That's why you can't lose weight. You were genetically designed to be fat." Dr. Lee beamed at her.

Becca put her head on the conference table and cried.

From *Direct Sales Daily*
Inspired by "Mummy Juice"

Melissa Cobalt's success story reads like a movie script. Over video chat, she tells us, "Call me Missy." Missy, her husband Milo, and her brother, Dr. Kelvin Pilz, now live in a sprawling compound somewhere in the Compass States. They would rather keep their exact location secret.

A few years ago, Kelvin, an archeologist, was part of a remarkable discovery many people may remember. As the water levels dropped in Hall Lake behind the Kimi Dam, artifacts of archaeological interest surfaced. Kelvin's Compass University North team was onsite to catalog the discoveries. The most famous of these was the "Red Sarcophagus," an out-of-place red stone block with unknown hieroglyphs carved across its surface. Kelvin's team opened the box under conditions as sterile as possible, finding it filled with partially dissolved human bones in a soup of reddish liquid.

A horror movie script, indeed!

Kelvin snuck his sister Missy and her husband Milo onto the site to see the miraculous box. When Kelvin told them the archeologists and other scientists on site believed the red liquid had odd fungal traces, inspiration struck.

Many edible mushrooms and fungi have remarkable adaptogenic and health properties, and as they talked, the three came up with a radically new idea: a fungus-based weight-loss system.

Missy claims, "It was as if a voice spoke in my head."

Missy, experienced in direct sales (having sold workout clothing and press-on nails in the past), knew their start-up should be a direct sales corporation. They jointly envisioned the products as weight-loss supplements and a total health-enhancing regimen geared toward women, who are the primary consumers of both direct-sales products and weight-loss supplements.

In a few short years, the company they founded, MyCo System, has spread from its humble beginning in a single pyramid-shaped headquarters near the Kimi Dam to over a dozen pyramids across the country, with a hundred thousand Body Management Partners whose levels in the MLM organization they named after precious stones: quartz, obsidian, diamond, sapphire, and hematite.

It's quite possible you already know someone who uses MyCo System products. If you don't and want to know more, check MyCo System's social media sites to get in touch with your nearest sales representative. There is still time to get in at the bottom of this fantastic, fast-growing pyramid.

CHAPTER NINETEEN

The punishing words flowed over and around Becca. Becca couldn't think of anything her mum or grand-mère had ever said that was as cruel as what had come from Dr. Lee's mouth. Genetically created to be fat? She wanted to kill herself.

And yet the doctor sounded excited—as if this was a good outcome.

Her stomach growled. Becca had felt ravenous her whole life. Now she could eat nothing but these stupid shakes, or she would vomit. The shakes did nothing to assuage that gnawing hunger. Everyone else lost weight, looked great, had sales. Everything was as it should be.

Fat Becca, she was a failure, as always.

Leila's big hand stroked her head. Leila's long nails burrowed into Becca's hair, scratching her scalp, comforting her even as Leila's voice rose and fell above her head. Whiffs of orange-scented smoke drifted across Becca's wet face.

Born to be fat.

Someone smelling of expensive perfume suddenly occupied the other chair beside Becca. A dark hand touched her face, trying to lift her head. The famous voice she had heard a thousand times on her TV said, "This is a tragedy. She fell through the cracks. How many others like her are out there?"

Becca raised her streaming face and gazed at Dr. Opal Knox.

Opal caressed Becca's round cheeks, the curving plumpness of her chin. "What a lovely girl. So soft." She turned to Salome, leaning across Becca and Leila. "Right under your eye, you stupid woman."

Salome set her jaw and huffed vapor from her nose. Those vape cartridges that never ran out of juice or battery power fascinated Becca. "I'm not sure what you're accusing me of, Opal. Or what this is all about. I haven't even read all those papers." She waved across the table at the folder holding their non-disclosure agreements and test results.

"Those NDAs don't say anything except to tell you not to say anything." Opal dismissed the folder. "But you know very well we are searching for people with lots of lovely soft fat. You found Leila for us, didn't you?"

Leila's hand on Becca's head stiffened, her nails digging into Becca's scalp at that revelation.

The two people in the gray scarves watched all this, motionless.

"Yes, and she's helped us already," Salome replied grudgingly. "But she's sick. She won't be able to maintain her weight."

"What?" Leila said.

"My dear girl." Opal kept stroking Becca like a new pet. "The whole point of MyCo System is to recruit the fattest people. Most get so skinny they don't need the supplements anymore. That's not what we want."

"What happens when MyCo System customers don't need the supplements and want to return to actual food? My most profitable job is mukbanging, and I can't do that right now." Leila cradled her belly. "I only agreed to the spot reduction to help my kidneys in case I need surgery. I don't care about being thin. Becca does. But I need to find out how to reverse my metabolism and go back to food soon, or all my fans will be gone."

"Maybe she isn't that bad of a candidate after all," Salome offered, ignoring Leila's concerns. "She wants to gain weight again."

"Why do you want very fat people?" Leila persisted, her eyes narrowed in anger and confusion.

"Well, to make money selling them weight-loss products," Dr. Lee said, "and also—"

Opal cut him off. "We are helping people. Look at all the people who have lost weight, made money, and improved their lives through MyCo System's wonderful products. And to develop those products, we need money."

"And—" Dr. Lee started.

"This makes no sense!" Becca eyed the doorway, thinking about leaving. But where could she go? She owned nothing but a spiky orange fish with a bad attitude. She depended entirely on Leila, who was deep into this MyCo System crap. Becca understood only now that it was a complete scam. Nothing worked. The pills were probably sugar. And she was part of this, selling this crap. Drinking it.

"She's gonna bolt." Dr. Lee aimed his pen at Becca.

Opal grabbed Becca's arm. "You're in this now. You signed the NDA."

"I can leave and not say anything."

"What will you eat?"

"I don't know. I'll go to a doctor and get checked out." Or they could just tell her and Leila how to eat again.

Opal and Salome exchanged glances. "That wouldn't be a good idea," Opal explained. "Especially for you. Now that we've done these tests on you and know what you are."

"I failed your stupid test!"

"No, you passed the MyCoLysis test with flying colors, as they say. You need nothing that's offered at the lowest levels. That's why you aren't losing weight. This program isn't designed for you at all," Dr. Lee explained. "You are an evolved human, as far as the test is concerned."

"Evolved human?" Becca couldn't keep the scorn from her voice. "Me? The human blob? What is so evolved about me?"

"Well, evolution works toward different things. And you were engineered for something different from other people. And you evolved toward one goal."

"No one should evolve toward being this fat." Becca set her mouth and glanced sideways at Salome, unsurprised to see her huffing dragon-breath everywhere. Salome would never think being fat was better than being thin.

"Why would anyone be genetically engineered to be fat? That doesn't make any sense …" Leila's voice trailed away. "I mean, if you want to be fat or are happy being fat, fine, but to force someone to be fat? Becca isn't happy being fat. Her mother practically disowned her."

"Essentially, she did disown me," Becca corrected. "She has gone non-contact until I'm thin enough to meet her standards."

"That's strange," Opal mused. "Your mother and father genetically should be quite large."

"I'm adopted, remember?" Becca pulled her arm from Opal's grasp and crossed both across her chest. "My mum is a stick-thin fashion model who thinks I'm disgusting."

"Yes, that's right." Salome tapped her pointy chin and allowed smoke to ooze from her mouth. "Your mother is—"

"No." Leila cut her off with a sharp hand gesture. "We don't talk about who Becca's adoptive mother is. That woman is evil and mean and doesn't deserve any recognition."

"Well, I know who she is, and she is indeed quite slim. Everyone knows her tiny silhouette."

Opal seemed intrigued. She squinted at Becca, as if she could figure out who her adoptive mother was by studying her.

Becca pulled a face. She despised people fawning over her mum. "Did you ever think maybe her 'tiny silhouette,'" she used her finger quotes, "is also genetic and therefore not of her doing, so why should you praise her for it? Just as apparently my fat is genetic and not my fault, and so I shouldn't be reviled for it?"

"My dear, your mother works hard to stay trim, I'm sure." Opal frowned.

Becca pushed her rolling chair away from the conference table and gazed out the slanted window at the dark parking lot. For once, it wasn't raining.

"Oh yeah, everything she does to be 'trim' is admirable because being skinny is great. Anything I do is terrible because being fat is disgusting. If I can't lose weight, I'm an awful person."

"Beck, no," Leila said. "I, for one, never thought that."

"I bet Salome thinks that." She twirled the chair around to aim her gaze at the skinny dragon bitch.

Salome stared at the ceiling, where a tiny cloud of vapor clung.

Dr. Lee sighed loudly. "Regardless of what might be better or worse, aesthetically, this is what Becca was engineered to be. And she is a splendid example."

Becca studied herself. Her chin almost rested on her breasts, which sprawled on the top roll of her belly, and the lower roll of her belly smothered the large poufs of her thighs. "Splendid?"

The doctor nodded and came around the table.

The gray-scarved people watched.

Dr. Lee held Becca's hand and palpated her arm. Her forearm was plump, her upper arm a mass of hanging fat mashed against her pendulous breasts. A fat roll across her mid-back mimicked her chest, and her shelf-butt was prominent enough that she could have balanced a glass there.

Opal was proud of being able to do exactly that, as she had done in a photo shoot with her boyfriend band, HaunTED.

"How did I get genetically engineered to be fat? Especially since I don't know who my parents are?" Now Becca sounded as if she was going to cry again. She was weak and useless, not the pinnacle of anything except failure.

"There have been additives in the water of the Collective States for years." Dr. Lee poked her broad belly, more curious than professional. "The problem is people have to be susceptible to the additives. Not every genetic line will react when exposed. Your genes expressed perfectly. So did the genes of generations before you. Epigenetic changes. Does this hurt?"

"Not really…You mean, this was intentional? Who put additives in the water for generations?" Unbelievable.

"Above my pay grade." Dr. Lee grabbed handfuls of her back. "And trust me, my pay grade is very high."

Becca stared at Opal, assuming her pay grade was also very high.

Opal raised her immaculate eyebrows and shrugged, which wasn't an answer.

She glanced at the silent watchers in their headscarves. Did they have pay grades?

"Additives in the water?" Leila asked. "But everyone drinks filtered water or spring water now."

"Yes," Dr. Lee said glumly, releasing Becca's back fat. "The plan was working well, and the needed genes were expressing. Then the bottled water craze started. People still use unfiltered water for irrigation and animals, though."

"You poisoned the irrigation water?" Becca's mouth hung open in disbelief. Her stomach growled, not caring about poisoned food.

"*I* did not." Dr. Lee drew himself up. "Above my pay grade. But yes, the irrigation water had additives."

"Even the most rudimentary water processing should filter anything out," Leila argued.

Opal watched the conversation avidly, eyes darting back and forth.

Salome blew vapor at the ceiling.

The watchers sat still.

The air vent covers rattled as the pyramid's noisy HVAC system switched on.

"Microplastics," Becca realized.

"What?" Leila stared at her.

Becca riffed on the idea. "There are microplastics in everything. Even in human breast milk and in deep-sea fish that have never seen a human. I bet that's how the additive got into everything. It's in the microplastic. Even filters can't remove it; it's ubiquitous and so very tiny." She nodded to herself and tried not to laugh. This was so absurd.

Dr. Lee guffawed, waving his pen. "Miss Becca, you are brilliant. Perhaps not far off from the truth. Although that's not the truth."

Leila covered her mouth, dark eyes bulging. "Poisoned microplastic?"

"You signed an NDA, Leila." Salome made clouds against the ceiling.

"But you are poisoning people," Leila said from behind her palm.

"An NDA is an NDA. And you have no proof."

"You all just told us," Leila argued, dropping her hand. The untouched black drink next to her fizzed.

Becca stared at it with hunger. She wasn't supposed to know what it tasted like.

"Are the powders that make up the drinks and supplements part of this poisonous microplastic?" Becca's stomach growled again. Not sugar pills. Microplastic pills. That was one way to recycle.

"There's no poisonous microplastic!" Salome shouted. "You have an obsessive, one-track mind. I don't know if that's your programming or just how you would be, regardless. Stop with the poison microplastic ranting. The drinks aren't plastic. The supplements aren't plastic. Take those thoughts out of your mind." She blew a rude, narrow stream of vapor into Becca's eyes.

Drinks and supplements were absolutely plastic. Becca nodded slightly, blinking back tears; the vapor was harsh. She turned to Leila. "What did you get me into?"

"You? I'm in this too! I have kidney failure. I'm trying to get healthier. Instead, I'm being poisoned." She glared at Salome. Her poor, already unhealthy kidneys were trying to filter microplastics out of her blood.

"You aren't being poisoned, either of you. Both of you are far too dramatic for words," Dr. Lee declared, pointing with his pen.

"You said you genetically manipulated me." Becca's mouth curved down.

"MyCo System genetically manipulated many people," he said flatly. "Don't take it personally."

"MyCo System did this? So you could get more fat people and sell them supplements to make money?" Becca felt herself getting hysterical. "Pardon me if that makes no fucking sense." This had to be a joke. MyCo System wasn't even around when Becca was born, not to mention generations before her.

Everyone stared at her.

"Oh, that's right, it's beyond everyone's pay grade." She waved her hands. Her upper arms flapped. "No one stops to think about how this makes no sense. What is the endgame? Do you want fat people, or do you want thin people? Can someone please explain this to me? I'm addicted to your damn drinks. They taste awful, yet I can't eat anything else. Now you tell me I can never ever lose weight, no matter what, because I'm a fucking experiment."

The two figures with the gray headscarves conferred so quietly she couldn't hear a word and then left the room together, walking in silence.

Becca felt like she had just failed a test. She set her arms on atop her boobs and clenched her jaw. "Now what?"

Level 5: Hematite Body Management Partner

Founder's level: the ultimate level

Your Team: Black Sapphire Body Management Partners, Red Diamond Body Management Partners, Rainbow Obsidian Body Management Partners, and Quartz Body Management Partners

You sell: We do not expect Body Management Partners to sell products at this level

Your nutraceutical program: Red Gill-Tea™ Pleasure drink, Red BubblyBoost™ drops

Your headscarf: Gray

Your meeting location: Pyramid Pinnacle

Your perks:

- 55% discount/commission on Shroomshee™ smoothie shakes and Cosmic Cleanse Caps™
- 35% discount on Black Gill-Tea Pleasure™ and Red Gill-Tea Pleasure™ drinks, Red Fun Gi-Up™ and Black Fun Gi-Up™ Drops, and Red BubblyBoost™ and Black BubblyBoost™ drops
- 35% discount on ShroomSlim™ and FungiFuel™ custom supplements
- Free LipoGest™ spot reduction treatments
- 30% of your downline's sales
- 15% commission on MyCoLysis™ and SporeCode™ testing fees and 30% commission on ShroomSlim™ and FungiFuel™ custom supplements

CHAPTER TWENTY

"You need to level up," Opal decided. "Although you haven't got the sales to support it."

Becca waved her hands. "I'm about to fling myself into the harbor. But I'm so fat I would float instead of drowning."

"Well, moving you up without sales isn't above my pay grade. Or even Salome's. Salome would benefit from having someone else at a higher level under her, not that she would notice one more person. She's the boss-babe queen, after all."

Salome snorted steam. Becca couldn't tell if Opal and Salome were friends or frenemies.

Leila leaned toward Salome, scratching her neck. "All the while, when I told you how Becca was suffering and failing and needed help, you said she needed to work harder and do the program better. You could've helped her?"

Salome shrugged. "Most people fail at this. At least eighty percent, to be exact. I can't help them all. I won't help them all. This is very much a business of 'the gods help those who help themselves,' no matter what gods you worship. And I'm no god."

Becca bet evil Salome was best friends with Willow LeNoir. They were perfect for each other. Both skinny evil cunts. Whatever duplicity was going on here, Salome had masterminded it for sure.

"Funny, when you recruited me, you said the exact opposite." Leila's voice burned with resentment. "How you do so well at direct sales and what a great boss-babe you are because of how much you care for everyone in your downline, how you want them all to succeed and will do anything to help them."

Salome snorted dragon fire. "I lied. Sue me."

"I wish I could."

Opal removed a folding tablet from her bag. Becca wanted it. The gorgeous piece of hardware undoubtedly had more memory and better programs than her creaky old laptop. It had a nicer screen, and a stylus slid into the hinge. Then again, Opal had money from all her TV appearances, plus her rich rock-star boyfriend. Who knows how much her MyCo System commissions were on top of all that? She was more than a boss-babe, more than an influencer.

"Salome, didn't we write someone off last week or the week before? She wasn't one of yours, I don't think."

Salome did a long, slow exhale. "I think so. She had just leveled up. Good prospect, didn't last at all. Very disappointing."

"Where is her downline?"

"Unassigned, unless someone has asked for help. It wasn't a huge downline."

Opal pushed the tablet to Salome. "Assign them to Becca."

Salome frowned. "Becca doesn't know how to manage a team."

Opal shrugged. "Leila can manage her team if needed."

"I can do what now?" Leila glanced back and forth.

"Manage Becca's new downline. Which automatically becomes your downline as well," Opal explained.

"What just happened?" Becca asked, confused. "I have a team? Of what?"

"Of ladies. Um, and one man. You are now officially a boss-babe, Becca," Opal said. "Welcome to Rainbow Obsidian."

Rough translation of pictographs on a sacred hide, presumed to be of Desert Bloom origin, excerpted from 'Folklore of the Desert Bloom Nation: New Translations from Pictograph Artifacts," ***Compass Archeology*****, retrieved from online archives:**

During the Goose Moon, a star fell from the sky. When it hit, it smashed and spilled mushrooms. This was in the valley of the antelope. The following summer, the antelope were very skinny and few in number. Giant mushrooms filled the valley, sometimes looking like antelope or people. They moved. One mushroom ate a man called Fat Beaver. Left behind sludge and bones. People had strange holes in their bodies. People shriveled up and became skin and bones. People heard sacred god voices saying the mushrooms were good to eat. People grew fat eating mushrooms. The mushrooms ate the fat people. The few remaining people made a container from sacred stone, gathered all the mushrooms, and sealed them inside the box to rot with the bones of the last of their victims. The star-borne walking mushrooms cursed the valley. No people should live in it ever again.

CHAPTER TWENTY-ONE

Money poured in, commissions from the new people under Becca.

At the next meeting, as Leila tottered off for her third spot-reduction treatment, Becca headed to her private session to be introduced to the black drink with about a dozen other people. She didn't argue with the presenter, who talked about all the hard work they had done to get themselves to the Rainbow Obsidian level.

Becca had done the opposite of hard work.

The presenter's red headscarf slipped. As the woman pulled it up, Becca saw she had a scar on her neck, much like the spot Leila constantly scratched. That was strange. What were the odds?

It surprised Becca to see everyone who had leveled up was fat. She figured it would be mostly the thin people who advanced. After all, who would buy weight-loss products from a fat person? Although when Becca did *the thing*, she saw she was still the fattest.

The woman droned on about the advanced Black Gill-Tea Pleasure drink. One's body had to be acclimated to the ingredients by drinking a good quantity of Shroomshee smoothie shakes first. Then one could "upgrade" to the more potent Black Gill-Tea Pleasure drink and the more powerful Red Fun Gi-Up supplement drops that went with it, accelerating weight loss.

Becca thought about microplastics. She wasn't cut out for this direct sales stuff. It was so dull. She pulled her hair over her shoulder, twisted it, and tried to stay awake.

"Part of the upgrade ritual is a short meditation session."

Becca rolled her eyes. Quasi-religious headscarves and now meditation?

The leader handed each Rainbow Obsidian candidate a clear capsule filled with multicolored globules. The capsule tasted like dirt. They swallowed them with sips of shake.

The leader herded them into the black hallway and pointed Becca to one of the unmarked offices. It was just big enough for a generous leather chair, like the kind used for gaming, and a small shelf for her bag and shake, with extremely dim lighting.

The leader instructed, "Sit in the chair and breathe deeply. Meditate if you know how. Be thankful, be grateful. When you exit the room, I'll issue you a headscarf, and you'll officially be a Rainbow Obsidian. Expect the unexpected, and whatever happens, just roll with it. But if you feel too uncomfortable, call out."

This was seriously weird.

Becca placed her messenger bag on the shelf and settled into the chair. It felt dirty. The leather had a strange consistency, almost squishy. Maybe vegan leather? Knowing this place and their affinity for everything fungal, they had developed a way to make mushroom leather. The strangely designed chair held her head at an uncomfortable angle. The touch of the weird leather felt awful along her bare arms.

The dim lights in the windowless room snapped out a moment after the door closed. Although Becca had never been in an immersion tank or sensory deprivation chamber, this felt like one.

The pseudo-leather seemed to bond with her skin. She couldn't tell where her arms ended and the chair began. Were her eyes open or closed? Becca blinked furiously but couldn't tell. Her hands felt welded to the chair arms, her palms sinking deep inside the soft material. She could grab a fistful. It was the same temperature as her body. Even along her back, she felt the chair molding to her precisely through her shirt. It was creepy, yet comforting.

The chair was hugging her.

It took a few minutes for Becca to realize the leader had drugged her. The capsules with the rainbow beads, what had they been? She leaned her head back. Or the chair grabbed her head and pulled it back. She couldn't tell where she ended and the chair began.

How come Leila hadn't warned her about this? Was this a ceremony? Who had to go through something like this to level up in direct sales?

Becca didn't know how to meditate. Close your eyes and think of nothing; that was the basics. It had never worked for her before, and it wasn't working now.

The reclining chair's leg area wrapped around her calves.

The chair engulfed her.

They had fed her hallucinogens. Weren't there hallucinogenic mushrooms? MyCo System cornered the market on every conceivable use of fungi.

She was tripping. That made her angry. No one should take a hallucinogen alone with no warning. Becca had always thought if she experimented with anything like that, she would do it with supportive friends or pay to go to a professional shamanistic retreat.

The headrest embraced her head and neck in a way she didn't like. Becca hated being confined. Enormous, she always feared getting stuck in a small space. Was she having a waking nightmare?

The chair had her. It tightened around her head and neck, causing actual pain.

"I want to leave!" Her voice seemed muffled because the chair covered her ears. It crept across her throat.

No one turned on the light or entered.

"Hey!" Becca yelled.

The chair extended and enveloped her, leaving only her eyes, nose, and lips exposed. She felt as if she was wearing boxing headgear. The chair hugged her whole body. It was impossible. She was much larger than the chair. Nonetheless, she was drowning in it.

"Help!" she tried to call out, but the chair had immobilized her lower jaw.

I don't like this at all. She couldn't get to her phone to message Leila for help. The phone was in her bag by the door. The chair had her hands incapacitated, anyway. She was tripping. Her best bet was to ease herself into it, see what it was about.

Why the fuck would MyCo System drug their Body Management Partners, lock them up, and make them hallucinate?

A sharp pinch bit her neck, as if someone had nicked her skin, or caught it in a buckle. Something like a finger entered her mouth and probed her cheek. A fat, squishy finger. It was also filthy. She touched it with her tongue and tasted the ubiquitous dirt. The finger withdrew. Her neck ached.

The darkness hurt Becca's eyes as she strained for the slightest hint of light. Shouldn't her eyes be adjusted by now? Shouldn't there be a slit of light along the doorway?

Nothing.

She didn't like this at all. Awful. Pointless. She couldn't speak because the chair still held her mouth open. What was this supposed to teach her about selling? How long was this supposed to take? How long had she even been there? She tried to think back to sitting in the meeting room, but her mind wandered off down the hallway into nothing.

She closed her eyes and surrendered. She couldn't fight the darkness; she couldn't fight the ravenous chair.

CHAPTER TWENTY-TWO

When she opened her eyes, the leader stood in the doorway, smiling. "You look relaxed, Becca. I think you fell asleep."

Becca inspected her surroundings. Just a big leather chair. Well, not genuine leather. She had left sweaty handprints on the arms, which she tried to wipe away as soon as she noticed, but the leader laughed and flapped a hand. "Oh, someone will wipe down the chair after you leave. We are spotless here."

That didn't sound right. Becca hoisted herself from the chair and turned to study it. It had an unusual design, like a gaming chair with extra support pillows, but it didn't look dirty. In the dark, hadn't she thought it was filthy?

She lifted her messenger bag. Her bare lower arms were red like she was sunburned. Her mouth felt dry. The hinges of her jaw ached as if she had just been to the dentist. The side of her neck hurt. Her eyes were crunchy-dry.

Becca moved her tongue around, touching her teeth, aware of her bad shake-breath. If it meant she was in ketosis and losing weight, that would be good, but it was the taste from the shakes she couldn't brush away. Mouthwash and flossing didn't touch it. It clung. It felt extra thick now, worse than morning breath, and the inside of her cheek was sore, as if she had bitten it.

The leader took Becca's arm and led her to the conference room. Everyone else was already seated around the table. "You looked so peaceful, sleeping in the chair, that I left you for last. Please tell us what you experienced. It's sharing time."

Becca sat, blinking. What had she experienced that she wanted to share? "Um, I'm still processing." The chair was weird leather. No one would care. Then what? It had been too dark. She had felt scared and claustrophobic in the too-small chair. She could mention that. They needed to be more size-sensitive. The folding chairs downstairs were a comfortable size, yet this chair was so small she felt smothered. But had that been it? Becca rubbed her sore neck. And then she had given up, hadn't she, frightened of the dark and being constricted?

Others shared their experiences. The dark had been enlightening. They had felt touched by gods or by angels. A god was trying to whisper in their ears. It had been very spiritual. Loved ones from beyond the grave had embraced a few. The dark had been so comforting, enabling them to confront their own failings and flaws without the light getting in the way. They felt worthy and empowered.

Everyone chose a scarf. At Rainbow Obsidian level, they could have any color other than the reserved colors of red, black, or gray. These were reserved for Red Diamond, Black Sapphire, and Hematite, in that order.

Becca mostly wore black, so she chose a dark purple one with black border stitching. The scarves had tiny mushrooms on them so they could recognize each other. To the uninitiated, the prints might appear to be dots or splotches.

That was the trademark of selling for MyCo System: the mushroom headscarf. "Of course, you don't have to wear a headscarf if it makes you uncomfortable or feels too religious. But it is a way for new customers to find you in public. So, it's up to you if you want to lose that opportunity," the rotund leader said, touching her red scarf. Now Becca recognized the mushroom pattern on it. How had she not noticed the mushrooms on Leila's? She had never looked closely at it.

The leader showed them how to drape the scarves. Just around the head, like a headband, with the loose ends flowing down the back. Or framing the face. Wrap the loose ends around the throat. "It's handy because, after weight loss, the throat can be a problem area. The headscarf is perfect for covering that."

Becca used hers as a headband.

"What was your experience in the Black Chair?" the leader asked again, and Becca could hear the capital letters.

"I felt subsumed, taken away from myself, and I had to force myself to relax and go with it. I guess the metaphor would be I shouldn't fight?" Becca reminded herself they thought she had gotten to this level legitimately. They didn't know Becca had played leapfrog and didn't deserve to be here. Maybe her Black Chair experience had gone so poorly because the chair had rejected her. Becca shuddered.

But the rest thought her bullshit was a brilliant answer.

The leader explained the Black Gill-Tea Pleasure drink to the new Rainbow Obsidians. "It's more concentrated; it's purer. Not flavored like the Shroomshee smoothie shakes." She brandished a handful of thick black straws. "You shouldn't think of it as a shake or a smoothie. It's not thick. It hasn't got that consistency. In theory, you don't even need the water; you could just pour the contents of the straw down your throat. But once you've gotten to the Rainbow Obsidian level, drinking plain water can be difficult, and it's easy to become dehydrated, as you might have figured out, so it's best to mix the contents of the black straw with water. Many mix it with ice water."

"My roommate makes hers with cold water and then adds a lot of finely crushed ice," Becca volunteered, eying the woman's handful of straws. She realized the leader had never introduced herself.

"Yes, that works too," the woman agreed, smiling at Becca. She didn't know Becca was technically an intruder who hadn't earned her place at this conference table.

The leader passed out small boxes of straws, bottles of red drops, clear MyCo System-logoed tumblers with a spot to snap in a straw, and little MyCo System logo tote bags.

"You don't have to drink through the straw. Discard it once you've mixed the powder into the water. The straw is biodegradable pseudo-plastic," the leader continued, "So it goes with compostables."

Becca hadn't known. She threw Leila's used straws in the regular trash. Oops.

"The design idea was to make the Black Gill-Tea Pleasure drink a real treat. Pop the end of the straw and pour it into the water, adding the Red Fun Gi-Up drops. The drops fully activate the compounds in the Gill-Tea." She demonstrated the process and then drank. "Something fun."

The leader put her almost-empty tumbler down. "Some of you have heard that innovative technology is coming down the pike here at MyCo System! For now, it's only available at Red Diamond level. I'll give you the thumbnail version to quell the rumors."

Becca sipped her dirt drink and listened to the woman launch into her sales pitch as the darkness shifted in the corner.

"MyCo System is rolling out the MyCoType product line, designed to detect and enhance each person's unique nutritional and weight-loss needs. We will issue a hand scanner to every Red Diamond and Black Sapphire. The scanner detects elements and properties of people's blood through their skin and is used to create custom supplemental formulas. The scan is called a MyCoLysis test. The supplements that are custom blended based on the results of the test are called ShroomSlim. There is also a blood test, the SporeCode test. It's more refined, but more expensive, and offers an even more precise formulation for the custom supplements, which are called FungiFuel. We have a doctor on staff who will do telehealth visits for the bloodwork, should you choose to go this route. We will offer people at Rainbow Obsidian level first access to have the tests done for now."

Becca's head swam with all the product names. Even though this was her second or third introduction to them, she'd never be able to keep them all straight. Having two different tests and sets of supplements struck her as too complicated to market effectively. What was up with that, anyway? Just a way to sell twice as much. She thought many of these people must agree with her that this was all a bunch of bullshit, but they were hoping they got into it soon enough to still make money. They didn't care about helping people lose weight or get healthier, but they would undoubtedly lie and say they did.

They had to see the scanner was just another gimmick to separate people from their money. Especially since the supplements prescribed by the tablet and the blood tests, unlike the shakes, were just microplastics.

"Our marketing department has come up with a few new ideas," the leader continued. "We will put subscription plans into place."

Someone had been listening to Becca. Were those silent watchers marketing people?

"Obviously, we want to push those. You might think you won't be making as much money because of the discounted price. But people forget to cancel subscriptions."

Everyone nodded, their eyes big.

Brilliant, Becca thought, using mental finger quotes. Her stomach growled. She wondered about microplastics again.

"MyCo System had the tablets specially manufactured in limited numbers, so we don't expect them to become available to Rainbow Obsidian members soon, if ever. You need to level up to Red Diamond to take advantage of selling this great new program. You've already proven yourselves by rising from Quartz to Rainbow Obsidian. Only twenty percent of Quartzes make that move. You are elite!"

Becca remembered Salome saying nonchalantly eighty percent of people who joined MyCo System would not advance.

The presenter explained what to do with any leftover shakes: sell them or give them away as party samples. "Shroomshee smoothie shakes won't help you as much once you switch over to Black Gill-Tea Pleasure."

They already did nothing for Becca.

They stirred in unison, swishing the long, black plastic-looking straws.

"You should have called this the galaxy drink. It's out of this world." Becca stared into the side of her glass, turning it so the logo wasn't in the way of seeing the swirls.

"Why?" The presenter frowned at her own almost-empty glass.

"The swirls look like a galaxy." Becca tilted her head, glancing along the table. Every glass had a different galaxy brewing.

"Is yours contaminated? There aren't any swirls." The leader lifted her glass to the light. The galaxy in her drink eddied with red and purple, dancing around the straw.

Everyone stared at Becca.

She squeezed her lips. "Oh. Maybe it's just the lighting over here."

Her galaxy separated into two counter-swirling ones. She didn't want to move the straw, so she hooked it into the holder.

"Is everyone ready?"

Becca stared into the glass from above. Through the crushed ice, she saw the glow. Why couldn't anyone else see this? It must be something in her weird DNA, like people who had extra color perception. Was she seeing microplastics? She could tell Dr. Lee. *Hey, I can see galaxies in the black drink no one else can. That might be a simple test to administer.* But fuck him.

After a moment, everyone lifted their glasses in unison. A few placed their lips on the rims, but most sucked on the straw.

The leader sipped the dregs from her straw, and everyone followed her lead.

Becca watched their faces. Most seemed amazed at the flavor, making joyful noises, groaning, licking their lips. She sipped hers, although she wanted to gulp it. It tasted better than the shakes, not chalky, but it still smelled of dirt with a hint of moldy leaves.

For the first time, Becca didn't have to take a miserly lick of black drink before handing the rest to Leila. She put the straw into her mouth and pulled deeply. The galaxy shifted, came together, and flowed up the straw and down her throat. The glow hit her stomach. It calmed instantly. It soothed the hollow growl that had plagued her for months. She closed her eyes, wrapped both hands around the glass, and drank, not giving a shit about poison microplastics and bio-engineered DNA.

Much too quickly, the open-drain sound of the empty straw in a glass of damp, glowing ice caused her to open her eyes. Everyone stared at her.

The taste wasn't great. Whoever invented flavors for MyCo System just didn't get it. This was a foul combination of licorice, generic cola, and dirt. Unpleasant. But it was filling and satisfied her gnawing hunger.

Everyone marveled at how delicious and refreshing the Black Gill-Tea Pleasure drink was and how they loved Becca's crushed ice idea.

No one said the drink tasted like dirt scraped from under a pile of poop.

Some hadn't finished theirs. Becca wanted to grab those half-empty vessels and suck them dry. Her eyes widened, and she wondered if others could hear her thoughts. She would go home and drink half a dozen of these. No. Put three straws at a time into each glass.

She put her empty down carefully and half-raised her hand. "Can someone overdose on the black drink? Or red drops? Is there any danger to this?" Now she thought about microplastics. Ever-present poison, engineered to make her fat. Unless that was part of the lies MyCo System was peddling. If that horribleness was the lie, how bad could the truth be?

"This is an adaptogenic nutraceutical. You can't overdose on it, only on the water you put it in."

Becca nodded. Got it. Add more powder to less water. The words *nutraceutical* and *adaptogenic* were bullshit marketing terms she ignored.

"Children? Animals? I live with a cat and a fish."

Someone snickered.

"You shouldn't let your fish swim in Black Gill-Tea Pleasure drink." Everyone tittered. "And no, the cat shouldn't drink it. It's formulated only for humans. They tested none of this on animals, so we don't know."

It was the first time hearing something had not been tested on animals sounded menacing. They had tested it only on people. Becca was one of the test subjects. Accidentally, after generations or longer of trying to breed a certain kind of fat person, there she was. And now they were going to throw everything at her and see what stuck to her fat.

"And children, no. If there is a very obese child, just Shroomshee smoothie shakes. Eventually, testing on the tablet."

"How many shakes does it take to equal one black drink?"

The others perked up when Becca asked. It was a good question.

"It's not mathematical. They each have unique properties. Black Gill-Tea Pleasure drink has different adaptogenic nutraceuticals than Shroomshee smoothie shakes. More advanced ones. Shroomshee smoothie shakes are a beginner's drink. People who don't need to lose a lot of weight won't need anything else."

Becca tilted her head. "But once they've lost the weight, how will they return to regular food? I tried eating a bite of pizza a while back and got seriously ill. My upline told me I might never eat food again."

The leader frowned, lips pursed. "That's not entirely true, and she shouldn't have said that to you. You are far from needing the reversing protocol, but there are ways to guide you back into eating regular food. If you have customers who need it, we will make it available by special request. It's a unique set of supplements."

No doubt pricey, and nicely weighted to give her a good commission. Why didn't Leila know about it?

"Please don't spread rumors about depending on the shakes and unable to return to food."

"I don't spread rumors. But that's what I was told by my upline. How can I know if I get bad information from someone inside the organization? How do I know, for instance, what you are telling me isn't also false?" Everything MyCo System told her was a lie. She felt like a mushroom: kept in the dark and fed shit.

The presenter snapped, "You need access to better promo materials. Have you ever logged in to the marketing database to get the materials to promote your business? Your upline should have set you up with an account and password."

Becca shook her head. "I copy posts. Of course, I change them a bit, so they are coming from me. My marketing background is coming in handy."

"That's probably why you're so good at it," the presenter said, "even without all the up-to-date information."

Becca didn't correct her. No one was supposed to know she wasn't here because of all the work she'd put in. Although was it hard work to lie to fat people about weight-loss drinks?

The people here were fat but also loose-skinned, Becca realized, as if they had recently lost weight. Unlike the horrible weight-loss meetings her mum had forced Becca to go to in the past, they hadn't exchanged the unholy numbers: *How many calories do you eat a day? How many hours do you exercise a day? How much do you weigh? What's your BMI?*

Thinking about it, Becca shuddered. She gazed into her MyCo System glass, where the ice had melted from the heat of her clutching hands. The galaxy glinted at the bottom. She sucked. The drink was icy. She had had a brain freeze before from eating ice cream, but this gave her stomach freeze. That would take care of her hunger if her stomach went into stasis from being frozen. She would think that was the black drink's secret if she hadn't been satisfied with a few sips in the past without the belly-freeze effect.

One woman, with loose skin and underlying fat pads, asked about the LipoGest Spot Reduction treatment. "I heard someone died after having it."

The presenter twisted her mouth. "Who told you that?" She glared at Becca as if Becca was on SeenIt, making social media posts all day about it.

Becca shook her head. Whether the woman took it to mean she hadn't told or she didn't know, Becca didn't care. But was it true? Had it killed someone? It did seem to hurt Leila badly.

"Spot reduction?" Others immediately grasped the concept, although they hadn't heard of the procedure. Obviously, they hadn't read their onboarding materials carefully. Many, including Loose Skin, hadn't finished their black drinks. They didn't seem interested in the black drink, only in making money. Becca hated them. She weighed as much as any two of them, even though they were all fat.

The presenter said grudgingly, "When you level up to Red Diamond, you get the option of a special spot-reduction treatment called LipoGest. There is nothing more to talk about right now, including death, which I'm sure I would have heard about had it happened."

"I know someone who has gotten it, and the results are amazing, but she can't tell me details!" The red-headed woman next to Loose Skin said sotto voce.

Leila had been in so much pain each time. An amazing amount of pain, that's for sure. Was that true of everyone?

"What about the testing tablets? When can we get those?" Becca asked, to change the subject.

"You just got to this level." The presenter sighed and threw up her arms.

Becca explained, "We need to have a goal, whether it's getting access to the tablet for testing or the spot reduction treatments for ourselves. We need to think, 'just this much more in sales' or 'this many more people under me,' and I get this reward. And then we can beg for sales appropriately."

The presenter glared. "You can't mention the spot-reduction treatments in your social media posts!"

Becca said, "No, but there are teasers I could say about the MyCoLysis and SporeCode testing. I could say, 'If I sell x number of shakes this month'—any number, who cares, I could lie—'I can bring something amazing to all my people buying from me! This is something never seen in any weight-loss company! It will revolutionize weight loss, and I want to bring it to you. I have experienced it, and it is amazing! But I can't bring it to you yet. Help me reach my goal and get a free four-pack of shakes.'"

The presenter stared. "Where did you get that script from?"

"In my head. I just came up with it on the fly. I used to work at a magazine doing marketing and advertising, designing ads."

"Who would pay for the free four-pack of shakes?" Loose Skin demanded, frowning.

"Well, you would structure the promotion to make more than enough profit to give away four-packs."

"I don't want to give anything away. I work hard, and I want to keep all my profit."

Becca shrugged. "Then don't give away anything. Or have a contest and only give away one four-pack to one customer. People fucking love contests."

A few looked appalled at her language. Becca had forgotten how many religious people were part of the organization. She didn't understand the overlap between a business that was tantamount to swindling, and people who worshipped gods. Leila made regular trips to the temple of Bast on behalf of herself and Nyx. Becca had moved around a lot and never really settled on any god, not finding a use for one. Her French grand-mère had Jewish heritage, but Becca wasn't blood-Jewish, so her grand-mère hadn't bothered to teach her any of that, and Willow LeNoir had long ago become agnostic.

"People love contests, and you're free to run your own as long as you pay for your own prizes," the presenter said. "That's a great idea. Becca, I'm curious; how long did it take you to level up with all those wonderful ideas?"

Becca's eyes widened, and she shrugged. "I didn't work it as hard as I should have at the beginning." Which wasn't a lie. And didn't answer the question. "But I had a great mentor. Finally, we straightened it out, and now I'm here where I belong." All the truth, all completely misleading.

"I still want to know about spot reduction." Redhead returned to the subject.

"It exists and it's not available at this level. Nothing else to say. Don't let me catch anyone posting about it on social media." Again, she looked at Becca.

Becca shook her head.

"And the tablet?" Redhead refused to give up.

"As I told you earlier, eventually, you may be eligible for the tablets at the Rainbow Obsidian level, but there aren't enough. So right now, they're for Red Diamond level only. They are specialized pieces of equipment and are very expensive. You need to be a top seller with lots of people under you generating high sales to afford one. Even at that level of sales, you still need to pay out of pocket for the tablet, but you make the money back if you can order enough tests."

"What are the tests, again?"

"This isn't the time to talk about the tests. This meeting is about the Black Gill-Tea Pleasure drink."

"How much profit do we make selling the drink?"

The presenter stilled, her eyes on Redhead. "You don't sell the Black Gill-Tea Pleasure drink."

Becca nodded to herself. That was illegal, she was sure. Totally pyramid scheme territory.

"The Black Gill-Tea Pleasure drink is a reward for reaching this level. It's a carrot to get your buyers to sign up as sellers and your sellers to sign up sellers underneath them."

"I thought we weren't supposed to talk about the black drink?" Becca asked.

"You aren't."

Becca just stared.

The leader looked uncomfortable, shifting in her chair.

Finally, Becca said, "How can the black drink be an enticement to get people to sign up as sellers and to get others to sign up as sellers underneath them if we aren't allowed to talk about it?"

"Well, the same way you phrased your clever little pitch earlier, but this is something you would do in person or at an in-person party for someone who loved the shakes and was losing some weight, but not enough. Someone like that is perfect to pitch this to. An ideal candidate."

Becca nodded, seeing the pitch in her mind, but waiting to see what the presenter would say. *You've lost some weight, that's great*. That would always be your opener. Even if they haven't lost over five pounds.

That described Becca, still, after all those months.

"If you already signed them up as sellers to get the Shroomshee smoothie discount, tell them if they sign up some buyers under them, they will get even more of a discount. That's always wonderful, but if one or more of those buyers turns into sellers, you can introduce them to something really amazing that will speed up their weight loss even more."

Becca wobbled her head. Wishy-washy. Not what she would have crafted. Too long, not punchy. She could work with it.

"If they are still only buyers, you should just urge them to become sellers and get the seller discount at first." That was standard, first-day advice.

"You're just moving them up the chain," another woman remarked.

"Yes, but you are giving them an extra reason besides making money," the leader countered.

"What if the person is already thin?" Redhead wondered.

"You use the money as the carrot. But weight loss is a better carrot," the leader said.

"People will see you are making money off them. Isn't that going to make them unhappy? They will feel as if you took advantage of them." Someone else who thought like Becca spoke up. This woman had a foxy, mixed-heritage face.

"Most people don't think that hard," *and you shouldn't either,* was the unspoken end of the sentence by the leader. "They will see first how much they can save if they sell the shakes to themselves instead of buying from you."

But they would still be buying from Becca because Becca would always get a cut. And Leila and Salome. Possibly Opal Knox. The shakes probably cost the company a dollar to make, if that. The rest of the money poured into the upline from every sale.

"Hm." Becca made a polite noise.

"Then they will want to sell to their friends and get that profit for themselves," Foxy said.

"That's what I don't understand," Becca complained. "I'm making my customers into my competitors."

"The chances of you signing up any of their friends are slim. This way, you are bringing all these people into MyCo System, and you can oversee them all, even if it's not directly." The leader looked annoyed. The meeting was out of her control.

There was a flaw in her reasoning, but Becca couldn't explain it. Her stomach growled, out of habit more than hunger, she thought.

The presenter laughed and used that to change the subject and diffuse the tension. "Your tummy likes the Black Gill-Tea Pleasure drink? Have another!"

Becca added a black straw to her melting ice and more water from a metal pitcher rimmed with condensation. In went the red drops, tiny dark jellyfish sinking into a glass filled with galaxies. No one seemed to notice but her. She sucked on the straw, watching the galaxies reform, wondering if she was a mythological black hole in the glass's universe. Wasn't that some kind of trope, tiny universes being carried around in everyday objects? Crystals, glasses of water, and whatnot?

Her phone beeped. Leila was done with her third treatment.

She was in awful shape. They had bandaged her now-reduced buttocks. She could barely walk and had to lie across the back seat of the tiny car on her side, sobbing in pain, crying for the black drink with the black additive.

OPAL MAGAZINE ONLINE

MODEL LIFE: A Candid Interview with Supermodel Willow LeNoir (excerpt)

Opal Knox: You've never married or had a child. Do you have any regrets?

Willow LeNoir: Never is a long time! And currently, there's a remarkable man in my life. I wouldn't want to risk my figure or take a year off from modeling to give birth, but we have discussed adopting a child. But I've heard horror stories about the quality of children some people have adopted. It's like getting a used pet from a pyramid; you never know what kind of horrible beast you'll end up with. (Laughs) Or perhaps I'll consider some type of surrogacy.

Opal: You had planned to adopt a child at the beginning of your career, hadn't you? You were going to raise the child with your mother, your manager at the time.

Willow: (Laughs) That wasn't me! I have no adopted child.

CHAPTER TWENTY-THREE

"The Black Chair experience didn't seem right to me. It was intrusive and creepy. I think they drugged me. What happened to you when you sat in that Black Chair?"

Leila shrugged as best she could. Her breathing seemed constricted; the bandages across her hips twisted her torso forward into an awkward slump. "It was just a chair. I sat in the darkness. I felt a little woozy. The table I lie on for my spot-reduction treatment is similar, and so is the pill I take beforehand. It's a drug, but it's not nefarious. Maybe your attitude going in influences what you experience."

"It was weird. When it was happening to me, everything seemed so real and crisp, and I had such firm ideas of what was going on, and now it's mostly all gone. Like when you wake up from a dream, and you're gonna remember it forever, but you still want to write it down, but you have to pee, and by the time you leave the bathroom, you've forgotten there was even a dream you wanted to write about."

"It didn't seem like that big of a deal for me, just dark. I sat for a while, disorientated from the sensory deprivation—"

"Yes! Sensory deprivation! I thought that too!"

"—and I sort of drifted off into my thoughts. It was pretty relaxing, though after a while I felt like I had a headache. Then the leader came to get me. I got my very first Rainbow Obsidian headscarf out of many—I picked an orange one—and had my first Black Gill-Tea Pleasure, and the headache disappeared." Leila lolled her head toward Becca. "I have a belt in a similar shade of purple I made for someone who never paid for it. You can have it. It will look nice with all the black you wear, plus the scarf." She inhaled deeply. "Can you go to the fabric store for me if I give you a list?"

"I don't have your eye for colors …"

"I'll order for pickup. Help me into the sewing room."

Becca remembered a new expansion for her favorite VR game was available only at the gaming store downtown. She considered stopping there, too.

She buckled the purple elastic belt around her broad waist. Her body kept its apple shape; no belt could change her to an hourglass, but combined with the headscarf, she looked nice enough for someone her size. She adjusted the scarf to cover the sore spot on her neck that had been plaguing her since her Black Chair experience.

Once Leila was face down on the couch with Nyx, the TV remote, and a black drink nearby, Becca set off to the gaming store. She was behind a few expansions in her game and, for once, could afford them all. Not eating saved a lot of money. Once she would have made a beeline for the pretzel cart outside the store, but now she barely glanced at it, although it smelled heavenly. She wondered if Salome's vape company made pretzel or bread-scented vapes. A nearby vape shop drew her eye, but Becca resisted. She enjoyed having lungs. Breathing in Salome's secondhand cloud was terrible enough.

People were feeding pretzel crumbs to squirrels and pigeons by the cart. Becca couldn't decide if that was a waste or not. Lucky rodents and birds, she decided as she entered the gaming store.

Becca grabbed the last box of the newest expansion and had to scrounge around to find the older two she had missed. She was bent over, broad ass in the air, going through a pile on the bottom shelf, when someone started laughing.

They aren't laughing at me. But she knew they were. She located the boxes she was searching for and had to brace herself to stand. Her vision swam. The laughter increased as she leaned on a shelf, clutching the three boxes to her ample chest with one hand and blinking.

"Who you buying those for, fatty?"

The teenage boy was tall, Ichabod-Crane thin, with a prominent Adam's apple and a blotchy skin condition flushing his cheeks red.

Becca breathed, staring at her feet.

"Why don't you take a walk instead of sitting on your fat ass playing games?"

"Excuse me," Becca muttered, and tried to push past him.

He planted himself in the center of the aisle. A blue-haired girl came up behind him and peered under his armpit at Becca.

"May I get by?" Becca looked at their sneakers.

"What's this fat lady doin' in our store?" the girl asked.

Becca could smell her breath from three feet away.

"Being fat in public," Ichabod answered. "With a snotty accent."

Becca tried to loop up another aisle, but they beat her to it and blocked that one too.

The girl showed Becca her yellowed, crooked teeth. No wonder her breath stank.

"If you move out of my way, I'll pay for my games and leave your sight."

"I think you'll buy us some games," Ichabod said in a fake British accent. "You got money to eat yourself fat."

"I don't think so." Becca held the boxes tighter.

Ichabod and Yellow Teeth advanced. Becca backed up. Her hip struck a shelf, and boxes tumbled off.

The clerk, a college student with pink hair and a lip ring, ran down the aisle, yelling at Becca. "Hey! Clean that up!"

Becca stared at him. Ichabod and Yellow Teeth fled.

"You made a mess; clean it up. Or I'll call security." He sneered.

Becca laboriously picked every game off the floor and replaced them haphazardly on the shelf. When she paid for her expansions, she felt no joy. She didn't think she would ever play them. They were spoiled now.

She walked two blocks toward the fabric store through the pedestrian mall. As she passed the pretzel cart again, a woman said, "Hey, is that a MyCo System scarf?"

Becca stopped and turned her head.

A chubby woman with brown hair holding a pretzel approached her. "Is it?"

"Um, yes, it is."

"You sell MyCo System?"

Becca nodded.

The woman glanced down at her pretzel and at the muffin top spilling over her jeans. "Well, I need some. I'm Evangeline. Can we talk?"

CHAPTER TWENTY-FOUR

During Leila's fourth treatment, Becca searched for her. She wanted to find out what the hell they were doing to her friend. Because she felt like they weren't just sucking the fat out of her—they were sucking out her life.

Leila appeared sicker and sicker. She canceled appointments with her nephrologist. Becca knew it was because the news would be bad, and Leila didn't want to hear it. Leila's face was hollow, her eyes surrounded by black. She scratched herself constantly. The red headscarf did an excellent job of hiding the turkey wattle under her neck.

Becca spotted a table of mixed headscarves by the stage and grabbed a dark blue one. Under the weird reddish lighting, it appeared black. She wrapped it around her head with zero style and walked past the stage as if she belonged back there. She kept going, eyes wide, dragging her right leg slightly, scanning. Her excuse would be she was searching for a bathroom. In reality, she was going up if she found stairs or, better yet, an elevator.

Backstage, the smell was more potent. Raw dirt and fertilizer, like driving by a farm on a muggy day, except she was inside on a fall day. Becca's knee screamed at her. For no other reason, she would like to lose weight to shut it up. She couldn't help limping.

It was darker back here. Not all the lights were on. Mostly unlabeled doors lined the outer walls. A few had numbers.

One read, *Stairs*.

She grasped the knob, figuring it would be locked.

It turned, cold under her fingers. A cloud of dirty odor rolled out, almost visible in its horridness. Becca gasped, trying not to choke, and waited for the air to clear before stepping inside.

The stairs inexplicably led down.

She hadn't known the pyramid had a basement. She thought about it. Leila never actually said she went upstairs for her treatments. Becca had assumed she did because it never occurred to her there could be a downstairs. The upstairs may have been for meetings, offices, and conference rooms. That meant treatments could be downstairs.

The dark, grungy concrete stairway had no exit sign, no emergency lighting. It seemed like a strange way to get to a medical setting. Especially as there were no stairs heading up to the higher floors from here.

Becca pulled out her phone and activated the flashlight, holding it with one hand and clutching the thin, dirty railing with the other. The metal was damp. Grit balled under her palm as she slid it along the railing step by step. She climbed down her usual way, one right foot at a time, unable to bear her full weight on moving, bending knees.

Becca didn't think Leila was down there, but kept going anyway in case she was wrong. How deep was the water table this close to the harbor? How deep would the stairs go? The air was damp as well as stinky. The basement couldn't be that extensive, not bigger than the footprint of the pyramid. Every twelve steps, the stairway rotated around a landing. The gritty steps lacked padded treads. Had she ever been in a filthier place?

On the next landing—the third? The fourth? Becca moved the scarf to cover her lower face. It didn't block the smell, but she hoped she wasn't breathing in particles of whatever fouled the air.

When the stairs ended, Becca stepped onto a stone or concrete floor covered by a scattered layer of dirt. She shined her phone's light into the gaping black entranceway. Stinky racks of soil stretched endlessly before her, studded with fungus and mushrooms. The rows went on forever to either side in the moisture-soaked air and dim light. This must be one of MyCo System's mushroom farms. That made more sense than a medical wing.

Far away was a strange greenish light. Becca moved toward it to get a better look. The light had motion in it. If it was a worker, they'd catch her. Her "I'm looking for a bathroom" story wouldn't hold up. She was sixty or more steps down. She had to have known there wouldn't be a public restroom here. This was snooping. It was exactly like her favorite VR game, but in real life.

If she were in a movie, something terrible would happen to her now. Becca was alone in a place she shouldn't be, and it was very dark. But she was an experienced video game player, and there were no other players to come along and mess up what she was doing. She had this, whatever it was. It was her quest.

The aisles were too narrow for her wide body, and her knee was screaming from the stairs. She would have to climb back up all those concrete steps, which would be even worse. If only she had her slim game-character body.

She moved closer to the green light and the shifting movement. The smell had hints of ammonia. Someone cleaning an empty mushroom bed, perhaps? She could just say she had gotten lost. The door had locked behind her.

What if it actually had? Oh, gods. Calm down.

If Leila messaged her, it wouldn't come through. She was too far underground. Whatever Becca was going to do, she'd better do it fast.

Becca grabbed a wooden rack and leaned, taking the weight off her knee, eyes on the greenish glow. She tried to remember if a person could die from inhaling ammonia. The odor was powerful.

She pushed forward. She was getting accustomed to the low brown notes of the mushrooms and their substrate; it was the same as upstairs, just stronger. The high ammonia scent dominated the air. Another smell crept in, one she associated with handmade soap. Her grand-mère had been into artisanal soap for a while. This smelled like inferior cheap soap. Becca shook her head and snorted into the scarf, huffing to get the burning from her nostrils.

"I should go," she whispered. She checked the phone screen for the time but couldn't remember when she had begun exploring. Leila's procedure would finish soon. How long would it take Becca to climb sixty stairs? Were there sixty stairs? Or more? She hadn't counted. There could be seventy-two. Eighty-four.

The green light and movement were right ahead. Becca would have to do all this over again to find out what was going on down here if she fled now, and just thinking about it, she groaned inwardly. She physically couldn't get Leila down here with her. Leila was too weak, and admitting that was upsetting.

The shelves of mushrooms seemed to end at a central atrium, which, by her calculations, was nowhere near the pyramid's base. Maybe they were under the harbor or the highway? The twisting stairs had discombobulated her. She didn't have a compass app on her phone or the signal to download one, and her GPS app couldn't lock onto a satellite from underground.

Becca stopped at the aisle's end and gazed into the atrium. She didn't understand what she was seeing.

The stone floor was scooped, or melted, into immense, irregular pools, and in them lazed big blobs of … something. Giant fungus. Storage for colossal mushroom caps? But even in the terrible light, Becca could tell the things were moving.

She snapped her wrist to shut off the phone's flashlight. The weird green glow emanated from overhead. Luminescent fungi. Was this a natural cave MyCo System had found and built their pyramid over? It had to be well underneath property belonging to other businesses. She could be standing underneath the diner for all she knew.

She studied the mushroom caps, wafting the smell of rotten soap and ammonia as they shifted. Tentacle-like things formed and flattened from their flesh.

One cap moved forward, heaving a wave of itself toward her. An eye formed. She ducked back into the row. Had the eye seen her? She couldn't tell through the shelves of mushrooms. Holding the frame, she eased toward the floor, her knees creaking and screaming in protest. If those things could make eyes, they might be able to make ears and hear her joints. She pulled the dark blue headscarf higher across her face, except for her eyes, and peeped.

The mobile mushroom blob slid from the rock pool and undulated in her direction. Eyestalks formed and dissolved along the front edge as it searched for her. The eyes it created were disturbingly human-looking. The thing was huge, at least twice as large as Becca. It didn't crawl like a slug; its motion was more rolling. Its front end constantly formed tentacles and eye stalks that searched for a way forward and pulled it along. For a fungus, it moved fast.

Becca backed away. This was too much like her video game. However, she didn't have her thin, robust, flexible video-game body. She had her fat, clumsy, easily hurt one that barely fit down the rows. She had no extra lives and no magic potions to drink. She couldn't respawn fully healed out in the parking lot if this went badly.

Keeping her shoes flat on the dirty, uneven stone floor, she slid her feet backward, holding the rack. The fungus monster rolled toward her, flowing its bulk into the narrow passage between the racks. It seemed ancient and implacable. The other mushrooms made long eye stalks and pointed them in her direction. She was a reality show for fungi. One was enormous, the size of a military SUV or small tank. It seemed content to watch from the wet pool. Two or three other ones, about the size of her pursuer, were smooshed together in a single pool. Perhaps they were the children of the big one.

She slid back a few more steps. The mushroom followed. She banged painfully into the sharp edge of a shelf, hearing her shirt tear and feeling the coldness that meant she was bleeding. How many steps had she walked from the stairs? She had no idea. If this was her game, she would have all kinds of information in her heads-up display. In real life, nothing.

Her shirt tore further as she backed up again, leaving a piece of cloth behind. Great. The strap of her messenger bag caught and almost choked her. As she disentangled herself, trying not to drop her phone, the mushroom creature crawled closer, squelching wetly, a big living spore-sponge.

The leading edge was almost close enough for Becca to touch. The thing had the texture of a mushroom, meaty and vegetable-like, with the flexibility of an octopus. It was the kind of creature that would stalk her in her video game, but this was real, and it was going to get her.

Becca backed up again. In the dim green light, the ripped piece of her shirt flapped on the shelf. She was hyperventilating. Her vision was graying. This would be a terrible place to faint. The scarf was too tight across her nose and mouth. She didn't want to breathe the unfiltered air this thing was exhaling. It was breathing, wasn't it? There seemed to be a regular heaving pulse along the underside of the cap, where the gills were. Gills, how ironic, Becca thought.

A few more steps. The mushroom ball was almost even with her torn shirt. One of its tentacles touched the small piece of cloth, while a beautiful blue eye with long lashes watched Becca inch away. As the tentacle examined the cloth, the eye widened at Becca. Without a face, she couldn't really read its expression, but it seemed amazed. The eye blinked and turned into a wide, sharp-toothed mouth that called "li-li-li!"

The tentacle stuffed the cloth into the screaming mouth. Another mouth formed and fastened onto the shelf where the fabric had caught. The mushroom focused all its attention there and seemed to forget about Becca.

Becca raised her phone and triggered the camera a few times. The shutter noise seemed very loud. Becca backed away from the green fungus light and the octopus-armed mushroom. As the harsh ammonia scent faded, she hobbled as quickly as she could back down the row. Fifty stairs, seventy-five, however many. She had to get to Leila and tell her what was in the pyramid's basement.

CHAPTER TWENTY-FIVE

Leila, surrounded by ice packs on the emerald couch, was in no mood for conversation. "You left me waiting!" she moaned. "You know how much I hurt afterward."

The spot-reduction treatment had flensed her upper back.

Becca's back had heft to it. Leila's hadn't.

Leila lay face down, head to one side. Nyx sat on the couch arm, green eyes huge, in gargoyle mode.

"I'll get your drink, but you need to listen to why I was late. It's important."

Becca mixed two perfect double black drinks, one with red drops and one with fizzy black. She delivered Leila's to her mouth, holding the straw so her friend could drink the healing concoction. The black cat eyed her owner's glass.

"No, Nyx, not for you. I'll give you gooshy wet food in a minute."

When Lila turned her head, Becca sucked her own drink dry and pulled over the sapphire ottoman.

"I snuck into the pyramid's basement." She held her fingers to Nyx.

Nyx sniffed, lips pulled back to expose her teeth. She was absolutely a gargoyle in a cat's body.

"What are you talking about? The pyramid doesn't have a basement. It's built on a slab. I drove by when they started building it. I hoped it was gonna be an Anubis temple. We need one. The Temple of Bast is overwhelmed."

"Really, Lee, there's a basement. I was searching for the stairs to find you. So I could sit with you during your treatment."

Leila patted her head. “That’s not allowed. You’re too sweet.”

“I wandered behind the stage and acted like I wanted to find the bathroom. I found a door marked stairs, but they led down. So, I went down.”

“I’m delighted you want to entertain me with silly stories. Drink?”

Becca held the straw to Leila’s lips and explained the long twisting staircase, the lack of emergency signs, the mushroom farm.

“You believe they are growing the mushrooms right there for all the drinks? There wouldn’t be enough room.”

“The ‘room’ underneath,” finger quotes, “—it was a cave. No, a cavern. Gigantic. Way bigger than the pyramid. And in the center, there were these things.” Becca paused as Leila stopped drinking and started moaning.

“Do we have more ice?”

“I can put ice into plastic bags from the fridge dispenser.” Becca rinsed her empty glass, filled a plastic bag with ice for Leila’s back, and wrapped it in a cloth. She stroked her friend’s bandaged back gently with the ice bag as she continued her story. “There were these things, like giant mushroom caps. But moving. They sent out these tentacles. Some had eyes on them. Or a mouth.”

“Don’t make me laugh, Beck; it hurts too much.”

“I took pictures! Wait!” Becca fumbled one-handed for her phone, rubbing ice on Leila with the other. When she unlocked the phone and navigated to the photo roll, she saw darkness with green blurs. She left the ice bag on Leila’s back and used both hands to enlarge the blur where the mushroom-octopus thing should have been, but everything was still blurry. She showed Leila. “They didn’t come out. Bad lighting.”

“Good try. My back is so cold. Can you move the ice?”

Becca rubbed the ice. It grated on the bones in Leila's back, even through the swelling and bandages.

"They are going to do my legs next," Leila said, groaning. "Then I guess I'm done. But they were weird about it. Like, once I'm done, I need a replacement? You better get to leveling people up."

"What do you mean, a replacement?"

"I don't know." Leila sounded fretful. "That knockout drug really messes with my head. I thought they were joking, but it's like I have to ensure a supply of fat or something."

"What? That's gotta be a joke. You probably misunderstood while you were out of it. They just want you to level people up to Red Diamond by incentivizing the spot reduction treatment." Ugh, the marketing jargon that fell from her mouth sometimes.

Leila reached for her glass, and Becca held it to her lips. "I have a lot of fat I'm willing to donate to whatever cause. They are the ones who say I have to do it on their schedule."

"Hmm." Leila finished the drink. Nyx climbed onto her back, and Leila yelled. Becca moved to scoop the cat off, but Leila went from being tense to relaxed as the cat sprawled across the length of Leila's back. "Maybe she is trying to heal me. As long as she doesn't use her claws, let her stay."

"I'm going to bed now. Yell or message me if you need me." Becca put Leila's phone near her hand and removed the empty glass.

CHAPTER TWENTY-SIX

No internet research turned up any giant mushroom creatures that smelled like ammonia and bad soap and moved like octopuses, not that existed in reality.

Becca found plenty of similar beasts in fiction and myth. Horror writer HP Lovecraft's shoggoths, for instance, and it surprised her to find a creature called xoggotli[2] in Mesoamerican mythology that seemed similar, though smaller. Maybe Lovecraft had based his fiction on the Native myth. The shoggoths seemed too different from what she had seen, though. Since overzealous Christians had destroyed much of the records of ancient Mexico, there were few contemporary mentions of xoggotli. Historians had only translated a few primary sources, from their native languages and hieroglyphics, into Spanish, which she didn't speak. AI translations were less than helpful.

From the rough translations, she figured out the basics: Something came from space in a rock. A protoplasmic something. It could transform briefly into anything else and was also capable of mind control. But the xoggotli didn't seem like fungus creatures; they appeared to be more plant-like. Becca was positive the indolent blobs under the black pyramid had been mobile and semi-intelligent fungus. Fungus-based xoggotli.

Fuggotli, she thought.

---

[2]*Encounter a xoggotli in* Formless, *the second Mickey Crow adventure, or* Murder One, *the Mickey Crow omnibus, available on Amazon.*

Fungus shoggoths. That could mind-control people. That stunk of ammonia and cheap soap.

Becca thought about cheap soap. Soap was made of two things: lye and rendered fat.

Excerpt from:
ORIGIN STORY: MYCO SYSTEM.
UNAUTHORIZED
Source: The Industrial Secrets Site, where companies come to die.

… Missy, wife of Milo Cobalt, founder of MyCo System, explained her brother Kelvin smuggled the dark-red liquid from the sarcophagus at the archeological dig and brought the samples to Unieda Corporation, a private lab she knew of from her many MLM direct-sales gigs.

After seeing the liquid up close, Missy says it was as if a voice spoke in her head, and Kelvin felt the same way …

Most of the archeologists agreed the red liquid wasn't at all mysterious; liquefied human remains, perhaps with adipocere (also known as corpse wax), mixed with groundwater from microscopic cracks in the red stone.

The siblings felt differently about the liquid. Their story becomes unclear here. Unieda Corporation claims they lost the untested red sarcophagus samples during an incident where several of their biological specimens escaped, killing several employees and causing a fire. Missy insists she locked Unieda's test results in an industrial safe.

Based on these findings, whether real or imagined, Missy and Kelvin prevailed upon Milo Cobalt to found MyCo System, a direct-sales company to help people lose weight through proprietary drinks and supplements. The voices in her head directed her to do this, Missy claimed. Later on, Milo also claimed to have heard the voices. Kelvin left his wife and family to move in with Missy and Milo to help run MyCo System.

No one has seen Kelvin in public in some time, including his wife and children. He didn't respond to our interview requests.

The family started small, with a single mushroom farm. Some claim they fed the fungus with unique extracts derived from the red liquid. This happened at the same time as the *#drinktheredjuice* social media frenzy, and there's a possibility they may have spawned that hashtag themselves for publicity. Later on, the Cobalts built their first pyramid headquarters and moved all manufacturing there, along with the farming operation for mushrooms and other fungi, some of which appear to be rare and even unknown types many mycologists would give their eyeteeth to study. But they remain proprietary, patented strains.

Neither the Pharmaceutical Industry Oversight Administration (PIOA) nor the Department of Agriculture and Food (DAF) have approved any of their products for human consumption. Since MyCo System markets their products as supplements, not medicine, there is no agency oversight. The products are also not food, although the company's salespeople, aka Body Management Consultants, appear to subsist entirely upon them.

Kelvin left his archeology position when he joined MyCo System. Kelvin's former employer, Compass University North, refuses to comment on him. Perhaps the university fired him. There were allegations of theft, misconduct, and even talk of experimenting on humans, which is highly unusual for archeology, not to mention scientific ethics.

The MyCo System products started small and local soon became an enormous hit with social media influencers …

CHAPTER TWENTY-SEVEN

The ringtone of Leila's phone woke Becca, and she limped barefoot into the living room over the warmed floor. The phone, tossed aside, showed a missed call from the kidney doctor. Nyx was curled up on Leila's back. Leila was sleeping so deeply she might as well have been unconscious.

Becca fed Apep, watched him eat, and mixed herself a black drink. She plunked in Becca's chair and unfolded her laptop to visit the MyCo System website. On the site, everyone was full of praise; the same crap she heard at meetings. Delicious shakes, weight loss, improved health, earning opportunities. The shakes were mutagenetic, epigenetic, counteracting an obesogenic environment, nutraceutical, bioceutical, all the excellent health buzzwords that doubled as hashtags. Before-and-after pictures. Opal's face and newly slim body were everywhere, her hands filled with the three flavors of shakes. As if Opal Knox had ever drunk a lowly brown shake to lose weight.

Becca moved to a search engine that didn't track people and looked up what others said, people who weren't MyCo System Body Management Consultants. She had done some of this before on her phone, but this was a deeper dive. She even tried to find information on the black drink. Nothing seemed accurate. Nobody mentioned galaxies. People postulated the black drink was an exceptionally strong version of the brown shake, perhaps dark chocolate instead of milk chocolate. It was far from the truth.

Although the company's product sheet listed both Red Gill-Tea and Black, Becca knew little about it, although she wondered if the red drops were similar. The only red drink she found related to the Red Sarcophagus was from when the hashtag *#drinktheredjuice* had been circulating. That search eventually led her to an unauthorized MyCo System origin story on an industrial secrets site.

Becca was drinking the red mummy juice, she just knew it. The spores from the sarcophagus grew the unique fungi that went into the supplements. Mixed with microplastics. That was it.

Becca gagged. Corpse juice. Human bones, liquified human flesh, and human fat were mixed in that juice. MyCo System had made her into a cannibal. Gross.

The behavior of Milo Cobalt, Missy, and Kelvin reminded her of something. There was a fungus that caused infected ants to crawl up grass stems to get eaten by birds. Maybe the red mummy juice infiltrated their brains the same way. The voices Milo, Missy and Kelvin claimed to hear could be the controlling fungus.

Could fungus control humans—any mammals—that way?

Becca resumed her research. Nyx left Leila and curled against Becca's leg.

The zombie fungus couldn't control humans, only insects. Becca waved that aside. The closest thing she could discover in humans was toxoplasmosis, which some researchers believed infected almost every cat owner. It perhaps made a person more susceptible to liking and owning cats, but it didn't control them. It didn't make a person into a robot governed by cats.

While Leila and Becca adored the spoiled Sphynx , Nyx certainly did not control the house, or she would have eaten Apep by now.

If this whole fungal enterprise was being run by a temple of Bast or Anubis, or another animal god, it would make more sense. But it wasn't. Even the pyramid shape made no sense.

Toxoplasmosis is a parasite and not a fungus, Becca found. Still, the same concept of being infected by a foreign body that controls you to that foreign body's benefit. Or a third party, like cats. But actually, so toxoplasmosis could move between humans and cats.

Was MyCo System run by fungus zombies?

She checked on Leila, who might have been sleeping too soundly. Becca drank another black drink standing in the kitchen. She inspected her Red Fun Gi-Up drops. They probably had extra-concentrated mummy juice in them.

Becca brought a black drink, mostly crushed ice, to Leila and left it by her. Nyx slept, sprawled on Leila's narrow bony back, naked black flesh on bandages. Becca had thought hairless Sphynx cats, although by far the most popular cat breed, were creepy before she met Nyx, but she found Nyx's skin unbelievably soft and warm. Nyx needed baths, but the cat loved them. She ran a hand over Nyx's sleeping, hot body, and the cat made a purring grunt and curled her front paws without waking.

Becca poked her own belly. It hadn't gone down. She hadn't lost weight. Her stomach had changed consistency, though. It was softer, looser. She could pull her pants tighter. She could lace the purple corset belt's edges closer together than ever before. Pretty soon, she wouldn't need the modesty panel under the laces.

In her bedroom, she unbuttoned the fitness tracker and plugged it in to charge, then stood on her scale. Still the same weight. It made no sense.

She researched what it meant when your fat became super squishy, but you weighed the same. She found nothing.

On the private MyCo System Body Management Partner message boards, she logged on to the Rainbow Obsidian channel. Everyone ranted about great their sales were, how much weight loss they and their customers had achieved, how they were looking forward to the next meeting, how they were signing up people to sell, and couldn't wait to move up to Red Diamond. No one said anything negative about anything.

But eighty-twenty, Salome had implied. Only twenty percent leveled up. So, either everyone was lying, or only twenty percent of Rainbow Obsidian Body Management Partners posted on this board. Perhaps all those failing and wanting to quit weren't on the board, or admins had booted them. She searched for "failing" and "leave" but found nothing, same with "quit" or "get out."

On a whim, she searched for "shoggoth," "monster," and "basement."

Her connection to the message board failed. Just like that.

When she tried to log back in, she got an error, a problem with her credentials. She wasn't allowed access to the message boards.

She went to a different channel and logged in to check her sales, and the same credentials worked just fine.

Well. Becca was forbidden from trying to find out what the monsters in the pyramid basement were.

Becca started a private metered connection, one she could thankfully now afford, and downloaded a dark-web browser with a built-in private search engine. She started a deep dive into whether there were real-life shoggoths or xoggotli made of mushrooms.

What she found was pure science fiction or fantasy. Nothing like an actual living, sentient blob.

Well, except for actual fungus. The largest living creature on the planet was a fungus. But it wasn't sentient, not how the blobby stinking things in the pyramid's basement seemed to be.

Becca had never heard of any fungus that could spontaneously grow and retract limbs. Some fungi looked like penises and bloody fingers and other crazy things, but that was their fixed shape. They couldn't make that shape and then unmake it how the fuggotli in the basement had made eyes and limbs.

These basement monsters were advanced fungi.

Could they be aliens?

Becca returned to the Native stories. She tried to find out anything more about the red box that had spent so much time under the bottom of the reservoir, and the Desert Bloom tribe who abandoned the place, why they might have left and cursed the valley. A meteor was how she interpreted the story. A rock fell into the valley where the Desert Bloom lived happily. Then people started acting crazy, and others got sick and shriveled up.

Becca looked at Leila.

People had heard voices in their heads.

People had strange marks on their bodies.

It was unclear if the same things had happened to the same people. Did some hear voices, some have marks, others get shriveled up, while others acted crazy, got sick, and died? There was a reproduction of a sacred hide with drawings detailing that terrible time, an illustration of a picture. The person doing the sketch of the hide obviously hadn't understood the symbols. It was like someone copying a computer printout with many fonts without understanding different fonts and slightly different shapes represented the same letters and words. Without speaking the language or knowing the alphabet. Or knowing any alphabet. And what she was looking at online was an uploaded scan of a photocopy of a poor photo of the bad drawing of the original hide.

In considerable detail, the original drawing could have shown how to create gold from lead, and Becca wouldn't be able to follow it. *Creating Gold from Lead 101* on a bison hide. Making gold from dirt.

She scrunched her fingers together and apart to zoom, but the images were poor resolution. That was a blob, sure, but in the original, it could have been an ostrich. And those things sprinkled around could have been mushrooms or poorly drawn lollipop-shaped trees. Maybe that was a mammoth or a pyramid with an anaconda. There was no way to know. A museum fire destroyed the original bison hide long ago. The only thing anyone could have ever figured out from these terrible reproductions was that a meteorite struck the area.

Radiation poisoning? Becca knew nothing about the subject, but none of the symptoms seemed right. Maybe the getting sick, losing weight, and dying part. Not the hearing voices or the going insane part.

She stared at Leila. Leila didn't have radiation poisoning. It made people's teeth and hair fall out. And didn't people throw up? Leila never vomited that Becca knew of, but she always scratched herself and smelled bad around her leaky bandages. Becca had only puked that time she had eaten at Poppa's. Her mouth watered, remembering delicious pizza from the past.

The upshot of the sacred bison-hide story, as far as Becca could discern, was that something had fallen from space. People had gotten variously sick in body and mind, or both. The Natives had imprisoned a body or bodies in the red box, sealed it, and buried it. And then they had utterly abandoned the area, although it had been a pleasant valley. When the white men arrived, the Desert Bloom people told them not to live there, although they hadn't remembered who cursed the area and why, and it ended up being ideally situated to be dammed up for a reservoir.

Or had a voice in someone's head somehow suggested that too?

Just how sealed had that red box been? If the juice inside had been super concentrated and slowly leaking out into the water for a hundred years …

From SeenIt s/anti-MLM

Has anyone heard these rumors about some kind of weird liposuction that people are getting at higher levels of MyCo System? Because allegedly, a few people have gone in for this lipo and died. Not many people, but any number of people dying from a fucking MLM are too many. I'm trying to verify if this is just a rumor. Everyone heard it happened at a different pyramid, never the one they go to. Is this real? It's bad enough these places prey on people, lie to them, and cause them to go broke, and, with MyCo System, ruin their health. Now that they are dying, it makes it much worse.

~~The most I can say is, yes, some people associated with MyCo System have died, and they have been upper level, and it's been hushed up. It's not like they died in a car accident or something. Supposedly, they died in one of the pyramids, getting liposuction. And it's not like these pyramids are licensed medical facilities where people should get procedures done. The families know they died, and I don't know what the families are told or if there is any compensation. Do the families keep getting the money from the downlines the dead people built, I wonder, like a consolation prize? I'm glad you brought this up because I heard this from a friend who was in MyCo System and trying to quit. It is difficult to get out of selling and drinking this utter crap.

~~This is crazy. This is an MLM that is killing people? How can it still be in business?

~~Is there a place we can report this to?

~~~Report what? You have details of deaths and proof that MyCo System was involved?

~~Does anyone actually know of anyone who has broken away from MyCo System successfully who we can talk to? Can we do an AA (ask anything) with them?

~~~I have never heard of anyone getting away from MyCo System except by not joining in the first place.

CHAPTER TWENTY-EIGHT

Becca's phone beeped with the ringtone set up for orders. She rolled over. Nyx made an indignant noise at being squashed.

"What are you doing in my bed instead of with Leila?" She stroked the cat's downy flesh. Nyx purred, grunted, and headbutted Becca. "Is Leila okay?" The cat curled into a fold of the blanket. "I guess you like me now?"

Becca pushed herself upright and swung her swollen legs toward the heated floor. She adjusted the sweatpants jammed into her crotch and the t-shirt twisted around her armpits. The cat was already fast asleep, a black velvet ball. She hoped Leila wouldn't mind.

Becca headed for the bathroom and flicked on the light switch. When she had relieved her full bladder, she ran cold water in the sink and splashed her face. Her image looked back at her from the mirror, puffy cheeks and double chin, same as always. At least the mark on her neck was healing.

Becca checked on Leila, who was propped up on the couch, leaning on one elbow, face knotted.

"Your kitty is in my bed. You need the bathroom?"

They took care of that, which wasn't easy or fun. Leila appeared bony; her color washed out. "Why don't you call the kidney doctor back?" Becca suggested, settling her friend on the couch. "After breakfast. He'll be happy you lost weight. He can rerun your numbers."

"I'm afraid," Leila confessed, scratching her neck. "I think I'm sicker, even though I'm thinner."

Becca fed Apep and added fresh water to his tank. He needed a water change. She made black drinks and counted out pills.

Leila looked terrible. But if it had been her obesity causing all her medical problems, shouldn't her doctor be happy? All the custom MyCo System supplements Leila was taking were alleged to include kidney support. Leila had gotten approval from the nephrologist for those supplements, right? Of course she had. Becca pushed away the nagging voice whispering Leila had not.

That same voice insinuated the pills were just sugar pills and poison microplastic with a side of dried mummy.

Doctors were obsessed with their patients' weight once it exceeded a certain BMI, like with Becca and Leila. Leila's weight was way down. Why wouldn't Leila just call him with the good news?

Becca put Leila's morning supplements in a dish and brought them with her shake, handing her one capsule at a time and helping her wash it down with a sip of black drink. Becca's stomach growled. When Leila finished, Becca washed the dish and glass and brought her own Black Gill-Tea and pills into the big chair.

"Why do you think you're sicker?"

"I hurt all over." Leila hugged herself and then scratched her neck. The sore wasn't healing. "I didn't know the spot reduction would be so broad, would be done on my whole body so quickly."

"I think you should skip the spot reduction for a while. You don't need it anymore."

Leila's eyes widened. She looked old with no makeup. Her naked brown eyes were small and tired, ringed with dark bruises. "I can't stop once I start."

"What do you mean, you can't stop? Say you don't feel well and can't come to the next meeting. I'll go alone and tell them you're sick."

Leila shook her head. "That's not how it works. You don't understand yet. Once you level up and start your LipoGest treatments, you will understand. And honestly, I hope that's soon." Her words had a strange intensity.

Becca frowned. "It sounds like you're saying you can stop your treatments when I start. Like I would take your place."

The rotting soap smell of the mushroom creatures in the basement wafted through her memory.

Leila's mouth trembled on the edge of a smile. "That would be silly. How would that work? Don't think that way. Can you hand me my tablet? I want to get back to making corset belts now that you've brought all that material from the store. Maybe you can help? I have fabric and embellishments to sort, and requests for custom belts coming in, thanks to Opal."

Leila had put her mukbang channel in vacation mode. Her biggest fans were still sending her money and frantic private messages, enticing her to return, trying to figure out why she had "temporarily" stopped doing her profitable food binging. She still posted messages, telling her fans she hadn't forgotten them and would be back as soon as her personal emergency was over. She put up pay-per-view outtakes of previous mukbangs, but that didn't bring in the income of fresh new ones or of eating live on demand.

Luckily, Leila made decent money selling MyCo System and corsets, and had few ongoing expenses. She had paid off the car and the condo. Eating until she was enormous had financed a good lifestyle.

"Oh, that reminds me, I had a sale or something. My mobile dinged. It woke me up. I almost squished Nyx because I didn't know she was in my bed." Becca returned to her bedroom, enjoying the warm floors under her wide, bare feet. The cat was still there, curled into a tiny ball, half under the blanket. She grabbed her phone from the charging dock and retreated to the living room, plopping in the overstuffed, oversized recliner perfect for Leila but a bit much for her, designed for a tall person, not a broad one. If only Becca were made of taffy, someone could stretch her to Leila's height.

She would still be fat.

She checked the MyCo System private message channel and saw a post from Evangeline, the pretzel lady.

Hi Becca, I've been thinking. I'm doing great with my weight loss. I want to sign up to sell the shakes. I have many friends in other cities, so I wouldn't be butting into your territory. Of course, I would ask my friends here in Newhaven who already buy from you to continue buying from you and not switch to me, if that's what you want. Some of my friends want to sell in those other places. We could get our own little group going.

Becca stared at the chat.

"Who's it from?" Leila asked, fingers busy on her tablet. "Big order?"

"Remember Evangeline, the woman I met when I went to the fabric store? She recognized my headscarf and started buying MyCo System from me on the spot." Becca's lips went numb. "She wants to become a Rainbow Obsidian; she already has friends who will sign up under her in other cities."

Leila stared. "Seriously?" Her thin-lashed eyes widened.

"Seriously. I could be a Red Diamond soon!"

CHAPTER TWENTY-NINE

Evangeline moved fast. By the next meeting, she had leveled up to Rainbow Obsidian and was sipping on a green shake in the auditorium. Leila didn't attend, and Salome stormed up to Becca, demanding to know where Leila was, glaring, breathing vapor like an angry dragon.

"She isn't answering my messages." Salome snorted steam into Becca's face.

Becca adjusted her purple headscarf to block the cloud and cover the sore on her neck. "She's sick. She said to tell you that."

"I had scheduled her tonight for a LipoGest treatment." A vapor cloud momentarily obscured Salome's wide, panicked eyes. She raised one hand to her narrow waist and pinched at it frantically. "Someone else will have to take her place."

Becca cocked her head. She had plenty of fat but wasn't volunteering for anything that would help Salome. Plus, she wasn't a Red Diamond, although she wanted to know what happened at these strange fat-reduction treatments everyone wanted so badly. Including Leila, who also dreaded them.

Becca shrugged. "I can barely get Leila from the couch to the bathroom. I'm not dragging her out to the car and to this meeting, and you can't make her have some weird medical treatment without a doctor's supervision."

"Doctor Lee supervises." The vapor du jour smelled like cotton candy, sickeningly sweet.

"Doctor Lee?" Becca scoffed. Doctor Lee was obviously some sort of supervillain. He was even growing a goatee. Becca was almost positive he lived in the pyramid and never left it. He sold blood tests through video meetings; how creepy was that? He was the lab work equivalent of a pill mill. Not someone who inspired trust. If Dr. Lee had prescribed anything besides the non-pharmaceutical sugar and microplastic pills, Becca would suspect him of sampling the goods. As it was, she wasn't sure if he partook of the shakes and drinks, but he was undoubtedly complicit in whatever weirdness was happening.

"Anyway, I must get back to my Rainbow Obsidian meeting. Good luck with finding someone for the treatment." Becca headed up to the boring meeting. She wasn't cut out for selling. She enjoyed making sales materials look good, laying out web pages and print materials, but pushing someone to buy something, ugh. That was boring. And these meetings were all the same, endless pep talks.

We are BOSS BABES (and the occasional boss bro). MyCo System has freed you from your awful nine-to-five job. We work on our phones, from anywhere, making UNLIMITED MONEY! MyCo System allows us to LOSE WEIGHT and help everyone else lose weight too! Everyone we encounter needs better health, and it's our responsibility to help them get better health. Obesity might limit opportunity in almost every way, but not in MyCo System! You are the living inspiration. Proof MyCo System works! Help everyone fight fat discrimination while getting thin!

Becca heard the truth underneath: *If you don't offer people better health, you're a monster! Don't be a monster! Help keep fat people from being discriminated against! Help fat people become thin!* Because you can't discriminate against what isn't there. Becca's head ached from listening to the leader talk in exclamation points and capital letters.

She wondered how Evangeline was doing with her introductory meeting and the Black Chair.

The leader gushed over unveiling more new flavors, orange and grape, as well as mint.

Becca snorted.

Next on the agenda: auto-shipments. Everyone thought that was the best idea ever. No one gave Becca any credit. She sniffed but was okay with being ignored.

The mysterious gray-scarf people had taken Becca's ideas seriously. MyCo System would roll out new drink flavors once per month for the next three months. Auto-ship and auto-billing would begin sooner; everyone was to push it. Customers tended not to cancel subscription products.

Becca sipped her black drink, a galaxy in every straw, as they talked about skin-fold-testing, how the Rainbow Obsidians could access it for themselves, but they couldn't offer it to others. If someone asked for it, take their information and get it to your upline immediately. Becca tried not to yawn.

Leila had gotten her testing tablet delivered, but she was too ill to use it. Becca needed to level up so she could do the testing for both of them. Too bad they couldn't share a tablet. Rules at MyCo System seemed idiotic.

The leader laid out a timeline for every Rainbow Obsidian to be tested by their uplines. Becca was on the list despite her previous testing. She didn't offer a correction.

"Upstairs in Red Diamond training, they are being given this same information," the group leader, a specially trained and quite plump Red Diamond, explained. The group leaders rotated so they didn't miss their own meetings. This one had introduced herself, but Becca had deliberately ignored her name.

"We want all Rainbow Obsidian Body Management Partners to be tested and to understand how the testing works, so when you level up, as some of you will, you will require less training." The leader touched her scarf.

Becca, bored, excused herself to use the restroom. In video game mode, she crept down the back stairs to the basement door. Legs burning, she lowered herself down the dozens of winding stairs to the mushroom farm, intent on getting clear photos of the giant mushroom creatures to show Leila. She would not let them see her this time, though. She wouldn't get pursued.

When she arrived at the bottom, legs quivering like noodles, she found a brand-new fire door, locked.

Glancing up, she noted a security camera above the door, blinking red. Becca wasn't capable of fleeing on her rubbery legs, but she did her best. Had someone seen her down there before? Did the creature somehow tell someone? Did they know it was her? At the top of the stairs, behind the door, aimed down the staircase, was another camera.

Now they knew it was Becca who had been creeping around in the basement.

Becca mixed with the crowd in the Quartz Auditorium, heart pounding. Would they come for her? What would happen to Leila, sick and alone?

But they did not come for her.

Dear Miss Becca Gifford:

Thank you for contacting us about Willow LeNoir. Having been Ms. LeNoir's solicitors for many years, we are well aware of your relationship with our client. However, we cannot divulge the contents of her private papers or beneficiaries of any wills or trusts.

We can verify you appear on the secondary list of people to contact if something unfortunate happens to Ms. LeNoir.

The secondary list contains those people we are to notify after the private funeral and reading of the will, but before the public service.

As per your request, we will forward your correspondence to Ms. LeNoir.

CHAPTER THIRTY

Becca threw away the fitness tracker and smashed the glass scale. No wonder she had gotten no money from her mum when she had hit eleven pounds lost.

That fucking bitch. Telling her solicitor not to notify Becca first if she died. Laughing in interviews about how she had no children and how adopting a child was like getting a horrible used pet.

She was heartbroken but not surprised.

Leila came from a large family—goofy family photos hung all over the walls—and while they didn't approve of some of her lifestyle choices, like the mukbanging (which she wasn't even doing anymore) and the BBBW escort stuff, they never shunned her. Leila couldn't understand what it was like to be alone.

Leila watched as Becca sobbed and hugged poor Nyx much too tightly. When she finished crying, Becca ordered a bigger tank for Apep with a mountain of plants and toys to put in it, along with a side of cat treats and catnip toys.

"You don't need anything I can buy you," Becca said to Leila. "So, I'm spoiling your cat."

Leila was still in pain and bandages from her last treatment. "I need you to help me," she said. "I'm glad you're here and delighted you're about to level up and join me in Red Diamond territory."

True to her word, Evangeline's friends progressed to Rainbow Obsidian in their separate towns, which lacked pyramids. They attended meetings by telepresence, except for their first Rainbow Obsidian meeting, where they had gone in person to the closest pyramid to undergo the Black Chair ritual.

"What did you think of the Black Chair?" Becca asked Evangeline, trying to be casual.

Evangeline shrugged. "Weird little meditation ritual. Made my neck hurt." She rubbed her throat through her new orange scarf. "But that Black Gill-Tea Pleasure drink—wow, that's delicious! I've already told all my friends they must level up and get it."

After Becca's red scarf presentation ceremony, Becca led Leila up two slow flights of stairs to the Red Diamond Balcony.

Leila kissed Becca's cheek. "Shine on, my crazy diamond," she whispered. "I'll be with you again soon." She headed to the main Red Diamond meeting, her shoulder against the wall for balance, steps measured and slow.

Becca watched her go, worried. Leila was skipping her spot-reduction treatment again; she had promised.

Becca entered the training room with another new Red Diamond, a bottom-heavy man named Mateo, shaped like a triangle, flesh dripping from his shoulders as if from a hanger. Becca thought she might have seen him once before. He wore his scarf like a bandana around his neck.

It annoyed her to discover Salome was training them.

"I know you're both excited to be Red Diamonds and to get your first LipoGest spot-reduction treatment." Salome blew a cloud of cherry-scented vapor. The sweet scent of her pen's exhalations did little to diffuse the deep, awful smell permeating the space.

Becca stared at the skinny dragon bitch. "Is that all Red Diamond is about? The spot treatment?" Salome moved stiffly. There appeared to be something bulky under her clothes around her waist. The realization hit. Salome had found no one to take Leila's place. Did this mean Salome had to do the LipoGest treatment? Becca didn't dare ask where they had found fat on her cadaverously thin body.

“That’s why most people want to advance to Red Diamond, yes. Even if they have lost some weight, the LipoGest spot-reduction treatment takes care of loose skin too. Have you ever priced liposuction or skin removal, Becca? You get it free here. That’s why people are clamoring to join MyCo System. Weight loss and body contouring. There is nothing else like it in the world.”

Becca cocked her head. “That’s how you got so thin, then?”

“Oh no, I’ve always been thin. But with middle age comes droopiness the spot reduction helps with.”

“So why join a weight-loss scheme if you’re naturally thin?”

Salome blinked slowly and expelled a large amount of cherry smoke. “For the money, of course, my dear. And because they begged me to jumpstart their new company from the top.”

“While everyone else claws their way up from the bottom?” Mateo asked. “Seems unfair.”

“That’s how direct sales works. At each level, only a few people move up.” Salome opened a wide-mouth black bottle on the sideboard and shook out two clear pills. “These are for your LipoGest spot-reduction treatments. They will help you relax. You might remember a similar pill from your initiation into the Rainbow Obsidian level. These are stronger.”

The pills were also bigger, with more rainbow bits inside. Salome turned away from Becca and Mateo and expertly mixed black drinks, adding black fizzy drops. She pushed the MyCo System branded glasses across the table. “Drink up, take your pills, and I’ll get you settled in your treatment rooms.”

Becca’s galaxy appeared different with the fizzy black drops. The darker flavor stuck to Becca’s tongue and coated her mouth. Large as the tip of her finger, the capsule choked her as she gagged it down, gulping the black drink to unstick it from her throat.

Next to her, Mateo also struggled with the giant pill. "Should have been a suppository," he joked, coughing.

Salome must have pushed a button because another red-scarfed person entered and brought Mateo into the hall. Of course, Salome would want to oversee Becca. The taste of black-drop-infused black drink flooded Becca's mouth, mixing unpleasantly with the cherry smoke and dirt scent. Feeling woozy, Becca swooned against the doorway as she exited into the hall.

Without sympathy, Salome put out her hand. "Careful. The pills are strong."

Luckily, the treatment room turned out to be only a few steps away. Becca wondered if Leila had ever been in this room. Salome had Becca lean back against a tilted table and secured her with straps across her ankles, thighs, chest, and wrists.

"I don't like bondage." It was supposed to be a joke, but it fell flat as Becca's words slurred.

"It's so you don't fall off."

The padded, wide table was covered with the same faux leather as the Black Chair, what Becca had decided was mushroom leather. The single ceiling light swirled and distorted as Salome operated a switch that tilted and lowered the table until Becca was lying almost flat.

"What happens? Do you suck the fat from me, or does Dr. Lee do it, or does someone else?" Becca was scared. The leather felt awful against her skin, but there was something else it reminded her of. She struggled to remember, her brain treacle-thick from the rainbow capsule.

Salome unbuckled the gorgeous red belt Leila had made her for tonight's induction ceremony; she put it on the shelf next to Becca's messenger bag. She pushed Becca's shirt to her chin, exposing her giant bra. She shoved at Becca's leggings and underpants, pushing them down until Becca felt uncomfortably exposed.

"I don't like this." She felt embarrassed about Salome seeing her lolling pale abdomen spreading across the table. It covered her pubic area, but it was an invasion to be restrained and have someone she disliked pulling her clothing off.

"Some of this will be gone soon," Salome grunted, pulling at the fat, moving it around, putting it on display. Her touch was impersonal, not sexual, but still a violation.

"I don't like this," Becca repeated, worried, but her voice was failing. The room wasn't sterile. Nothing was stainless steel, and what operating room had a leather table? The usual dirty funk hung in the air, not a trace of soap or disinfectant, just cherry vapor.

"Nothing not to like," Salome panted, arranging Becca's enormous gut. "Free liposuction. Best deal ever." The vape pen hung loosely from her lip, and for once, no clouds spewed from her mouth. Salome's brow was damp with sweat. She appeared unwell. "How is that pill treating you? Are you feeling it yet?"

"I don't—" Becca answered. "—know." Her brain was plodding, her eyes heavy. Odors hung thickly. Her mouth didn't close properly.

Salome stepped back and wiped her sweaty face on her shoulder, almost dislodging the vape. The cherry glow had gone out. She sucked in, but nothing happened. "Take a last look at your belly, Becca. Say bye-bye."

Becca tried to lift her heavy head. The sore on her neck hurt. "Bye-bye, Bella," she slurred. "Bella belly."

Salome snapped off the lights and retreated. The odors intensified.

Becca sank into the reclined table. The curved headrest embraced her face, forcing her mouth shut, holding her jaw in place, and squishing her cheeks against her eyes and nose, impeding her breathing. She remembered this now.

Everything was dark, like the paint that absorbed all light, the blackest of blacks. What was it called, black-hole paint? Her head would have fallen to the side if it could move. Her cheeks pinched her nostrils. When had her cheeks gotten so plump?

Not enough air was getting in, yet it seemed like a breeze blew across her exposed belly. She never understood the amount of sex Leila had. Becca didn't like to expose herself to anyone. Were there infrared cameras aimed at the quivering pale mass Salome had arranged like an offering between her bra and her yanked-down underpants? It felt obscene. The tight straps holding her to the table—for safety!—only emphasized how broad and floppy that fat belly was.

When would Dr. Lee come in and do the procedure? He would knock her unconscious first, surely.

Becca felt woozy but wide awake. Not numb, not one bit. The leather rubbed against her bare back. She felt both exposed and claustrophobic. The powerful scents of shit and dirt made her want to gag, but the headrest around her face meant if she vomited, she would choke.

"Hey," she tried to say, but the padding around her fat neck kept her from speaking up. However many chins she had all choked the life out of her. "Dr. Lee?"

Something touched her belly.

Someone. Not something. Someone, right?

"Dr. Lee?"

Had he been in the room all along, and she hadn't seen him? Why would he be standing in the dark?

She tried to say, "I'm scared. Can you turn on the light?" but only something garbled came out.

A hand stroked her belly. A sweaty, sticky hand, rather cold.

Becca sucked in her abdominal muscles but couldn't move her fat enough. The hand grabbed her skin, pushed it around. The headrest further constricted her face and neck. How was the headrest moving? It was even over the top of her head. She felt like a drowning person. Were her eyes closed? Only her nose was poking out of the headrest now. This big padded thing, eating her head and face, leathery and stinking. She choked and thought, *don't puke, don't puke*.

She vomited into her mouth.

A fat, dirty finger probed her mouth. Déjà vu, familiar and horrible. The finger sucked up her vomit like that tube at the dentist. That's what it was, a suction device, not a finger. A medical tool. It retracted when her mouth was clear.

The hand dug its fingers deep into her side. It hurt like a charley horse, a big cramp. The hand twisted. Becca sank deeper into the gross leather.

She was inside the table.

The hand yanked on the handful of fat.

She didn't believe this was Dr. Lee.

Becca yelled inside her leather prison that tasted of dirt and vomit. Mushroom leather? She thought of the lolling things in the basement. They were more than big enough to be made into leather.

The hand twisted again. Was it even a hand? She couldn't hear anyone else breathing. She couldn't speak. Something like an animal was burrowing into her side. This didn't seem like liposuction. She had seen lipo on TV. It was violent, with a small vacuum hose stuck under your skin, but she heard no machinery, and this didn't feel like a hose. And she shouldn't be awake. Did they forget to do the anesthesia?

Spot reduction. What did that really entail?

The metallic smell of blood joined the other awful odors. Becca felt the unique weirdness that signaled she was bleeding. It didn't hurt. The hand remained against her side. Perhaps, Dr. Lee had injected local anesthesia. Nice job with the painless needle, if so.

Why did this have to be done in the dark?

Her middle felt strange. She listed to the side like a deflated balloon. Becca was being emptied. Something was sucking out her fat. Couldn't important things like veins, arteries, and intestines be sucked out too? This seemed wrong. Why was she awake in the darkness? Wouldn't being asleep in the light be better? In a sterile operating room?

Leila had been through this four times and said nothing about how terrible the experience was. Becca must be doing something wrong. Perhaps she was supposed to be asleep? Maybe the pills weren't strong enough for her body weight? She tried to will herself to sleep. She inhaled through her crunched nose.

She imagined she could smell the cheap, fatty soap smell of the weird mushrooms in the basement, but here beside her. The stench didn't mix well with her blood or with the thick shitty dirt smell. Or was the smell dirty shit? Could shit get dirty?

Becca tried to picture herself with a smaller stomach. She would have to take it easy for a few days. At least Leila wasn't getting a treatment at the same time. They wouldn't have to figure out how to care for each other.

The hand moved from her belly.

Becca heard an out-of-place sound. It took her a while to realize what it was. It was like seeing the bank teller at the grocery store and not being able to figure out who they were.

The sound was so familiar: the slurping noise of sucking through a straw from an empty cup.

CHAPTER THIRTY-ONE

"What do you mean?" Becca, breathing heavily, stared at Leila's keys in her palm.

Salome blew vape smoke in her face. "I couldn't allow Leila to skip her LipoGest treatment. She's staying here tonight since she's not recovering well. Go home, and she'll see you tomorrow or the next day."

"Why can't I see her now?" And why had Leila allowed Salome to bully her into another treatment?

"Because you need to get home and recover. This is your first treatment, so we don't know how you'll be feeling when the pill wears off. It's better you go now while you can drive."

Becca wrapped her other arm across her smaller, lopsided middle. It ached. It hurt so bad her whole body was shaking. She didn't have words for the pain she was already in. She had expected Leila to drive. Now she had to go home alone.

"You are the last person still here tonight besides Leila, and she's asleep. Go home. She has her phone."

Becca made her way to the stairs in the pyramid's corner. Clutching the railing with one hand and her middle with the other, she limped down, right foot, right foot, right foot. It felt like someone was slicing her with razors under the elastic bandages. The leaky feeling wet feeling around the bandages happened, as if she was bleeding. Leila hadn't bled like this.

The edges of her vision rounded and darkened, and Becca sat in a padded folding chair by the stage and tried to breathe. Her face and neck were sore from being buckled in the padded headrest. Dark marks across her arms showed where the straps had been. The empty Quartz Auditorium seemed huge. She had to cross it and the parking lot to get to Leila's car. All while being invisibly stabbed.

She hauled herself to her feet, feeling the bruised strap marks across her thighs. Becca crept up the aisle, holding onto the chairs. Someone turned out the lights when she was almost at the door. She had to make the rest of her way by the orange emergency light.

When she finally climbed into Leila's car and adjusted the seat, she pulled up her shirt and studied the bandage, damp with blood. She was smaller. Spot reduction worked.

If only she could make it home without passing out.

CHAPTER THIRTY-TWO

Becca shouldn't have been driving, but she wanted to get home, and she didn’t want to leave Leila's car in the lot. Her sluggish body felt wrong, heavier, even though she was technically lighter. She wished she hadn’t smashed the scale, wondering how much fat they had removed during that dream-like procedure.

When she blinked, her eyes stayed closed. If she had been reading or playing her game, that would have been her cue to go to sleep. But she had to drive; it was only a few blocks.

She forced her eyes to open and lifted her head.

The car was in the wrong lane. She swerved back to where she should be, overcompensated, and almost hit a parked car. This was terrible. The swerving, the abrupt motion of her arms on the wheel, ripped at her side. She felt more of the wetness that signified part of her was leaking out.

“Deep breaths.” Her vision rounded and darkened again. This was an awful place to pass out. Drive faster? Drive slower? She couldn't put her head down, although she wanted to.

The stitch in her side was more like a rip. Why did they call it a stitch, anyway? It was the opposite of that, a tearing, an opening. Did they liquify her fat? Was it leaking out into the bandages even now? She could smell it. It smelled rotten. Nothing from inside her body should smell like fatty meat left in the sun. At least it wasn’t summer, or she would attract flies.

Her eyes drifted closed. The little SUV’s bumper kissed a parked car, and Becca jerked, snorted, opened her eyes, shook her head. *Fuck.* She should stop, check for damage …

Which car had it been? Now she was a block away. It didn't seem important. She opened the window and allowed the frigid air to dispel the seeping odor and wash across her face. That would keep her awake, she hoped. She rolled through an amber light as it turned red, her eyelids heavy. Almost there, right? She wasn't sure which intersection this was. Her brain was foggy, as if filled with Salome's damn vapors.

The car slowed. The front tire bumped the curb. She blinked. Was she home?

She was not home.

A flashlight shone through the window. Becca squeezed her eyes shut against the painful brightness. Someone with a deep voice shouted at her. She lifted her hand to block the light and shook her smoke-filled head.

The door opened. If she hadn't been belted in, she would have fallen out.

The police officer covered his face with the hand not holding the flashlight. "What's that smell, lady? Did you shit yourself?"

Becca tried to look at him with her eyes closed. "It's blood," she explained. "I had a—" she searched for words in her thick head. "A procedure. The stitches may have opened. I'm trying to get home." She pointed to her side.

"Your car stinks. Get out." He dropped the hand from his face to his gun.

"What did I do wrong?"

"You were driving erratically. You stopped in the street."

"I'm just trying to get home. I have bandages and medicine there. And my friend." The implication was that her friend was at home. Which was a lie.

She unlatched the seatbelt and swung her swollen legs from the footwell. The police officer stepped back as she dragged herself from the car, groaning, holding her side. Because her shirt was black, the blood wasn't visible.

"Why is your head wrapped up? You a religious nut?"

"What? No, it's just pretty." Her breath whistled through her nose.

He forced her to assume the position to be frisked. She had thought that was an urban legend. When he arrived at her middle, she yelped. When the frisking became rougher, she screamed. The officer swore and pulled away his hands.

Becca dropped her arms from the car and turned around laboriously.

The officer examined his hands. One was bloody. "Are you shot?"

"I told you: I had a medical procedure and the stitches are opening up." Inspired, Becca yanked up her shirt, displaying the blood- and fluid-soaked bandages.

He recoiled. "You need to go to the ER. I'll call paramedics."

"No, I can handle it at home. I have bandages and stuff. I just need to get there. Please."

"Why do you stink?" The officer looked around like he wanted to wipe his hands. He finally scrubbed them on his uniform pants.

"I was in a place that burned incense. A meeting," she lied. If only.

"Why were you at a meeting when you're bleeding?"

Why was this cop so dumb? "I wasn't bleeding until I left. I had to use the stairs. That pulled something." Did that sound plausible? She couldn't tell him she was driving directly home after some fucking scary liposuction that happened while she was awake.

"That's some stinky incense."

"They are very new age. That's where I got my headscarf." Becca pulled her shirt over the bloody bandage and leaned against the SUV. If she closed her eyes, she would fall asleep standing up and fall over. Then she would really rip herself open, and the cop would call the ambulance. She still had no health insurance. Becca forced her eyes wide.

"How about if I follow you home? How far is it?"

Becca stared at the officer. She didn't know where she was. "I can do it. It's not far."

"I think I should give you a ride home and leave your car here. In the morning, you can get a ride from your roommate to pick up the car."

"We share this car."

"A ride-share then. I don't think you should be driving."

He was correct. Her knees buckled. "Follow me home." Becca had to hang onto the door to get back into the car. As she did, she tried to read the street signs. It was too dark. She turned on the nav system even though she was just blocks away. Probably.

Leila had done that safety thing where you don't program in your actual address, but one nearby in case someone steals your car and your keys. Even negotiating her way through those few buttons—current location to "home"—taxed the deep fog in her brain. Already Becca had forgotten what lies she had told the officer. The ache in her side was deep and thrumming, and if she took too deep a breath, it felt like she was being knifed.

Becca was further away from Leila's flat than she thought, or Leila had programmed *home* to be farther away. She longed for a glass of black drink. As soon as she got home, she would make a double. She needed the black fizzy drops for healing. She would have thought Leila would have messaged her by now to tell her what was going on and why she wasn't coming home tonight. Although both of them in this condition would have been impossible to manage.

She drove slowly, the police car behind her, following the car's prompts. With every inhale, her eyes drooped and wanted to stay closed. Just a few more minutes, she told herself, and then you can have your black drink and go to sleep. Change the bandage in the morning. Wrap yourself in an old towel first.

The blinks were getting longer and longer. Her foot kept slipping off the pedal. The sat nav showed several more turns she didn't think she could manage, but she realized the entrance to Leila's building was right there. She carefully turned the blinker on and ventured into the lot. She located Leila's designated spot, which was further away than Becca liked. The cop pulled up behind her. Becca crawled out of the car, her eyes barely open, messenger bag dangling, shut the car door and beeped it locked, and aimed herself at the building's door.

The cop, stupidly muscular and fit, jogged up to her and took her elbow, grimacing.

"I'm good."

"You're limping."

"I always walk like this. My knees are broken glass inside."

The cop walked her into the lobby and to the lift, which thankfully was operating and already at the lobby. He contorted his full lips and squinted his eyes as the elevator doors shut between them.

CHAPTER THIRTY-THREE

Becca guzzled a double black drink with fizzy black drops. Nyx meowed and headbutted her, screaming for Leila.

Becca threw her stinking outfit, including the headscarf, into Leila's washing machine, and stood in her underwear, unwinding the damp elastic bandages from around her waist. Soaked with blood and fluid, they stunk like the pyramid's deep basement. She tossed the wet bandages into the machine with her bra and panties. Under the bandages was a disgusting layer of once-white gauze, now red and brown. She wasn't supposed to change it yet. The odorous wet gauze stuck to her. She pressed more folded gauze over the worse filth, gagging and grimacing. Leila's aftercare hadn't been so bad. Becca rolled a fresh elastic bandage around her lopsided waist. Immediately, it darkened.

She added detergent to the washer, started a quiet cycle, and chose which sweatpants and t-shirt to stain while she slept.

Still no message from Leila. Nyx howled, but Becca couldn't pick the cat up to comfort her. She wasn't supposed to lift anything. She made kissy noises at Nyx and climbed laboriously into bed. Her bed had never seemed so tall. She debated sleeping on the floor, but even uninjured, she couldn't get down there, or get back up, for that matter. The couch had become Leila's domain, and even though Leila was away, she felt weird sleeping there. Leila's chair didn't fit Becca comfortably, either.

The world didn't fit Becca comfortably.

Even sleep didn't fit her tonight.

CHAPTER THIRTY-FOUR

Her phone was dead in the morning. Becca plopped it on the charger and expected the message icon to light. Nothing from Leila.

She fed Nyx and Apep, made herself a double black drink, and avoided the empty couch.

Her wound stank. Breathing hurt. She had more empathy for Leila now, who had gone through this so many times in just a few weeks. But Becca was smaller! Once again, she wished she had kept the scale. She considered how strange it was that there was no scale or place to weigh in at the pyramid. Most weight-loss groups were obsessed with weigh-ins. The Body Management Partners were, but MyCo System didn't seem to care if you lost weight. Only if you consumed the supplements, sold them, and recruited people to sell more and drink more ad nauseam. The building's pyramid shape was a troll. A nose-thumbing.

When her phone had charged, she messaged Leila, asking how she was and when Becca could come to get her. *I want to talk to you about my first spot reduction session! It was wild!*

The texts remained unseen. Probably Leila was sleeping.

Becca pulled on her old VR rig and dived into her game, loading a new expansion. She hoped it would keep her mind off her aching side. The non-player characters might be old, fat, or ugly, but all the players' avatars were young and beautiful. For her avatar, Becca could choose any skin tone from albino to pitch black, any natural or unnatural hair color or eye color, even ridiculous-sized mix-and-match breasts and genitals, but every character had a chiseled, perfect, youthful body. She could not choose otherwise for the avatar options.

At first, Becca had enjoyed being part of a level playing field, but now she found it annoying. The avatars were generic, only different on the surface and in how the players made them act. When she interacted with avatars, they treated the non-player characters who were old, fat, or ugly as bad or worse than they would those people in real life, beating them and yelling slurs.

Becca wondered what they would say to her sexy avatar if they knew the body piloting it weighed over three hundred and fifty pounds.

The puzzles and mysteries she solved in-game were the best part. As much as possible, she stayed in single-player mode and only interacted with semi-scripted AIs. In this expansion, her avatar was hunting for a shipment of fake pharmaceuticals that, after extended use, turned patients sick in ways that couldn't be reversed, almost a Jekyll and Hyde situation. Becca wondered if they made the drugs from fungus. She could relate.

She couldn't concentrate. Nyx crawled all over her, distracting her, wanting attention, bumping up against her wounds, which responded with sharp jolts of pain. Becca missed simple clues and had to keep backtracking when she came up against dead ends. Other players were searching for the same shipment, and if they found it first, they would get a better in-game reward.

When, once again, Becca misunderstood a reference and searched the wrong warehouse, wasting a huge amount of time, she paused the game and flung off the VR rig. She checked her phone. Leila had seen her messages but not answered. Maybe she'd woken up and gone back to sleep. She'd become increasingly tired after each treatment, Becca had noticed. Poor Leila.

Nyx headbutted Becca. Becca rubbed her velvet skin. With her other hand, she scrolled to her sales dashboard. Evangeline and her downline were bringing in sales, but not enough for Becca to live independently. At least, not yet.

She had a message in her corporate inbox about the DNA tests.

MyCo System had found her birth family.

Becca glanced around Leila's living room. She wanted to share this news with her friend. She checked the message queue again; still no reply. She sent a new message: *Hey, I got DNA results, and they found my birth family! Should I wait or look? I don't want to wait but you aren't here!*

She waited. Petted the cat. Watched Apep battle his reflection in the floating mirror.

The message remained unread.

Becca clicked into the DNA database. She found nth-degree cousins. A few had accounts. If she wanted to pay an outrageous monthly sum, she could have full access to their information. For now, she used the free limited-access account bundled with the custom MyCo System test.

And there was her birth mother: Laurel Anne Mitchell, deceased.

Why did that hurt?

Someone she hadn't known existed until two seconds ago continued not to exist.

No headshot in the limited database. Laurel Anne Mitchell died not long after Becca's birth. Under her name were paper icons, links to scanned documents: Laurel Anne's birth and death certificates. Didn't look like she had ever been married, so Leila's fantasy had been wrong. Her mother had been thirty-three when Becca was born and thirty-four when she died. At least Becca's birth hadn't killed her. Probably.

Becca clicked the obituary link. Heart disease had killed her birth mother. It was a simple death notice, not a proper obituary.

Becca's maternal grandparents had been living twenty-five years ago. Locating them was possible. Having a mother who died so young worried her. She wanted medical records.

Back to the search engine. She plugged in her mother's name to see if Laurel Anne Mitchell had done anything noteworthy, like having a blog or winning an award. Things stayed on the internet for a long time, although twenty-five-odd years was a lot to ask.

Becca found Laurel Anne on a D-list celebrity site. She had been a reality TV star in a way that certainly qualified using finger quotes. Becca's adoptive mom was a famous model, and her real mom was a reality TV star. Meanwhile, Becca remained an unemployed, horrible, fat blob.

What reality show had Laurel Anne been on? One of the marriage or dating shows? They were still on TV, people willing to hook up on camera. House renovations? Makeover? She hadn't been married, so it wasn't a show where a guy had a dozen wives and forty children unless she was one of the forty children. Restaurant critic?

As she hovered over the next link, Becca tried to imagine what it could be. It was Schrödinger's reality show. Every reality show at once. Once she clicked, it collapsed to one show, Laurel Anne's actual show.

An alien archeology program? Medical oddities? UFOs? Bigfoot hunters? Not that it mattered. Her mother was long gone.

Maybe there were episodes online in some black hole on the dark web, sailing on a pirate sea.

Or maybe her mother had been in one episode of one show, once. But then she wouldn't come up on this old list, right? Not a one-timer.

Becca inspected her phone's messages. Leila hadn't seen the newest one. She sent another. *My real mum was a reality TV star! I'm going to find out more!*

She clicked open another link.

CHAPTER THIRTY-FIVE

Laurel Anne Mitchell had appeared on three episodes across three years of a popular reality series about people weighing 750 pounds or more. She had dropped out because she was pregnant.

"Pregnant with me," Becca told Apep. "I was on TV."

Apep flared his gills and dove into his new faux-rock cave.

Becca searched for and devoured the three episodes' synopses.

In Season One, Laurel went to a specialty bariatric doctor, desperate to lose weight, hoping for weight loss surgery, weighing 762 pounds, barely mobile. She lived alone in a double-wide trailer in the floodplain near the banks of the Kimi River. Her brother Arnold modified the trailer so she could get around more easily. A trucker, he lived nearby and was also obese.

His daughter, May Anne—Becca's cousin!—who was also quite large, helped her aunt, but she went off to college and left Laurel alone, which prompted her to seek out Dr. Please to lose weight.

Laurel lost a little weight; Dr. Please approved her for surgery. Once she had it, Laurel stopped losing. That was Laurel's first season; a year of weight loss condensed into two hours, further summarized into the couple of paragraphs Becca found archived.

Was this gripping, must-see TV? Or a modern form of circus sideshow, gawking at the fat people? The series had been on for over a dozen years with several hundred morbidly obese "stars."

The following year, in season two, Laurel started gaining weight.

Becca understood how her mother died of heart disease at thirty-four. This was Laurel's most gripping season with the most audience engagement, as Dr. Please told Laurel she would die. He put her in a rehab facility to get her physically stronger and force her to eat healthier foods. She met another morbidly obese patient in rehab, Dwayne Legare, a man who, as it turned out, lived right near her, but because of their homebound lives, they had never met. The two lost weight working out together. Fans adored this two-ton love story, and there was talk of a spinoff reality show about them. Laurel and Dwayne left rehab and moved into Laurel's trailer.

Becca leaned forward, staring at her phone, eyes wide, wanting the details even though she already knew the ending. She searched desperately for the next synopsis.

In her third and final season, Laurel and her paramour Dwayne had gained back all their original weight, plus bonus pounds. Laurel was no longer interested in following Dr. Please's weight-loss program. When Laurel announced her pregnancy in a video call, Dr. Please declared it was unhealthy to be pregnant at her weight. Laurel refused any further medical advice from him, which was the end of her being Dr. Please's patient and her TV stardom.

The spinoff reality show never happened.

"That was me," Becca told Apep, finishing the poorly written synopsis. "My birth parents were so huge they were on a reality show for fat people. No wonder I'm obese."

Before she thought about it, Becca forwarded the three links to Willow LeNoir. *These are my genes. I had my DNA tested. These are my birth parents. I will never be as thin as you. I can't do it.*

Her adopted mum might have some sympathy now. It wasn't Becca's fault.

When the phone beeped a little while later, it wasn't an answer from Willow but an auto reminder that Leila had scheduled a MyCoLysis testing party at the condo the next night. Becca was supposed to make sure the place was clean.

Becca checked her messages. Leila hadn't seen any more. She sent another.

Hey, we have that MyCoLysis thing here tomorrow. Am I canceling? I can't operate the MyCo tablet without you. You have your mobile with the customer list. And I don't know the password for your tablet. Can you at least send me that?

Not seen. Nothing.

Just in case, Becca limped around the living room and kitchen, cleaning. Not that they were messy. Well, she was, but Leila kept her in check. Leila's place was so lovely Becca hated to get it dirty. Food and eating generated mess, which they didn't do anymore. The black straws were biodegradable, and the empty glass jars of drops got returned to MyCo System for recycling.

Becca rechecked her phone.

The long string of unanswered messages to Willow LeNoir now said, *this caller is unavailable*, and everything was gone. Either her mum had changed her phone number in the last hour or had blocked her.

Becca didn't know how to feel. She hadn't spoken to Willow LeNoir in years. But she had hoped. Maybe it was just a phone-number change, and she would get a message with the new number shortly. Since her mum was quasi-famous, someone might have gotten hold of her number and was stalking her, annoying her, leaving her no choice.

Or that annoying someone was her adopted child.

She clicked over to the messages she'd sent to Leila. Nothing. Not seen.

Shit.

Thousands of potential dollars of tests were happening here tomorrow night. Leila had booked a video call with Dr. Lee for the SporeCode section. What should Becca do?

Her side ached. The bandages stank. She should change the gauze and rest. Take another hit of black drink and black fizzy drops.

Her fucking mum had blocked her. There was a tiny chance it had been a coincidental number change, but Becca didn't think so.

Bandages smelly and damp around her sore middle, she opened her laptop, signed up for a free online-only phone number that accepted messages, and tied it to a temporary email address. She sent her mum a calculated piece of fake spam through the browser pop-up: *Your friends think you look old and tired. Try our new YungSkin rejuvenating formula sold only at V-Mart stores!*

She waited for the error message stating her mum's phone number didn't exist.

The spam slid into her mother's account like a hot knife through canned ham, returning no error.

She canceled the temporary phone number and email account.

Her mum had blocked her for having fat birth parents.

Shitty fatphobic bitch.

Still nothing from Leila.

She logged into her MyCo System account and, after a search that was more difficult than it should have been, contacted her least favorite dragon bitch, Salome.

Leila has a huge MyCoLysis and SporeCode testing party scheduled here tomorrow, and she still hasn't returned from her spot reduction last night. I'm here alone, and I would run the party myself, except I don't have access to the testing protocols on Leila's tablet. She has over twenty people booked, and I'm not sure how to get in touch with them to cancel. She also has a video appointment with Dr. Lee to prescribe blood draws. Please advise.

Becca didn't know how often Salome checked her messages on the MyCo System page or if her alerts went to her phone. Or if Salome hated Becca enough to allow Leila's business to burn, even though Leila was one of her stars.

She made another black drink, chugged it, then changed the bandages over the gauze. Her side was leaking more, stinking more, hurting more. If Salome solved the testing problem, Becca would ask about the leak, too. Leila had pain after her LipoGest, but not this level of leaking.

Becca's phone rang. "Leila is still here," Salome said. "I will move her party to the pyramid and see if I can invite more people to it."

Becca pursed her lips. Leila had been counting on that money, and therefore, so had Becca. Salome must have heard her thoughts or guessed them. "I will make sure all the original people's testing commissions go into Leila's account. Why don't you come along and shadow me? This could be good training for you."

"Can I see Leila?"

Salome breathed heavily, no doubt vaping. "Perhaps. But we have some other things to talk about with you."

Were they going to kick her out? Oh no! Had they finally checked the basement cameras? At least she had gotten one spot-reduction treatment. She tensed in fear, and that made her side hurt worse. "Okay, do I need to bring anything? I have a lot of shakes; we were going to use them up as samples at this party since we don't drink them anymore."

"Sure, you can bring them." It didn't sound like Salome was listening to her. "I can get into the party details through the site. I will tell everyone to come to the pyramid instead and try to get more people, offer some incentives. Come a bit early, like 6 p.m. Bring your extra Shroomshee smoothie shakes if you like."

CHAPTER THIRTY-SIX

Becca spent the next day unsuccessfully messaging Leila and trying to find the three episodes of her birth mother's reality show. She found some partial excerpts with other people, but none with Laurel survived. From the clips she could find, the show seemed awful and exploitative. The doctors working with the patients were mean; they hated fat people. Dietary science had changed in the last twenty-five years or so, but what the bariatric clinic put the people through seemed barbaric.

Becca drank a black shake with fizzy drops as she scrolled.

Laurel's genes were likely messed up, like Becca's were, through epigenetic changes. No wonder her mother hadn't lost much weight and had quit when pregnant. Becca thought MyCo System might not be so bad after watching and reading about what her birth mother had gone through.

That MyCo System was doing gene-based weight-loss therapy really was incredible, especially if it was real and not based on lies and microplastic. Even if it was direct sales and a pyramid scheme, it was helping people. Maybe someday they would break away from this structure.

The eighty-twenty rule Salome claimed was so important would fall apart in the free-for-all that was the open market. Everyone would want to start with the potent Black Gill-Tea Pleasure drink that wasn't for everyone, and who knew what would happen if everyone drank that first, without the unworthy eighty percent being weeded out twice? If you gained fifteen or twenty pounds in college, you didn't need the black drink. Most people didn't need the black drink. Everyone would also want the spot-reduction treatment, even if they weren't eligible, even though eighty percent of the Black Gill-Tea Pleasure people had to be removed first.

Milo Cobalt seemed wise for structuring it as a pyramid and building actual pyramids to house the company. Because as you moved up, it became more rarified. Not everyone could cut it, nor should they.

Laurel might have washed out, never leveled up. The black drink may have proven ineffective.

The little voice in Becca's head wondered about the addiction to the shakes and not eating actual food. Was it worth being thin if you could never eat food again?

Becca sprinkled fish treats into Apep's tank. It was possible that part only happens to twenty percent too? Some people would just merrily go back to food. That's one way of weeding people out.

Their slogan should be, *are you part of the twenty percent?*

CHAPTER THIRTY-SEVEN

A few minutes before six p.m., Becca dragged two tote bags of shakes into the pyramid. They weighed too much for her to carry. Her side ached. Her shirt was wet. She had wound a double-thick elastic bandage under her black shirt, but it still leaked. She worried she smelled terrible, but the whole pyramid's interior stunk.

Two nights before, she'd dinged the side of Leila's car. She hadn't messaged Leila about that yet. She wondered how the cop had missed that.

After arranging her shake offerings on a side table, Becca searched for Salome. The basement door remained unlocked, but knowing about the cameras and the locked bottom door, she didn't even try to go down. The gamer in her yearned toward that staircase, though.

The thick, sloping walls groaned and creaked. Did the contractor who built the pyramid know how to construct them at a slant? Who specializes in modern pyramid-building, anyway? This was a step-pyramid, unlike the smooth-sided ones built for Bast and Anubis. The walls always seemed noisy or inhabited, as if there were raccoons inside.

She smelled no hint of Salome's vape.

Becca dragged her legs upstairs, clutching the railing, one foot at a time. The Rainbow Obsidian meeting rooms were empty, unlocked. She checked over the banister. Still no one in the Quartz Auditorium. She climbed to the Red Diamond Balcony, where the smell was overwhelming. The meeting rooms and treatment rooms seemed abandoned.

Did she dare hike to the Black Sapphire level? Where would they have Leila? Leila must be in a hospital. She couldn't be in this filthy place. What if Becca stood at the railing and shouted? Leila had answered none of her messages. Had they taken her phone away? Was the battery dead? Becca hadn't thought to bring Leila's phone charger or a change of clothes.

And Salome hadn't asked for those things.

Becca studied the increasingly smaller upper levels in the stairwell. The odor was overwhelming. Becca hid her face in her elbow, afraid to cough because of how much it would hurt. She hadn't seen her bare skin yet, but it felt burnt and peeled under the gauze. And very sticky.

"Becca? Is that you?"

Another odor crept into her nostrils: sweet smoke. Becca glanced over the railing at Salome, in the doorway beneath her.

"What are you doing up there? The testing is in the auditorium."

"Searching for Leila. She hasn't responded to my messages, and I'm worried."

Salome expelled a cloud. Behind it, her face crunched, annoyed. "Leila is being cared for. I've told you that. Come downstairs and set up the testing with me."

Becca clutched the handrail with white knuckles and descended. "Where is Dr. Lee? Is he taking care of Leila? What is wrong with her? Is she in hospital?"

Salome clicked down the stairs on her heels, not touching the railing, alternating her feet, trotting effortlessly. Becca hated her.

By the time Becca caught up with Salome, she was already putting out a testing tablet and leaflets. "These are new. You don't allow people to take them home."

Becca, panting from climbing downstairs, nodded.

"It's not proprietary, but we don't want this all over the internet."

Catching her breath, Becca said, "What about mobile photos?"

"We'll make a game out of taking away people's phones. You haven't had a party yet, have you? Taking away phones at the beginning is part of it. Then nothing can get recorded at all. That way, we keep closer control on the way the MyCo System brand is presented to our customers."

No fact-checking allowed, in other words.

Salome picked up the rubber-coated tablet and opened the app. She explained everything Becca had already learned at least three times. Becca could have done all the testing herself; except she didn't have biometric access to Leila's tablet. "When will MyCo System allow Rainbow Obsidians to test people?"

Salome exhaled sweet lemony vapor and waved her free hand. "Perhaps never. We want to keep it elite. The twenty percent of twenty percent thing. Give people something to strive for."

Becca nodded, still surprised Salome was so upfront about the failure numbers.

Another set of heels clicked into the room. The expression on Salome's face moved from annoyance to awe, and Becca turned. Wearing a flashy waist-enhancing belt of Leila's design, decorated with peacock feathers, Dr. Opal Knox crossed the room, holding out both hands. A black headscarf with a blue mushroom design swathed her famous face. A color-changing knit dress hugged the rest of her body, shifting between black, blue, and green as she moved. Her generous bottom bobbed behind her, and her breasts in front. She was an awe-inspiring sight. Photos of her appeared airbrushed or altered, but that was her actual body.

She didn't look like a doctor. She looked like an Opal, not like a Dr. Knox.

"Becca!" Opal called, taking her hands. "Oh, Becca." Opal's generous mouth turned down.

Becca cocked her head.

"You got here so quickly." Opal turned to Salome. "Did you go get her?"

Salome blew lemon vapor from the corner of her mouth. "We are having Leila's testing party here, since Leila is still indisposed. Her guests are due in twenty minutes."

"Oh dear," Opal said. "Oh dear. Well, Salome, you can continue the testing without Becca's help tonight. Give her account all the credit." Still holding onto Becca, Opal pulled her down the aisle away from the stage.

Opal's dazzling, birdlike eyes stared at Becca. Opal smelled of expensive, musky perfume. Becca wanted to bury her face in the woman's long brown neck to get away from the horrible odors of the pyramid.

"This really is terrible timing, my dear, terrible. I have a wonderful offer for you, and now it's going to appear as if I'm taking advantage." Opal squeezed Becca's hands.

"Opal, I am sure I don't know what you are talking about at all." Becca tried to pull herself away.

"My dear. I am so sorry. Leila's dead."

CHAPTER THIRTY-EIGHT

Becca sipped the black drink Opal had brought her. It tasted odd. She wondered if there were other colors of drops besides black and red.

Or the peculiar flavor could have come from her crying into the glass.

She was back to square one, even worse off: homeless with no proper job, and her best—only—friend was dead.

She was fat as ever. Her mum had gone no-contact.

If Becca had been physically capable, she would have curled into a ball and howled. But she had too much flesh and wasn't flexible enough, and even if it was that flexible, her body ached from the spot treatment.

Amid the waves of sobbing tears, a horrible realization swept over Becca: She had no one to turn to. Opal, even though she was sitting next to Becca with a thin, manicured hand on her shoulder, was not a friend. Salome was an enemy. Evangeline and her downline were random people Becca was taking advantage of, just like Opal and Salome were taking advantage of her.

"I don't know what to do." Becca might as well talk to Opal, who was, after all, a psychologist. "I live in Leila's flat and drive her car because I got evicted and sold my car. Leila has a cat, and I have a fish. What am I going to do? Where will I live? I don't make enough selling MyCo System supplements to afford an apartment and a car." And what she earned wasn't even real. Most was from the downline MyCo System had gifted her. It wasn't like Becca was going to grow it further herself. All a big lie.

Becca was worse than worthless, and now she was also being selfish, making Leila's death all about herself.

She sobbed and sipped. Her whole body shook.

Leila couldn't be dead. Colorful Leila had more life in her than anyone Becca had ever known.

Opal dug her pointed nails into Becca's soft shoulder. "I was going to offer you something, regardless. But now I look heartless or like I'm taking advantage of you when you're at your lowest, with your friend dead and all that you're going through."

Becca turned her round, wet face toward Opal's famous sculpted face.

Opal patted her damp cheeks. "Have you heard of HelSto cells?"

It was such a non sequitur that Becca stopped crying. "What? No. Why should I care?"

"They named the cells after Helen Stodge."

Becca wiped her cheeks on her shoulders and stared at Opal, who was clearly trying to distract her from her best friend's death. Opal didn't even know all of it, that Leila wasn't the only one she'd just lost. Willow LeNoir had cut her off because her birth mum had been a fat-lady reality TV star.

Opal didn't realize how alone Becca was. How vulnerable.

The smell in the room thickened despite Salome's lemony clouds, as if something foul was gathering in the corners.

"Many people, if not most, have HelSto cells inside them. HelSto cells are in all kinds of medicines and vaccines. Amazing cells that continue to live long after their donor died. They save lives and make the world better."

Becca wiped her nose on her hand and sniffed. Her eyes continued to leak. Great for Helen, she saved the world. Meanwhile, Becca was about to be homeless with a cat and a fish. A cat who didn't like her very much, but no way would she dump Nyx at the Temple of Bast.

"Probably as part of Leila's kidney treatments, she had gotten some of Helen's cells," Opal continued. "I really wish Leila hadn't kept her kidney failure from us."

"Is that what killed her? Was she in hospital?" Becca could barely speak, her throat swollen from sobbing.

Opal avoided the question, mouth pulled down with sympathy that seemed just a tad rehearsed. She stroked Becca's hair. "We need to go into another room before this presentation starts so we can keep talking."

Ladies filed into the Quartz Auditorium, talking loudly, grabbing the free shakes Becca had put out, not knowing she should have kept them to sell. She would need all the money she could scrape together now. Opal took Becca's wrist and pulled her toward the steps, seeming to understand Becca's lumbering one-foot-forward method of climbing.

They settled in a Rainbow Obsidian conference room. Opal offered a box of tissues.

Becca's life had torn apart. She couldn't really believe Leila was dead. No more Leila in the world. The incredibly designed corset belts. The sly, funny-themed mukbangs. The songs she sang to Nyx. All the time she spent online defending fat, LGBTQ+, and neurodivergent people, her firm belief others may exist and thrive just the way they are.

Leila never understood why Becca hated herself. Leila loved Becca just how she was.

Now that light was gone, and Becca was alone in the darkness.

"HelSto, as they affectionately refer to her in the medical world, never knew of her contribution," Opal returned to the previous conversation. "In fact, they never paid her. Doctors routinely sampled her cells during medical tests without realizing their importance."

Becca crumpled a wet tissue and pulled another from the box, barely listening. Why was Opal babbling about this? She didn't care. Becca was uninterested in medical topics. They boiled down to: *you're sick because you're fat. You're in pain because you're fat. Lose weight and come back, and then we'll figure out if something is really wrong.* Is that how her birth mother had died? Having symptoms and being sent away? Hearing that constant refrain.

If you're fat, it's your fault.

Somehow, Becca had probably killed Leila. Not forcing her to call back her kidney doctor. Not making sure she took all her prescription medicine. It was always Becca's fault for being fat.

"I knew she was getting worse. Are you saying I killed her?" She sniffled into a tissue. Her belly area ached. The fresh bandages felt soaked through. The room's odor eddied as if coming through the ventilation system. Becca experienced waves of dizziness and swayed in her chair.

Opal moved to the sideboard and fixed another black drink. Becca couldn't see what color drops she added. It lacked ice, but Becca drank it anyway. It didn't calm her thoughts. She really needed her anti-anxiety medicine, boxes of it. With no health insurance, she couldn't fill her prescription. Her veins fizzed with anxiety, and each inhalation of that damn dirt scent seemed to increase it a notch.

Leila was dead. Thinking of that made Becca want to howl. She hid her head in her arms.

"What do you mean?" Opal sat next to her and leaned forward. "How did you kill your friend? You weren't even here."

"She died here?" Had Leila really been recuperating here, in this dirty, smelly place? This was no hospital. The unsterile rooms where they did the spot-reduction treatments were terrible enough.

"You didn't kill her. How could you have?"

"She didn't always take the prescription medicine from her doctor," Becca mumbled. "I didn't make her."

"You aren't her mother."

Becca straightened and winced at the pain from the sudden movement. "Oh, my gods. I have to call her family. She has parents and a bunch of siblings. She's the baby! Someone needs to notify them. I need her mobile to get their numbers. Where's her mobile?"

Opal blinked and glanced away. "I'm sure it's around here somewhere with her other belongings."

"And where is she? Her, her body, I mean." Thinking of big, strong Leila as a cold corpse, when her friend had always been the most full-of-life person she had ever known, nearly broke Becca. She started bawling, on the edge of screaming.

"I think, um, I'm not sure." Opal glanced over Becca's shoulder. "Sent for cremation, probably."

"She worshipped Bast. She would want to be sent to the Temple of Bast for preparation. If you burned her …" How did you mummify ashes?

Opal bit her lip with perfect teeth. "I'm not sure. I'll have to ask. But usually …"

"Usually? As in, this has happened before? People have died here?" Aghast, she thought of her inherited downline. Had that person died and Opal transferred her people to Becca? Had she been profiting off a dead person without knowing?

"People die all the time. Doesn't mean we killed them." Opal stretched her neck, revealing a round scar.

"This is a new pyramid. How many people have died here?"

Opal pushed the almost empty glass at Becca. "Finish your drink. I didn't bring you up here to talk about people dying."

"Just about Leila dying." Becca drained the glass and slammed it on the table. It fell over, dribbling black liquid. A tiny nebula formed in the puddle. Becca dragged her finger through it, killing solar systems and their inhabitants in a great catastrophe. If she couldn't have her best friend, everyone could die.

Opal sighed and leaned forward, resting her breasts on the table. It must be challenging to have both a large bottom and large boobs. Her bubble butt kept her from sitting back in the chair. Becca had a moment of sympathy. Opal's back must hurt.

"Honestly, they authorized me to make this offer to you, regardless. Then Leila died, which makes it horribly awkward. And then this testing party." She waved her long, red nails toward the floor. "All those witnesses, not needed. I could have done without Salome there. She can be dramatic, but she brings in the recruits. She's a genuine believer in the system, if not the reason behind it."

"Salome hates fat people. She especially hates me. She got me fired from my last job." Becca wasn't whining, just stating facts. "She knows my adoptive mum. They might be in cahoots."

"What? What does your adoptive mother have to do with this?"

"She hates me too. She just went completely no-contact with me, changed her phone number. Salome was a consultant at my magazine job who interviewed me about what I did there and then recommended I get fired. After Leila brought me into MyCo System, Salome admitted it was because I'm fat and because I worked from home."

"But not because of your mother. Why would she know your mother?"

Becca stared at Opal and remembered Opal had once interviewed Willow LeNoir.

"My mum's in the same industry. Salome got me fired for being fat, even though I was doing my job well. I wasn't slacking off."

"She's not affecting you now. Salome's helping you."

Becca made a face at that lie. "She still dislikes me."

"That won't be an issue after you accept this offer."

"What offer?"

“HelSto.” Opal grinned her famous TV smile. In person, it was terrifying and false. She had a lot of teeth that seemed fake, capped, bleached, sharpened, or all the above.

“I don’t understand.” Becca played with the puddle, creating and destroying universes. Killing best friends everywhere. Could Opal even see the nebula?

“The reason we set you up so quickly for your first LipoGest spot-reduction treatment is Dr. Lee and others …” her voice trailed off, and Opal glanced around as if invisible others were in the empty room. “… wanted to look at your fat.”

The wind coming off Thin Island Sound, getting into the ductwork, shifted the walls.

“Look at my fat, how?” MyCo System was preposterous. Inspect her fat? Like, poke it with a stick and see if it was yellow and wobbly?

“Under a microscope and other tests. I don’t know much about the science.” Opal peered around again. The smell intensified, as did the sound of movement in the walls.

Becca wiped her leaking nose and eyes. “So, they checked my fat, whatever that means. Whoever *they* are.”

“They want you to be the HelSto of fat. Like Helen was the HelSto of pluripotent stem cells.”

“This makes less and less sense.” Becca closed her eyes. She wished she could breathe deeply to calm her racing heart and trembling body, but she couldn’t because of the overwhelming smell and the pain under her bandages. This all had to be a bad dream because Leila couldn’t be dead. Leila was home on the oversized green couch swathed in bandages, cranky because she wanted a Black Gill-Tea Pleasure drink and Becca wasn’t there to make it.

“There have been attempts to create humans with a certain type of fat for generations. Thousands of years. Most of those attempts have failed. In the last hundred years, it has been getting closer. And in you, it’s perfect.”

Becca pinched the remaining fat around her middle. "Perfect fat?"

"Yes, a certain composition. Resistant to weight loss. A few other properties. I don't need to know the details."

"Do I need to know?"

Opal shrugged. The smell moved around the room. Opal wandered to the sideboard and made herself a black drink.

While Opal was mixing, Becca said sourly, "Someone purposely bred me like a farm animal to be plump, and my fellow humans exiled and mistreated me for being fat." Except Leila, and now Leila was dead.

Opal gulped, leaving dark lipstick on the glass's rim. "That is unfortunate, but I'm trying to offer something to compensate for that."

"What can you offer me? When I go out in public, people scream at me that I'm disgusting. They tell me to die. My adoptive mother stopped talking to me because I hadn't lost weight. I'm lazy and stupid, that's what fat means. I lost my job and my apartment because I'm fat." Tears streamed down her red face. "Being fat is a choice! I choose to be fat! That's what I'm told. If I'm hurt or sick or in pain, if a car hits me, if I fall, it's because I'm fat and I chose it. I'm the victim, yet I'm always at fault." She punched the table; the nebula jumped and fell. Civilizations died. "Leila had kidney failure, and she died. All that will matter is she was a fatty-fat-fat person who loved herself, so she loved being fat, so she chose to die! Not that she loved people and loved her cat and made beautiful things like your belt!" Becca lashed out at Opal's middle. Opal jumped back in the wheeled chair, crashing into the next chair. "She was *fat*, so she *deserved* to *die*!" Becca screamed, her fists clenched. "I am fat, so I am *worthless*. My *mum hates me*."

Opal raised her hands defensively. "That's what I am trying to tell you. You're the opposite of worthless. You're precious and valuable. The apex of a pyramid that has been being built for generations."

Becca stared with swollen, irritated eyes. Many people had played tricks on Becca. It was fun to mock the fat girl. She shook her head. Teardrops flew into the nebula puddle. "I'm the lowest of the low. Don't tease me."

Opal stared at her, a famous made-for-TV look. "I'm not teasing you."

Becca shrugged one damp shoulder, sticky with tears and snot. "It doesn't matter. I've lost everything. I can live in Leila's flat for a while because it's on autopay, but the money in her account will run out, or her family will appear and boot me out for the squatter I'll be. They will throw her cat into the Temple of Bast and put my fish in a baggie and me on the street."

"Do you like Leila's cat?"

"I like her well enough not to give her back to the shelter. And she likes me. Sorta. If something horrible happened to me, Leila would keep my fish and not flush it." That reminded her again that something horrible had happened to Leila and Becca had decisions to make. She rubbed her streaming nose with her index finger. "I really have to call her family and inform them, which means they will come and throw me out. And if I don't tell them, I'm a horrible person. I can't win."

"I can call them." Opal cocked her head. "Where will you go? You have a small income from your downline."

Becca shrugged. "I'll have to use the internet from the library. Find a cheap place to live that will accept the cat and the fish. I'll have to downsize my fish tank again." She laid her head on the table, overwhelmed. The nebula puddle soaked into her dark-red hair.

"Surely your life would be easier if you got rid of the cat and the fish." Opal used her TV psychologist's voice.

"No," Becca said into her plump forearm. "I won't be alone."

"And your mother..." Opal's voice trailed off. "Should I contact her? Maybe there is hope?"

Becca raised her head and sat up. She laughed as tears poured from her eyes and nebula-filled black drink dripped from her hair. "How many spot-reduction treatments can you give me real quick to make me as thin as Salome, Opal? Only then would I be acceptable to my mum. Do you know why she cut off all contact with me? I found my birth parents! My birth mother was on a reality TV show about super morbidly obese people where she failed miserably to lose weight but hooked up with a big fat guy while at rehab and got pregnant before quitting the program. That was me in her belly, I assume from the dates. Doomed from birth, that's me. I prove nature overcomes nurture. If you knew who my mum was, you would see that."

"You keep hinting at that as if your mother is famous."

Becca laughed. It sounded shrill and hysterical in her ears. The walls shifted around her again. "You could say that. If I said her name, you would look at me funny forever. Not that you'll ever see me again after tonight, I'd imagine. Now that you're doing all this DNA and bloodwork, you'll find a better chosen one for whatever you want me to do. I'll fade into the sunset. Actually, can you help me get off these damn shakes and back onto actual food? I'm done with MyCo System." She ran her finger through the remains of the galactic puddle.

"You don't understand." Opal touched Becca's hand. "What you are is rare. You might be the only person on earth. We won't let you walk away."

"Are you going to give me Leila's mobile and her things? Her ashes, so I can bring them to the Temple of Bast?"

"Can we transfer her downline to you so you will have an income while you think about it?" Opal seemed much too eager.

Becca touched her damp finger to her lips, ingesting all those dead best friends. "There's nothing to think about. You people killed Leila with this last spot-reduction treatment. She was frail and weak from kidney failure, but Salome pushed her into going, even though Leila tried to beg off. Salome was furious when Leila skipped the previous one."

Opal snorted. The noise made her seem almost human. "Salome is angry because she isn't properly cultivating her downlines to book the required number of LipoGest treatments. She had to go for one herself, and she is already too thin."

Becca was tired and sad and didn't care. "I don't know what that means."

"She is responsible for bringing a certain amount of LipoGest treatment sessions into the pyramid in a set amount of time. Salome is good at recruiting people to sell, but she isn't good at moving them up in this organization the way she has been at others, and it's causing problems for her. That's why she is so thin. She brought Leila on because Leila was so large. And she was happy for the same reason when Leila brought you on and encouraged your rapid upward movement."

Becca's eyes ached, her throat was raw, her nose dripped. Her open side was oozing. She didn't care about Salome's problems. She said as much. "I don't understand why there's a quota on treatments. It's not like you're making money off them. Why do you need so much fat, anyway?"

She hoped Opal would give her the real reason, not some bullshit story like the one Dr. Lee had tried to sell her about genetic manipulation. Money and microplastics.

"We use it as fertilizer to feed the, um." Opal flailed for words, waving her hands. "The fungus that makes up all the products," Opal finished. "Human fat is the secret ingredient for the fertilizer."

Becca envisioned the enormous creatures in the basement. Back to bullshit. She would play along. "It has to be human? Why can't you get fat from animals? From rendering plants?" Becca spoke on autopilot.

None of this was real. It was a nightmare. She was still in the Black Chair.

"We get some from there, but the best results come from human tissue."

The walls slithered. Becca stared numbly at the undulations. She would never get back Leila's remains. Or if she received a canister of ashes, they would not be from her friend's body.

"What really happened to Leila?"

Opal shook her head with rapid, tiny movements. "Honestly, I don't know. I think she had an adverse reaction. She didn't wake up. Then she died." At least Leila had slept through her treatments and hadn't been awake, terrified, and tortured the way Becca had been.

"Can I ask you something weird before I leave?"

"I suppose. I'll answer if I can."

"You probably know from the cameras that I snuck into the basement a few weeks ago."

Opal blinked. "Basement?"

Becca twisted her mouth. Did Opal not know? "A doorway behind the stage marked 'stairs' leads down."

"I never noticed. I always use the corner stairway."

"When I was searching for Leila, I saw the stairs and got curious."

"Why would you think Leila would be downstairs? And why would there be a downstairs? I don't think there is a basement here."

Becca didn't explain about her video game and why she felt compelled to keep going, to pretend to be as brave in real life as she was in VR. "But it isn't a normal basement. It's a cave with racks of fungus."

"I thought we grew them off-site." Opal pursed her full lips.

"The basement is huge. It's not just underneath the pyramid. So, it's technically off site, I guess."

"What's your question? Whether the mushrooms you claim are in the basement are the ones grown with the fat? Probably."

"I didn't finish," Becca said, irritated. She swiped her swollen eyes with the side of her hand. "I saw a weird greenish glow through all the mushroom racks. In the center, I found an enormous cavern with dips carved into the floor. Giant mushroom heads filled the dips. It smelled terrible. Like what it smells like here, shit and dirt, plus cheap lye soap, but heavier."

"It doesn't smell like shit and dirt in here," Opal objected.

The odor intensified at Opal's denial, almost solid, wafting from the air vents. Becca felt as if eyes were watching her from inside the ducts.

"That's all I smell here, all the time. That's what all the drinks taste like. It's awful."

Opal shook her head.

"I can barely choke them down."

"All the drinks are delicious and delicately flavored, and the building smells like sweet incense," Opal argued. "I don't know why you think it smells bad and the drinks taste awful."

Becca huffed at being told again she was wrong. "Anyway, back to the giant mushroom caps of various levels of stink. I tried to tell Leila about them. She didn't believe me, either. When I made a noise, they moved in waves, like protoplasm. They made tentacles and even eyes. One seemed to see me. It chased me and ate a torn, bloody piece of my shirt, which distracted it. That's my question."

Opal's brows came together. "What is your question? You sound deranged."

"Did they tell you they saw me?"

"Did who see you?"

"The sentient fungus creatures in the basement!"

"Becca, I'm not sure there even is a basement. You are grieving and upset. You lost your best friend. Your life is in upheaval. I'm not allowing you to quit MyCo System. I'm transferring Leila's downline to you, giving you more income. Someone will find Leila's phone and purse and bring them to you. Do nothing rash. Think about our offer."

"What is the offer?" Becca had lost the conversation thread while remembering the terrifying moments the creature chased her through the green-lit cavern.

"You know what? Don't worry about the specifics. Just know there's an offer available whenever you want it. I'll give you my phone number, and you can call me whenever. I might be a famous person on TV, but I'm still a trained psychologist, and if you need to talk, I can help you."

CHAPTER THIRTY-NINE

Becca messaged Willow LeNoir. *Mum MyCo System killed my friend Leila please help me.*

Still blocked.

She sat on the couch, hugged Nyx, and they watched Apep swim in his new tank. The old tank was in a kitchen cabinet. She thought about downsizing her poor betta, downsizing herself back to a studio, or worse, a hotel room. She could bear it. The luxury of Leila's flat was Leila herself, and Leila was gone.

Becca wandered into Leila's workroom, where they had sorted fabric, elastic, real and fake leather, grommets, and lace for several new belts Leila would never finish. A couple of plus-sized mannequins draped with fabric waited in vain for Leila to finish their outfits. Becca should pack all this up, but she couldn't bear it yet. She doubted Leila had left behind anything like a will. No one under thirty had one. They were all immortal.

Becca sat on Leila's work chair, held an almost-complete rainbow-colored belt, and cried. Nyx came in to headbutt her. Becca pulled a feathered boa from the materials shelf and threw it to the cat to play with.

Becca would never be thin. Could never be thin.

Dragging the boa, she headed into the kitchen to make herself a shit drink. The cat gamboled after her, delighted. She drank standing at the counter. She couldn't quit MyCo System until she could get off the drinks; otherwise, she would have to buy them at full price. It would be cutting off her nose to spite her face.

She rigged the boa in a doorway for the cat's pleasure. Poor Nyx. She hadn't figured out her human wasn't returning.

Becca pulled on old boots and one of Leila's oversized puffy coats and took the elevator. She needed to breathe clean outside air. She needed to clear her mind and decide what to do with the next fifty years of her lonely life.

The park seemed like a suitable destination. It didn't require eating, although people spent too much time feeding the birds and squirrels there. Her knees hurt, her back ached, and the area under the bandages pulled and leaked. Walking wasn't a good idea.

The three pyramids of Newhaven pierced the skyline—the Temple of Bast, a Mexican multisyllabic one, and MyCo System. They made a pleasant contrast to the skyscrapers (which in Newhaven were short, more like sky pokers), the two cathedrals and various bell towers. A variety of shapes. Newhaven had never been an expansion setting of her favorite game, but she tried to imagine as she hobbled along the sidewalk she was a player character on an adventure, not fat Becca.

She couldn't. Her body was too real, too painful. Her life was too real, too painful.

If she could make it to the park, she could sit on a bench to think. Her mind could be at ease in the lovely environment of nature. Surrounded by traffic, bus stops, tall buildings, and shops, just as Mother Nature intended.

Becca realized she didn't know what weekday it was. Being part of MyCo System, not having a job, and living with someone who didn't have a job either had blurred the days. It was cold. She must have missed Samhain. Unless it was still October. It must be at least November.

She didn't know the date Leila had died.

She was sure Opal had lied. Leila had died during her treatment. There had been no recovery period. Dr. Lee had tossed her into that cavern, and those sentient mushrooms had devoured her beautiful self.

Becca's limping steps faltered. When the pain increased, she limped on both legs, so she appeared to be staggering. The park was still a few blocks away. No benches in sight. She leaned against a wall.

Which hurt worse, her body or her heart?

She had made it about halfway. She had to decide. Keep going, and be able to sit, but have to walk twice as far back after a rest? Or turn around now and head home with no sitting?

Under Leila's bulky coat, her bandages oozed, letting out their characteristic stink. She closed her eyes, just for a moment, and put her head against the rough brick wall.

"Hey! Fatty! You can't sleep here!" Someone leaned out of the shop door, an old Italian place. The potent odor of cheese wafted out. "No homeless here! You go be fat somewhere else!"

Becca straightened. "I'm not homeless. I hurt my leg."

The shopkeeper eyed her up and down in the coat made to fit Leila's six-foot frame. "You look homeless. You stink. You are disgusting. Get away from my cheese shop."

Becca pushed away from the wall and walked away, dragging her legs, breathing shallowly. The cloud of cheese and fermented milk followed her, along with the shopkeeper's derisive yells for "Fatty" to "go way," and as she rounded the corner, he said, with finality, "What a monster."

CHAPTER FORTY

Becca messaged Opal: *tell me more.*

CHAPTER FORTY-ONE

Becca, wincing, dragged Leila's oversized chair to the window and stared at a world in which she didn't fit. She messaged Willow LeNoir. Still blocked.

She cleaned the kitchen and found an ancient pizza in the back of the freezer.

An hour later, Becca was in the bathroom, vomiting, shitting, and crying. She ended up in the shower, hosing herself off. She replaced her bandages from the skin out and what she saw on her side was horrifying: a puckered, open wound instead of a clean slice from a scalpel, stitched shut by a doctor. Didn't liposuction involve slight cuts where they inserted the vacuum? This was a single, ragged hole. And it *was* a hole, not a neat slice. On that side of her abdomen, the fat had caved in. On the other side, the tissue had merely shifted in that direction, like an adipose avalanche. She touched the bruised, tender mess. The fat had liquified inside her and redistributed. Was that how liposuction worked?

Clear, pink, stinky fluid oozed from the hole. Not an infection, but not right. Shouldn't there be a drain catching this discharge? And stitches holding this shut?

She triple-padded gauze over the hole and put a single layer over the rest of her abdomen to hold it in place. The tight elastic bandage didn't help the bruising or pain. She couldn't believe Leila used to corset after her treatments. How Leila could keep doing this despite being doubled over in pain, almost screaming, afterward?

Only wearing bandages and undergarments, trailed by Nyx, Becca walked across the warm floor to the living room and checked her phone. She rolled her eyes at a message from an unfamiliar sender. Like Becca had time right now for spam or scams. Becca dropped the phone onto the ottoman and fed Apep, standing with her face close to the tank as he gobbled, so he knew she loved him. She felt far away from him in his big tank. In her studio, they had always been together. Bigger wasn't always better.

She touched her bruised middle and winced.

The phone beeped.

Perhaps Opal was getting back to her. She blew a kiss to her fish and turned, tripping over the cat. Nyx was becoming anxious without Leila, and Becca didn't know how to calm her. She had never owned a cat. She understood the basics: put in food and water, remove dirty litter from the box. Give pats, offer toys. But the cat was complex emotionally in a way the fish wasn't.

She scooped Nyx up, although it hurt. The warm, naked cat squirmed, looking at her with its vast alien eyes. "She's gone, buddy," Becca said, trying not to cry. "We're gonna have to figure this out together." She plopped into the chair with the cat and picked up the phone.

Same unknown sender, now with an urgent symbol.

"These spammers," she said to Nyx.

Nyx blinked.

She tapped the message to clear it unread, but hesitated. She had messaged Opal for information. Maybe this was it. A third party had sent it. She would glance at it. If it was spam, she would delete it immediately. She knew better than to click through.

Holy shit. The message was from Milo Cobalt! The guy in charge of MyCo System. She pulled Nyx against her shoulder so the cat could see. "Is this real?"

Nyx's big green gargoyle eyes said *probably not*.

The message was a link to a password-protected private message. Damn it. She had just agreed with herself not to click through any spam messages. But Milo Cobalt …

She fired off a quick question to Opal. *I just got a weird message that is supposedly from Milo Cobalt saying it's private and I have to click something and give a password. Looks like spam?*

Part of her was in awe that she could message Dr. Opal Knox, who had been on TV for years. The part that had grown up around her famous mum was a little less in awe. Mostly, Willow LeNoir had kept her shameful daughter far away from her celebrity friends. The perfect, slim, gorgeous model wanted no one to know her adopted daughter was a fat lump.

Opals' response was quick. *It's real. Your refusal was noted at the highest levels.*

That was strange phrasing, as if there was a level beyond Milo Cobalt. He did own the company, right?

Seated in the oversized chair, Becca went through laborious three-factor authentication to get into what turned out to be a video-call app. Milo Cobalt resembled a digital version of himself. Becca recalled what Leila had once told her about Milo. Like a robot, or maybe just neurodivergent. Yes, that, but even odder. He was in the uncanny valley. He held himself strangely still, with regimented blinks. As he spoke, his head didn't move. His neck might as well be in an unseen vise. His hands did not rise into the frame to accentuate anything he said. AI-generated fakes were excellent; AIs in her video game were more real than this guy.

"Hello, Becca," the floating head of Milo Cobalt said. It blinked.

Becca replied, but as Milo continued speaking, she realized it was a recording, not a video call.

"We're sorry to hear you're not interested in joining us at the highest level of MyCo System. What could we offer to make this more attractive to you? We deeply regret the death of your friend, and we would've prevented it if we had realized the situation sooner." Milo Cobalt's expression didn't change. The eyebrows didn't move, the mouth didn't turn down. Nothing showed sorrow.

Becca wondered who "we" were or if he was using the royal "we."

"We understand you need a place to live; we can offer that, equal to or better than where you live now. Full provisions for the creatures who live with you."

Becca trembled. In exchange for what?

"The only thing we can't acquire is your adoptive mother's attention. She is most recalcitrant. We hope that isn't a deal breaker."

Becca stared at her phone. Had they contacted Willow LeNoir? Before or after her mum cut her off entirely? And either way, why?

"We also can't promise you permanent weight loss. Genetically, that's not likely. But we can keep you healthy and ensure your life is long."

The two things she had wanted. To be thin and to be reunited with her mum. Both not possible.

"We recognize life as an obese person is onerous to you, and what we propose will help with that."

There was a long silence. Milo Cobalt's face froze. After a while, she realized the message had ended.

"That was unhelpful, Nyx," she told the black cat.

She disengaged from the secured server. A pop-up declared the video would delete itself. It was like something out of her video game, spy stuff. She clicked *OK* and sent a note to Opal.

What Milo Cobalt said wasn't illuminating. Can you explain what you want from me?

She buried her face in the cat's warm skin folds. Nyx needed a bath.

Come work for us. Opal shot back.

I thought I already did. I'm a Red Diamond, aren't I?

You know that's B.S. Work for the company for real, full time.

Becca stared at the words, wanting to scream. *Doing what? Sitting around being fat?*

Well, yes, but slightly more involved. Come back to the pyramid and talk. I'll be in Newhaven again tomorrow.

CHAPTER-FORTY-TWO

The usual odors hung over the parking lot. Even the chilly wind coming off Thin Island Sound didn't dissipate the smells. Oddly, the auditorium doors were locked. Becca found no door knocker or bell, but an electronic eye gleamed above the door.

Becca waved at it. "Opal told me to come down?"

After several minutes, Salome opened the door, puffing like an annoyed dragon. Becca wondered where she lived. She had thought the woman lived in the desert somewhere with cacti. Maybe she had left family behind. That could be why Salome was always angry, forcibly relocated to the Northeast from the Southwest.

Salome was probably just a bitch.

Salome blew so much menthol vapor into Becca's face her eyes watered. She looked like she had pinkeye already from all the crying. She wondered about the toxic, addictive chemicals in Salome's vape pen. Becca blinked, blinded, and put out her hand to grab the doorway.

"Get inside. It's cold."

It actually wasn't that cold. Becca stumbled in, and the enormous doors slammed behind her. She pulled off Leila's puffy coat, surreptitiously wiping her face with it. The lights were dim in the Quartz Auditorium.

"We're going to a meeting room upstairs." Salome walked away, heels clicking on the tile. Her hips were impossibly slim and rolled perfectly as she moved. Becca's adopted mum walked the same way, as if someone were always watching and admiring her.

Becca followed with her own wallowing, dragging gait. "You could at least pretend to be sorry," she shouted to Salome's slim back.

Salome stopped and turned. "What?"

"Leila's dead. She's probably been dead all along since that first night. You could pretend to be sad and say you're sorry to me. You brought her into MyCo System; you forced her into those treatments. You killed her." Becca wished she were more athletic. She would love to tackle Salome, sit on her, and smother her in fat for killing Leila.

"I didn't kill your friend. She killed herself."

Becca advanced, chin up. "She did not commit suicide. Leila loved life."

"Back off." Salome held up a slim hand. "She killed herself by not telling anyone about her kidney disease."

"You took all those blood samples. And that miracle handprint. You were there and saw the results of her tests. You knew she was in kidney failure. You just had to look at her to see how unwell she was."

Salome glanced away. "Many people appear unwell after beginning their MyCo System program. Dr. Lee didn't say additional LipoGest Spot Reduction treatments would be a problem after seeing her test results."

"You don't want to admit you didn't even wonder why she looked sick. You pushed her to get more spot-reduction treatments. Opal told me why. Because otherwise, you would have to get one after you let yourself get too thin."

"I am naturally thin, unlike you." Salome sneered.

"Well, I'm naturally fat, and people higher than you in the MyCo System ecology think that's wonderful."

Salome's phone beeped as she blew smoke at Becca. She glanced at the screen. "We need to get upstairs. They are waiting."

"You're the one standing around insulting me." Becca pushed past Salome. She could have shoved the older woman to the floor and stomped on her. Becca didn't enjoy having evil thoughts. She rarely wanted to stomp on people, knowing what it felt like to have people hate her. Only Becca was too big to be stomped on. Too fat to be kidnapped; that was her lame joke. *If I lose weight, someone will kidnap me.*

Well, she could go on social media and declare herself "safe from kidnapping for life" now. Fat forever.

Becca hauled herself up the steps one at a time in her time-honored method. Most people stopped climbing steps that way by about first grade. Not Becca. Her mother—her adoptive mother—had despaired of ever getting her fat, awkward daughter to walk like a lady.

"Keep going." Salome huffed smoke at the back of Becca's head when she paused at the Rainbow Obsidian level, where the largest conference rooms were.

Becca sighed, grabbed the next handrail, and pulled herself along. She had tried wrapping her knees and ankles. They swelled. Like most grossly overweight people, she had a touch of lymphedema, making her lower limbs stiff and extra heavy. The cure, of course: lose weight.

Salome and her menthol dragon breath goaded Becca to the third floor.

"Why don't you have lifts in this building?" Becca grumbled. "An organization built around fat people and losing weight." She panted outside the third-floor landing. "Seems rude."

"Because most people lose weight as they move up in the organization. Therefore, they don't need elevators."

"How do you get furniture up here?" Becca felt frustrated and wanted to delay this stupid meeting. They told her she would be fat forever. There was no way to lessen that sting.

"It doesn't matter, Becca. You won't be moving furniture for us. Move yourself through the door, please." A lungful of vapor accompanied the order.

Becca bent over, coughing, eyes watering.

Salome pushed past her into the hallway. Becca had the impression Salome didn't want their bodies to touch. She couldn't succeed in that quest, even with how tiny Salome's body was. Becca's oversized chest brushed Salome's bony back. Ugh, bones. Becca understood people might find a slender body more attractive, but seriously, having sex with a skeletal body had to be disgusting. Banging against all those bones must hurt. She had heard someone call a skinny girl "a bag of antlers" once. Salome qualified. Why wasn't one just as gross as the other? Why couldn't she scream at girls whose collarbones stuck out and tell them, "Go eat a fucking cheeseburger," the way people shouted at her, "Go on a fucking diet"? Give those bony bitches the side eye for eating anything low-calorie the way she got the side eye and the sarcastic "nice try, honey" when she ate anything resembling a vegetable in public.

Not that she could ever eat a vegetable again.

She stopped coughing and followed Salome down the hall to the far end, where the walls sloped. Pyramid insides were weird. It looked like they couldn't have lifts. A shaft in the center would mess up the layout of the Quartz Auditorium.

"What are you daydreaming about now?" Salome grabbed Becca's wrist. Her long fingers sunk into the soft flesh. "This is why you did so poorly as a sales rep. You can't keep your mind on track. This is why I told *Fast Fashion* to fire you. Your brain skips around like a wet bean in a frying pan full of bacon grease."

What did this skinny dragon bitch know about bacon grease? Becca's stomach growled loudly. It still didn't understand she couldn't eat food anymore.

Salome closed her eyes for a moment and then stared at the outline of the bandages around Becca's middle. "You seriously aren't hungry, are you?"

Becca nodded, feeling guilty. She started coughing again when Salome released another menthol cloud. Between the stomach rumbling and growling, she was afraid she would fart, and in this narrow hallway, it would echo. She squeezed her butt cheeks together.

"What are you doing? Can we enter the conference room, please?"

"I don't know," Becca admitted. She wished Leila was beside her. Leila would have laughed. Maybe if Leila had been there, Becca would have let the fart out. That reminded her anew Leila was dead and this bitch had killed her. She began to cry, leaning on the wall.

Salome threw up both hands, expelled a loud cloud, and pushed past Becca into the conference room. "She's having a breakdown in the hall. Are you sure she's the best candidate? She's really unstable."

The indistinct murmur sounded like Opal. Becca couldn't understand the words. The foul odor in the hall had increased when the door opened. Although the lights in the hallway were low and tended toward the red end of the spectrum, the conference room was even less well-lit. It was like a cave in there. It reminded her of the basement where the big mushroom caps had surged, created eyes, stared at her, then chased her.

She was positive the mushroom things had eaten Leila.

"Rebecca?" A man's voice. "Are you coming in?"

"My name isn't Rebecca. It's just Becca. My mum—my adoptive mum," she corrected. "She didn't like the full name, only the nickname."

"Well, Becca, you remember me. Come in. We won't hurt you."

"You killed Leila." She leaned on the door frame. The fart lingered in her butt area, wanting to come out and play. She thought cork thoughts and squeezed her cheeks.

"I didn't kill anyone." The male voice must be Dr. Lee. It had too much emotion to be Milo Cobalt.

"You all. All you all," Becca said in a snide, fake Southern accent, waving her free hand. "MyCo System killed Leila. And now you want me to work for you?" Her stomach rumbled loudly.

"Come in, Becca, and have a drink. Salome, make Becca a nice Black Gill-Tea Pleasure drink."

Salome grumbled wordlessly. Becca heard ice cubes. Her eyes hurt. She couldn't see into the dark, smelly room.

"Just come in." Opal sounded annoyed. "We need the door closed. If you aren't coming in, go back home. Or wherever you are staying once you lose Leila's condo."

That was a low blow. Becca felt her way inside and shut the door behind her. It was darker inside, warm, humid. Someone, Salome she supposed, pushed a cold, wet glass into her hand.

She smelled the black drink as she lifted it to her lips. The earthy, manure odor of the room overwhelmed her. She felt her way to a chair in the dark red light and eased into it. "Why is it so dark? Why does it stink so bad?"

"It doesn't stink at all. You seem overly sensitive to smells." Salome expelled menthol vapor.

"I figured that's why you vape constantly. To cover up the horrible odors everywhere in the pyramid."

"Unfortunately, Salome has proven to be heavily addicted to vaping, and we can't break her of the habit," Dr. Lee explained. "Somehow, those flavors don't bother her."

Becca snorted, sipped. "Maybe that's a new delivery method for your weight-loss chemicals. Vaping. It would bring in a new crowd, that's for sure."

Dr. Lee slapped the table. “That’s brilliant. This is one reason we need you on board. You have wonderful ideas. We brought in supposed experts from other direct-sales companies, but you, an outsider, toss out brilliant concepts.”

Salome huffed a gigantic smoke cloud that caught the faint light in the room. The walls seemed full of rats. Becca supposed it was the plumbing, working inside the slanted interior, or some other engineering thing. But why couldn’t they have insulated the walls better? The corner where the slope met the floor was entirely dark yet seemed to seethe.

Becca sipped and stared into that void. Was it Leila’s ghost? That was the best she could hope for. But the ghost wouldn’t pay bills or make sure Becca had a place to live.

“She’s gone again,” Salome said, sounding exasperated. “She just checks out. Is she brain-damaged?”

Becca blinked and turned her face toward Salome’s voice. “I’m thinking. Don’t you ever think about anything?”

“What are you thinking about?” Dr. Lee’s voice seemed too eager.

The corner drew Becca’s attention. “Why didn’t you insulate the walls better so everyone can’t hear the water moving inside them? And about Leila’s ghost.”

“The water moving in the walls? What?” Salome stared at the corner.

“Are you seeing Leila’s ghost right now?” Opal asked, speaking over Salome’s confusion.

“I see something in the corner where the slanty wall meets the floor.” She pointed. “Can’t you just turn the lights on? I don’t understand this meeting at all.”

“No lights,” Dr. Lee said. “It will be clear soon.”

Becca slurped air through her straw. She couldn’t see the swirling nebula, but she could sense its presence. She hoovered around the ice, making obnoxious noises.

"Do you want another?" Salome finally asked.

"Yes, please." Becca put her empty glass on the conference table, hoping Salome wouldn't be able to find it.

But she did, and she took it to the sideboard and prepared another drink.

The darkness in the corner shifted. Gleamed.

"What's in the corner, really?" Becca pointed. "I'm not stupid, I'm fat. Even in the dark, I can see it."

Dr. Lee huffed air through his nose. "All right. Let's get down to it. You understand you have some unique genetics, right?"

Becca took the sweating glass from Salome. "So you say."

"Part of the MyCo System mandate is creating fungus-based supplements."

"This seems like a non sequitur."

"No." The doctor's eyeglasses clinked onto the table. "It is not. We create fungus supplements that require a specific set of nutrients to grow. As the company grows, we need more supplements and, thus, more nutrients. We designed the eighty-twenty rule to keep everything in balance, to pace with the growth in resource needs, but the system is no longer in harmony. It isn't working as designed."

Becca drank loudly. "Why does this matter to me?"

"You need to sign this NDA." A sheaf of paper poked at her wrist. A pen wormed into her hand.

"Another one? I can't see anything to read it." Lots of tiny print and lawyer-speak. "Don't I need to have a lawyer go over this?"

"It's so secret we can't even allow a lawyer to see it."

Becca felt like sticking the pointy pen in someone's eye. Possibly her own. She found her name in prominent letters and scrawled something that may or may not have resembled her signature.

Opal took the paper and pen.

Becca drank and stared into the corner.

The corner stared back.

"I imagine you think," Opal continued where the doctor had left off, "that Milo Cobalt, his wife, and his brother-in-law started MyCo System."

"Well, that's the lore, isn't it?"

"They did, but they were only shaping its current form. It already existed."

"You aren't making any sense."

"The true mind behind MyCo System is a hive mind from another planet," Opal said in a rush.

The corner rustled.

Becca put down her glass and took a deep breath. She turned her head slowly, owllike, toward Opal's voice. "I'm sorry," she said in the politest voice and the poshest accent her mum had ever taught her. "I did not quite catch what you just said. Might you repeat that?"

"A hive mind from another planet," Salome said, whooshing a cloud of menthol.

"Aliens," Dr. Lee clarified.

Becca moved her face forward. The corner shifted. The smell intensified. She inhaled through her nose, exhaled through her mouth. "Aliens killed Leila." It wasn't a question.

"In a manner of speaking," Dr. Lee admitted, lifting his hand.

Becca's eyes were adjusting to the dark. "You allowed aliens to kill my friend."

"I didn't let—"

"What did they do to her?" Becca tried to keep her breathing steady. Every inhale brought in more stench. Her stomach rumbled. "They ate her, didn't they? I tried to tell Leila about the mushroom things in the basement." She was admitting the trespass. Whether or not the cameras were recording, now they knew for sure it had been her.

She wished she could see faces better. She heard throat-clearing. Everyone sounded guilty or in denial. That kind of throat-clearing. That British *harumph*, but the American version.

"When you give me a tin of cremains and tell me it's Leila, what will it actually be? Burnt wood? Something Salome knocked from her vape pen while cleaning it? It won't be my friend."

Dr. Lee said, "Well, we won't pretend. How's that?"

"You admit aliens killed and ate Leila?" All of this had to be a fantasy. Fat-eating mushrooms. Aliens. Couldn't be real.

He smacked his lips a little. "Well, what you imagine when you say that isn't how it happened. You make it sound like a pack of lions descending on a gazelle."

Becca raised her eyebrows.

The darkness in the corner shifted. If there were no aliens, what the fuck was stinking up the corner and staring at her?

"That stink in the corner; that's an alien, isn't it? Are you going to feed me to it? Is that your big plan?"

"Um." Salome's breath blew a cloud of vapor by Becca's face. "You keep saying it not quite right. You think we're bad guys, murdering innocent people, chopping them up, and feeding them to alien monsters."

"Please, enlighten me. And you, alien thing, come out." She humored them.

The alien thing did not come out. Becca wasn't sure if it spoke English. She wasn't sure it existed. She was likely drugged again.

That was it. Salome had put something into her black drinks.

Salome took several deep pulls on her vape. The end glowed. In the corner, many eyes reflected the red glow. When they noticed Becca looking, they vanished. They didn't close; no lids came over them like normal eyeballs. They just whooshed away.

Hallucinating. Drugged.

I didn't just see that.

"We need fat, human fat, of a certain kind," Dr. Lee explained.

Salome's menthol vapor snaked up Becca's nose and filled her sinuses, choking her. Although today's flavor was foul, it was still better than the shitty stench of the thing in the corner.

"Can't any of you smell that?" Becca cried, putting her hands over her face. "Gods, it stinks!"

"Salome, can you stop with the vaping?" Dr. Lee sighed.

"No, not the vape, although that is overpowering sometimes. I mean, the shit smell that lingers in here."

"What do you mean, shit smell?" Opal sniffed. Becca imagined her nose moving like a bunny's. "You said that the other night, too."

"This whole pyramid smells like dirt and shit all the time. The shakes taste like that. The black drink tastes like you stirred it with an actual piece of crap."

"There is no shit smell in here. I presume you mean literal excrement and not just something foul?" Opal sniffed again theatrically.

Becca held her nose and covered her mouth. "From the first day Leila brought me here, it's been overpowering. From my first sip of those shakes. I powered through it to lose weight. Now you tell me I never had a chance."

"Huh," Dr. Lee mused. "I wonder if this is some sort of genetic odor sensitivity to the fuggotli, part of what makes Becca special."

"No, they aren't really called *fuggotli*, are they? I invented that name for them."

That had to prove she was imagining all of this. She was still tripping in the Black Chair, a brand-new Rainbow Obsidian.

Chairs shifted as everyone leaned toward her.

"How did you come to make that name up?" Dr. Lee asked, voice low and urgent. His breath smelled of black drink. Evidently, he did partake.

"When I was researching, I found out about shoggoths and xoggotli and the fungus connection and just mashed it all together."

"She is the one," Opal whispered. "Who else could make that leap?"

"That's a fuggotli in the corner? Is it the one that ate Leila?" Her breath quickened. She remembered how quickly the one in the basement had pursued her. It could be on her in an instant if Dr. Lee ordered it.

"They have a hive mind. The fuggotli don't understand individuality. They all ingested Leila's body, and before that, they all feasted on her fresh fat. Just as they feasted on yours," Dr. Lee said in a rather pointed voice.

"What do you mean? They ate my fat?" Becca clutched her middle, where her side was still leaking. Opal had said it was used to fertilize the mushrooms.

Oh. Fertilizer was food, wasn't it? Becca covered her mouth with both hands.

"That's what the LipoGest spot-reduction treatments are," Opal explained. "Before each treatment, one of the smaller fuggotli crawls through the hollow pyramid walls into the treatment room. While you are out of it on the hallucinogenic mushroom substances in the capsule, it opens a hole in your fattest area and feeds."

CHAPTER FORTY-THREE

Becca bent over, choking. "It snuck into the room while I was half-conscious in the dark? How? Through the vents?"

"No, you misunderstand; it's already in the room with you. The fuggotli are protoplasmic. They can form any shape. You sit on it in chair form or lie on it in table form." Opal's voice was matter of fact.

The Black Chair, covered with weird leather, its headrest wrapping tightly around her face. She had been lying on an alien. That alien had eaten part of her.

Had eaten all of Leila.

Becca vomited black drink onto the table, her lap, and the floor.

Everyone else pushed back from the table in disgust.

Becca kept going, feeling much like she had after trying to eat pizza. Everything wanted to come out. The fart was back, and it snuck through her clenched cheeks in a squeaker. At least it was dry. She retched and coughed. Strings of saliva and black-drink vomit hung from her lower lip and out of her nose, dampening the front of her clothing.

The smell made her heave. She remembered Leila coming into the bathroom after the Poppa's Pizza incident. There was no more Leila to comfort her. Becca started crying even as she puked. The feeling of her abdominal wound ripping open was audible. More moisture flooded her clothes. She wailed.

No kind hand helped her.

The fuggotli in the corner writhed, as if it could smell her leaking fat. Its protoplasm banged into the sloping wall, and high-pitched noises came from whatever orifice—or orifices—it created to use as a mouth. "Li-li-li."

"Oh, sweet Anubis," Opal called from across the room. "Is it going to attack her?"

The red light in the room brightened slightly. Opal finally petted Becca's head, the only part not vomit-splattered.

Dr. Lee headed into the unnaturally dark corner. He had no weapons. He squatted and spoke in a hushed tone.

Salome handed rough, brown paper towels to Opal by the handful. Opal tried to clean up the table. Becca shoved back and dry-heaved into her own bosom, squeaking in pain as her side ripped. Salome pushed more paper towels her way. Obviously, mothering and empathy were not Salome's strong points. Becca wiped herself off, but she needed fresh clothes.

A loud noise emanated from the corner. The fuggotli made a tentacle and waved it threateningly over Dr. Lee's head. Dr. Lee braced himself with one hand on the floor and seemed to argue with the alien.

"I need clothes," Becca said to Opal. "I'm disgusting." She was spattered and filthy with vomit. The side of her dark shirt had to be soaked with blood and fluids. "At least a shirt? There have to be some MyCo System t-shirts around." She choked, bringing a hand to her mouth and nose. The skin on her hand stank, and she heaved again. "Bathroom?"

"Salome, upstairs, there are shirts. Grab her one. I'll bring her to the bathroom." Opal squinted. "You gonna be all right, Bao?"

"Well, they won't hurt me. They want her badly, though," Dr. Lee answered.

"And we're working on it!" Opal took Becca's arm and pulled her from the chair. "We need to move to a different room. Can you get them to move with us?"

Opal led Becca to an executive washroom. “I can give you wet towels for your pants. Your shirt you can throw away.” Opal turned her back.

Becca cleaned herself. Fluid and blood had soaked through her bandages. It hurt to breathe. She poked at the wettest area and hissed in pain. “I need new bandages or something? Gauze?”

“I’ll message Salome to swing by a treatment room after she gets you a shirt.”

Becca rinsed her mouth over and over. It didn’t surprise her that the water tasted terrible. Not that she drank plain water anymore, but this water was disgusting. Was it unclean?

She unwound the bandage.

“Salome is coming,” Opal half turned, saw Becca was in her oversized bra, and turned away again. Then she paused. “Do you need help with that?”

“Yes,” Becca admitted, holding up her hands. The heavy, soft flesh of her upper arms hung, weighing as much as a small child. She dropped her palms onto her head, feeling the skin swing. Opal unwound the wet, sticky bandage.

“I never had this much fat taken,” Opal admitted. “Just a token amount to shape my waist. It was painful, but I healed quickly.”

“They took a lot from Leila, and it hurt her bad. Before she healed, Salome had her back in giving more.” Becca winced. “That’s what killed her. Not her kidney disease, although I’m sure that contributed. Being gnawed on and weakened and never allowed to heal. And doing it all on practically no calories because she lived on the black drink.”

Opal dropped the sodden elastic bandage on the floor and started peeling away the gauze. “It was all taken from one side? That seems unbalanced.”

“With Leila, it was her front and then her back. But I’m bigger than her. Than she was. Maybe they took too much from one side. Ouch." The gauze stuck to the wound. "Too bad the fuggotli didn't choke on it."

"They aren't supposed to take so much. Too many deaths are suspicious."

"Too many deaths?"

"Leila isn't the first. Another person had an allergic reaction to the fuggotli, we think. She went home after her LipoGest treatment and died there. You got her downline."

Becca tensed as Opal used warm water to pry off the stuck bandage. "That really hurts," she complained. "You aren't much of a doctor."

"I have a Ph.D. in psychology. I'm not a medical doctor."

Salome knocked and handed in an orange t-shirt printed with psychedelic mushrooms and a few bandages.

"We can make this work," Opal said.

CHAPTER FORTY-FOUR

The new, smaller conference room was more well-lit, with no fuggotli in the corner.

Becca heard sliding in the walls, and she knew she hadn't imagined it all this time. "Where is the fuggotli?"

Dr. Lee pointed to a large grating. "Behind there, sulking as much as a sentient fungus can sulk."

Amazing, she was still high on hallucinogens even after so much vomiting. Instead of fighting it, she went with it. "They are sentient mushrooms."

Dr. Lee pulled his mouth down inside his goatee. "More or less. Except they do their best cognition, shape-changing, and creation of all these great compounds when they eat a certain type of premium human fat. Your fat, to be exact. And they are starving for it. You spilled some in the other room when your wound ripped open. There was a bit of a frenzy."

"I mostly threw up," Becca said.

"Well, they enjoy your DNA," Dr. Lee explained. "The room is pretty clean now."

Becca gagged again, and the other women looked a little sick.

"Tell me you are still calling for a cleaning crew?" Salome demanded.

Dr. Lee pointed at her. "Yes."

"If I fell over in this room and I was alone, that thing," Becca stared at the vent, the vague movement behind it, "would come out and feast on me?"

"Well, probably."

"It would kill me?"

"It doesn't want to kill you. They don't want you to die. Especially you. That's what we have been trying to tell you. They want you to live a long, happy, healthy life. If you want babies, they want you to have a lot of babies."

Becca's eyes widened. "They want to eat my babies?" Becca didn't want babies. Not after how her adoptive mother had treated her. She didn't know what healthy parental relationships looked like. But now she found herself desperate to defend these unknown, unborn, never-to-exist babies. Fiercely.

"No, they don't want to eat your babies," Opal soothed. "You are obsessed with creatures that eat people."

"Because I'm constantly being called a fat monster. People probably think *I* eat babies," Becca muttered. "So why do the fuggotli want the babies I won't have?"

Dr. Lee's mouth bent down. "Well, to breed more people with your special fat."

"To eat." Becca stared him down.

"They just eat the fat."

"Of babies!" Becca shouted, waving her arms, feeling them flap like flags. "You people are sick! You are cannibals!"

"We aren't cannibals." Salome blew a menthol cloud. "I don't have any taste for human flesh, special fat, or even unspecial fat."

"Then why are you helping them? What hold do they have over you? Just stop. Stop helping them, and they will starve to death. Lock the doors of the pyramid and walk away. Close MyCo System."

Salome and Opal exchanged a glance. "We're addicted to the black drink," Opal admitted. "And the cure is here, at MyCo System. We can't just leave. We understand you tried to eat actual food, so you know what happens."

No one had a cure for the addiction. It was a big lie. "Dr. Lee," Becca said desperately. "You are a proper doctor, right, unlike Dr. Knox?"

"Yes, I am a medical doctor," he corrected.

"Why are you part of this? Didn't you take the Hippocratic oath?"

He stared at the grate and the movement behind it. "Well, it's an alien lifeform, Becca. An intelligent one. First contact. With an alien. How could I say no? What person of science would say no? Of course, I want to be part of this. I want to know everything about them. And the only way I can do that is to help them."

"Eating people," Becca said stubbornly, fists clenched. "Eating babies."

He corrected her. "Eating fat. And they went about it so cleverly once they figured it out."

"Clever? Mushrooms?"

"They aren't really mushrooms. They are protoplasm that resembles fungus. Alien, remember?"

Becca realized what that meant. "So, every time someone takes a MyCo System supplement, they are ingesting something alien?"

"Well, yes."

She slapped herself in the face with both hands. "No wonder people lose weight, especially if you consider microscope monsters eat it right off their bodies! And no wonder Leila died. It's a wonder more people haven't died, and people aren't mutating and growing tentacles all over the place."

"Well, a long time ago …"

"I don't want to hear it." Becca put her face on the table with her hands over her ears. But was the table clean? Maybe fuggotli had licked it, just like they'd undoubtedly licked her puke off the table in the other room. Did they have tongues? They could make mouths; why not tongues?

Becca could smell vomit on herself. Leila remained dead, eaten by an alien fungus. Nyx was home alone. Tonight might be the night she ate Apep. And no one was home to break that up.

She sighed. "If I say no, what happens? I starve to death. You feed my fat corpse to the happy fuggotli. Leila's cat goes to the Temple of Bast, and who knows what happens to my poor fish?"

"Well, it goes beyond you." Dr. Lee pointed at her.

"Yes, don't be selfish," Salome said. "It's not about you personally. It's about your unique fat genes."

Becca raised her head and blinked.

Salome blew menthol vapor at her.

"You are very rude," Becca said. "In fact, you are a right bitch."

"It's a selfish thought," Opal concurred. "Think about others for once."

"I'm thinking about others. I'm thinking about the cat and the fish!"

The others stared at Becca.

She sagged. "Tell me what I need to know, then."

"Well, first, the fuggotli would eat their way through the world's overweight population seeking others with your delicious fat." Dr. Lee raised his index finger. "By force. If they no longer honor their agreement with MyCo System to make nutraceuticals, they will take all the fat they want and won't need to hide or be discreet. Right now, they are content for MyCo System to bring fat people to them in the pyramids. Without that in place, the fuggotli will go out on their own, seeking fat people, and they will grow in size and population, needing more fat. It's unlikely anyone they attack will survive to agree to any terms with them, like you are being offered. Here, we provide them protection from whatever government or military forces might try to stop them. Not that they could, but it would complicate matters. We make it easy for them to feed under the radar."

Becca waved away a cloud of vapor and tried not to imagine a horde of hungry, rampaging fuggotli seeking obese humans. "I don't understand the terms I'm being offered, although apparently I'm a survivor."

Dr. Lee continued, "The fuggotli don't just live in this pyramid in Newhaven. They live in every MyCo System pyramid. And underground, in stasis, in other places. They've been on our planet for thousands of years, trying to genetically engineer a creature with optimal fat to feed them. Humans have the best fat, but it's not quite right, because they are from a different genetic stock than the fuggotli, from a different original planet. Fuggotli are masters at genetic manipulation. They worked on a small population of Natives for over a thousand years, trying to get their adipose just right. Early humans beat them back and imprisoned them in the red sarcophagus. Now they are free. They found you, the pinnacle of their experiments. You are almost perfect. They have so many ideas about what to do with you. You just have to agree."

"What am I agreeing to? I don't want to be experimented on. I'm not a lab rat."

"No, you're selfish." Salome removed the vape pen from her mouth and glared at it. "You would doom humanity for your own pleasure."

"Pleasure?" Becca felt genuinely confused. "How is any of this pleasing to me? You killed my best friend, my only friend, and I'm about to be homeless again. She saved me from homelessness and dragged me into this MyCo System scam; now I am worse off. How am I getting pleasure from this? I should just sell my fish online, give the cat to Bast, and kill myself."

The movement behind the grating became violent. Becca wondered how much English the fuggotli spoke. Enough to understand her threat?

"Well, that's your choice." Dr. Lee's mouth bent down again, his default look. "We will keep searching for another obese person with fully expressed genes and hope we can sustain our population of fuggotli with the meager fat offerings we give them now."

Salome touched her slim waist protectively with one hand, the vape pen dead in her fingers.

Dr. Lee studied her. "Well, some might have to make the ultimate sacrifice, like Leila did."

"Everyone hates fat people," Becca said. "No one will care if monsters come out of the sewers and eat them all to the bone."

"She has a point." Opal's voice crackled with laughter.

"Some thin people will have to pay," Salome said, "for the sins of fat people." She rubbed her flat belly again.

"Fat people always pay, no matter what." Becca stood and stared at the fat-eating monster in the corner. "I don't think I want to do it, but I will think about it a little more."

CHAPTER FORTY-FIVE

Becca slept on the couch with Nyx. The upholstery smelled of Leila's strawberry shampoo. In the morning, she stared for a long time at Apep, who she'd had for three years. She didn't want to sell him or give him away. But if she was going to be homeless, she couldn't have animals. Checking the Temple of Bast on her phone, Becca confirmed they only accepted cats and occasionally dogs. She returned to the fish tank and leaned her cheek against the glass, sobbing, not knowing how to be homeless.

The fantasy of her and Apep on the streets, the betta in a plastic bag, was cute but unrealistic. The temple of Bast would find a new home for Nyx or pamper her until her life ended. There were no fish-worshipping temples. And who wanted an elderly used betta who spent his days fighting his reflection or hiding in his cave?

It was selfish of her ever to have had a pet. She was selfish. All fat people were inherently selfish. They couldn't keep jobs. They spent too much on food, on clothes—and whose fault was it their clothes cost more and were ugly as fuck? Designers like Leila tried with handmade garments for all body types, but handmade-to-order clothing was costly. Everything wore out faster when you were fat. Furniture, cars, bodies. Planets. The fuggotli were correct to want to exterminate all fat people. That was what they wanted, right?

The aliens would pour out from underground and tear through the obese population, searching for another Becca. Since the actual Becca would be homeless and unable to escape her fate, they would locate her, the original nay-saying Becca, and slurp her up like a black drink. They would hunt obese and fat people until no more remained.

Then all the skinny bitches could be happy, right? No more fatties taking up too much space they don't deserve.

MyCo System would go out of business with no fat people to sell to. Forgotten, the hungry fuggotli would return to hibernation. They would inadvertently wipe Becca's special genetics from the planet. A few fat people would be born only to die alone, freaks in human zoos. Perhaps, a fuggotli here and there would remain aboveground, hungry, to hoover them up as they were born, plump with delicious adipose.

Willow LeNoir would be ecstatic. All-you-can-eat restaurants, gone. All stores selling weight-loss supplements, gone. No more ugly fat people ruining the landscape. No more beached whales on the sand during shoreline photoshoots.

The world would be a utopia with everyone thin and perfect.

Becca studied Apep. If she flushed him, would he go into the sea? But he wasn't a saltwater fish, and that tale was told to children to make them feel better when their pets died. There was nothing else she could do. She couldn't say no to the fuggotli and drag the fish and the cat with her into the abyss of being fat and homeless.

She imagined Leila towering over her. What advice would Leila offer? Leila wouldn't want her to kill herself. Leila wouldn't want Becca homeless. She had proven that.

Leila had also written no will and left Becca worse off than she was that night she walked into the diner.

Becca hoisted Nyx. Nyx was so warm, she was almost alien. It was hard to cuddle with a naked cat. But Becca had gotten used to it. After all, she had never owned a furry cat.

"She didn't mean it," she told the cat's dark skin. "If she knew she was going to die, she would have done things differently." The cat purred, but her ears were back, and her tail lashed. Her legs bunched. Becca allowed Nyx to jump into

Leila's big chair. She would be okay with leaving all that stuff behind. She felt no attachment to Leila's material objects except the cat. And maybe her tablet. Leila's tablet was lovely, but Becca didn't know the password.

It wasn't about material things. The heated floor, great. The oversized shower, wonderful. But Becca missed Leila terribly. She had been so used to living alone, and now she couldn't stand it. She scooped the cat up again and got clawed. "Okay, I get it; I'm not her. I can't be her for you, and you can't be her for me."

She stood before the tank again. Apep fought his reflection in the mirrored toy, fins extended, gills out. Bettas enjoyed being alone. She dreamed of having a big tank of bettas but knew it would be a bloodbath of torn fins and dead fish. "I'm glad you're having fun." Tears dripped from her chin. Apep's new tank was huge. No one else would take a tank that big for a stupid little betta. He would end up in a cup or a vase with no toy or cave.

Even her pets were being punished for Becca's innate fatness. Her birth parents had been so fat her mother had been on television for it. Over twenty-five years later, Becca was homeless, and some random person would abuse her fish and send her friend's cat to the Temple. She didn't know enough about Bast to pretend to worship Her and become a priestess. Those jobs were almost impossible to get, even for real worshippers. Bast could tell if someone was for real.

"I could have worshiped Bast," Becca said to Apep. "If I had known it would come to this, I would have started years ago." But she had never owned a cat in her life. Even with Nyx, she didn't have that connection. She probably wasn't a fish priestess, either. Thousands of years ago, there were fewer people on the planet. And most reincarnated people living now had been no one important. The odds were against it. She wasn't a reincarnated ancient priestess. Even if she had an ancient soul.

Becca didn't feel ancient, just fat and unloved.

Seated on the couch, she watched Nyx lick her own butt. She opened her messages and tried her mum, but Willow still blocked her. She could search for "Willow LeNoir" news. Her mum had a website. But she wouldn't. Willow LeNoir had cut her off. She didn't care Becca was considering suicide because the other option was homelessness.

The third option was unthinkable: Working for aliens that ate humans. Were they cannibals? Cannibals were people who ate people. The fuggotli weren't people.

She messaged Opal.

Will it hurt?

CHAPTER FORTY-SIX

In yet another smelly conference room, Becca sat before a video call set up by Opal and Dr. Lee. They had banished Salome or not invited her. She wondered if they had fed her to the fuggotli for her sins. Any choice was acceptable to Becca.

Milo Cobalt's uncanny-valley face snapped onto the screen. Becca stared at him. He wasn't an actual person. She didn't believe that. Especially since now she knew the fuggotli could shapeshift.

"By agreeing to this, you will save lives." Only Milo's jaw moved when he spoke in his wooden voice. "You'll save the lives of your fellow overweight people."

"Some would say fat people don't deserve to be saved," Becca remarked. "We get a lotta undeserved hatred. Allowing the fuggotli to eat all fat people would be much more popular."

"Well, most people in the world aren't skinny," Dr. Lee pointed out.

"Not in the first world," Opal said.

The eyes on the video watched Becca, but it did not convince her Milo Cobalt wasn't a construct. The darkness writhed under a table that had been pushed against the slanted wall and emitted waves of foul odors.

"What is your final decision?" Milo blinked once, deliberately.

"Might I ask a few questions?"

Opal lowered her chin onto her hands. "Don't you know everything you need to know already, child?"

"I'm not a child," Becca flashed back. "I'm twenty-six." She turned to the screen. "What exactly will I be doing? Where will

I live? What will I do all day? And no one told me if it would hurt. Will I die from this, like Leila, eventually? Especially if I'm staying this fat, it's going to catch up to me medically."

Dr. Lee nodded and tapped his index finger on his scruffy villain goatee. "We will develop all kinds of new medicines. You should live another fifty years, at least."

"Doing what, though? In pain being used as a lab rat, strapped to a faux leather table that's really a fuggotli while it feasts on me?"

Opal shuddered.

"Well, no, not exactly. They will sample you, but more …" Dr. Lee searched for a word, waving his finger in the air.

"Delicately." Opal offered, but she was still shivering.

"I'm still a rat in a cage."

"Saving lives," Dr. Lee said hopefully. "You'll be the queen of MyCo System. The fuggotli will worship you. You will have anything you want or need."

"Not freedom?"

Dr. Lee shrugged one shoulder. "You probably won't want that after a while."

"Not being thin."

Opal shook her head, scratching her lips with her pinkie nail.

"Not my adoptive mother."

Opal sighed. "We can keep trying, but it's doubtful."

Becca remembered the interview where Willow LeNoir had told Opal she was childless. She wondered if Salome had told Opal Willow was her mother and if it even mattered anymore.

"My fish? Leila's cat? I can keep them?"

"Of course!" Opal said, perking up. "We can get you more pets. As many as you want. And we know how you love your video games. You can get a part-time job as a game tester. We can arrange that."

"In exchange for … letting the fuggotli sample me?" Becca touched her aching side.

"Well, yes, but they will try to grow your fat artificially in vats. Or grow clones of you to harvest fat from."

Becca raised her eyebrows. "I don't agree to be cloned."

Opal placed her slim hand on Becca's arm. "You already signed that agreement. And it's not a real clone, not a functioning one. Just adipose tissue, body parts. It's also a way we could give you spare parts if you needed them, a new liver or whatever."

"New kidneys for Leila?" Becca's voice was rough.

"Well, they would have had to clone Leila for that, and she wasn't a candidate. There was nothing special about her fat."

"She was my friend. She was special to me." Becca sucked her lips into her mouth.

Dr. Lee ignored her pain. "The fuggotli are natural scientists. Because they can mutate on command, they can create many compounds. They can change DNA; they can splice it and recombine it."

"So, these clones of me will actually be fuggotli?"

Opal rocked back and forth. "Fuggotli mutated into people."

Becca stared at the screen, where Milo Cobalt was frozen. "Like him?"

Milo blinked and froze again.

"No comment," Dr. Lee said.

"Will I turn into that? Controlled by fungus. Or turned into fungus?"

"You will be yourself." Opal eyed the darkness under the table.

"I see what I get out of this. What do the fuggotli get? What's their end game?"

"Well." Dr. Lee shifted in his seat. He glanced under the table. A long whip of tentacle snaked out and seemed to point at them. He nodded. "Well, they want the entire planet. Of course, they will share it with us, but they eventually grow enormous. And they get, well, they get *hungry*."

"Are we going to be their food or their friends?"

"We will share the planet with them in the way of their choosing. They will win, eventually, no matter what you decide. They win on every planet, always. You can help them, and they will reward you, or you can say no. Then they will eat you and everyone else who is obese. And eventually, everyone thin, too. Or you can preserve the status quo. Where fat people continue to thrive and survive, and gradually change the perception about obesity to being a valuable resource."

An aqua eye opened at the end of the tentacle and winked. It turned into a large lipless mouth that tried a terrifying smile and retracted.

CHAPTER FORTY-SEVEN

Becca lugged the cat carrier in both arms, with a clear plastic mixing bowl on top. Apep rode inside, gazing around. She kicked something shiny and metallic. She awkwardly craned her neck over her family of pets. The broken vape pen looked just like Salome's.

As Becca stood before the giant black step-pyramid for the last time, a man walking through the parking lot yelled, "Fat bitch!" at her.

She turned her head instinctively. He would be the last outside person she saw, perhaps forever.

It was Ponytail, the asshole from the diner.

"Fat monster!" Ponytail aimed an impolite pair of fingers at her. "Is that your lunch box?"

Becca shouted, "Fuck off and die, you skinny wanker!"

A thin whip of fuggotli tentacle snaked upward from a crack in the parking lot and knocked Ponytail down. He was screaming when the door closed behind Becca, cutting off the sound.

Inside the Quartz Auditorium, a sprawling fuggotli waited. It raised tentacles with eyes, mouths, and hands, carefully taking the cat and the fish from her. One chilly hand stroked her face.

"Greetings, queen," one mouth said.

The fuggotli slithered across the floor, bringing Becca, Nyx, and Apep toward their new forever home in the black pyramid.

Gevera Bert Piedmont is a neurodivergent cyborg swamp witch living on the edge of a frog pond in Connecticut with her spouse, cats, and an impressive collection of rubber lizards. She is the author of *The Maw And Other Time-Traveling Lizard Tales*, The Mickey Crow paranormal series (*Shiver*, *Formless*, *Metal*, and *Murder One*), co-author of *Airesford* (the other author is an actual zombie), editor of the *Necronomi-RomCom* Cthulhu Mythos duology, and co-editor of *Horror Over The Handlebars*, an anthology of Connecticut horror. Her next anthology, with co-editor Elizabeth Davis of Dead Fish Books, will be *The Atlas of Deep Ones*.

Bert has an MFA in creative writing and belongs to HWA, Connecticut Authors and Publishers Association, and New England Horror Writers. Her (very) small press publishing company is Transformations by Obsidian Butterfly, LLC, and at this time is only publishing anthologies.

Bert used to be mobidly obese, and in her younger and less wiser days, she was involved in not one but two pyramid schemes selling beauty products.

Connect with Bert at:

Facebook.com/geverabertpiedmont
obsidianbutterfly.com
https://linktr.ee/bybertabird
or her Amazon and Goodreads author pages.

Author photo by Athina Bellios.

ALSO AVAILABLE FROM NIGHTMARE PRESS:

JENNY'S SPOOKY LITTLE TALES: VOL. 1

The Frightening Floyds have been researching and writing about the paranormal and all things strange and unusual for ten years. To celebrate, Jenny has compiled ten of her favorite stories from the many books she has written with her husband Jacob. In this collection, you'll find ghosts, aliens, a cursed Porsche, a forgotten graveyard, a family home, Disney haunts, and of course, Waverly Hills Sanatorium, among others. We hope you enjoy *Jenny's Spooky Little Tales: Vol. 1.*

HEARTS IN THE HOURGLASS

by Jacob Floyd

The world broke, and he's been rushing to fix it ever since—piece by excruciating piece…

Prepare for a surreal and fragmented tale of madness and love living in nightmares and illusions; suffering, violence, fear, sorrow, obsession, and isolation fall through the fragile prison, tumbling through the quiet, chaotic catacombs of creation.

HEARTS IN THE HOURGLASS is a scattered story about the monsters of a man, a fighter who has failed, and the endless pursuit of an elusive force. It is a walk through a realm of space and time in the shadows of Cosmic gods, a broken soul, and a fractured mind where, underneath an existence where nothing makes sense, everything is as one.

The weird and wonderful meet good and evil, light and dark, and the gray ambiguous spaces in between, in this absurd unhinged journey through a wrecked world without boundaries or rules, seen through eyes with disjointed vision.

All is separate, yet all is one…

NOIR FALLING:
A BIZARRE MYSTERY OF ART AND THE MIND
by L. Andrew Cooper

Daniel Lowe, a presence but not a student at the prestigious University, keeps finding himself in strange situations, not sure how he got there. Color whorls devour people and places, a beautiful woman in a null space called The Blank asks him to save her from her corporate magnate husband, and dozens of missing students might somehow relate to these calamities. With companions such as Chuck Adair, a member of a philosophical Society that crams his head full of big ideas early on, and Voice, a young woman sprung from his head, he traverses hallucinatory landscapes, the interiors of famous paintings, and more on his quest to figure out both where a growing mass of "clues" will lead.

Noir Falling blends surrealism with dark noir, dark fantasy, horror, and philosophical speculation, taking Daniel on a wild quest to find out who he is while he tries to save an irresistible femme fatale from an international corporate conspiracy to traffic in the "substance" of art and humanity.

AMERICAN MYSTIC: THE LIFE, DEATH, & REBIRTH OF JIMMY WONDERFUL

by Coyote Wallace

American Mystic follows the daring exploits of gonzo journalist James Wozynski, renowned as Jimmy Wonderful, as he embarks on his final assignment: to bear witness to the fate of magic in the world of man. In a reality where magic is tangible and interwoven with everyday life, individuals with the ability to manipulate reality through The Word are known as Namebreakers. Feared and coveted in equal measure, these wielders of The Word are viewed as genetic anomalies, regarded by many as a plague to be eradicated.

Enter Roy Altenhofen, an enigmatic billionaire who has amassed his fortune by peddling the cure for magic. Now, claiming to possess the crucial elements needed to expunge the last vestiges of magic from existence, he convenes Jimmy and a select few at his compound in the desolate Salt Flats of Utah. Their mission: to make a final plea for the preservation of all that transcends the human realm.

American Mystic, narrated through Jimmy's unorthodox prose, delves into the climactic struggle for the very soul of the American ethos. As society hurtles towards a future stripped of wonder, where the peculiar is outlawed and the extraordinary hunted to extinction, Jimmy finds himself joined by Tek - a fierce Native American activist determined to thwart Altenhofen's machinations - and Moxley Allerton - a young, defiantly gay Namebreaker whose command of The Word may surpass all others in history. Their journey, rooted in the gonzo tradition, seamlessly merges with a contemporary fantasy landscape, offering a unique blend of irreverent storytelling and surreal imagination.

HORRIFICA

by Sheldon Woodbury

Imagine a place as infinite as the mysteries of dreams, just out of sight, hidden in our nightmares and lurking in the shadows. It's the place where all that's creepy prowls, a midnight scream away, where darkness is sacred, and the glory of horror abounds. This is where you'll find the trinity of fear, the misbegotten secrets that haunt our world.

The GROTESQUERIES are the freaks who rage against nature and order.

The MONSTROSITIES are the savage offspring of a blasphemous god.

The DEPRAVITIES are rarely glimpsed, their deeds so perverse they hide from even the dimmest glimmer of light.

Each reigning in a wasteland that worships the wicked above all else.

There is no map nor marker, for fear is no prisoner to the illusionary constraints of time and place. You can call it another dimension, or the nightmare realm; perhaps, it is the secret soul that dwells within you, hidden by the façade you wear every day.

Whatever distinction you choose, the macabre marvels of Horrifica haunt our world with their horror and fear, and you are about to enter the terror ahead.

JENNY IS THE STRANGE AND UNUSUAL
by Jenny Floyd

Thanatologist, ghost host, and paranormal author Jenny Floyd brings to you her journey from a small child seeing ghosts to an empath investigating the paranormal. Known as the Real-Life Lydia Deetz of Shepherdsville, she made her way into Louisville, establishing herself firmly in the paranormal community as an intuitive empath, also known as the Graveyard Girl.

Follow her life from the haunted homes in Shepherdsville, KY, to Joe Ley's Antiques in Louisville; from aspiring paranormal investigator to co-owner of two history and haunts tours; from researching ghosts to co-author of several books on the subject. You will see, herein, that Jenny's life truly has been strange and unusual.

DEATH AND LIPSTICK
by Jenny Floyd

Lipstick and a little bit of darkness combined with true crime, Old Hollywood, and ghost stories.

From the classic Lily Munster, celebrating her life in the shadows of a beloved Marilyn Monroe, to the tragedy of Carole Lombard, and Vampira's successful comeback; the sad and tragic murder of Sharon Tate, to the not-so-glamorous side of Bettie Page, I want you to sit back, put on a cool pair of shades (and don't forget the lipstick) as I tell you about some of the scream queens and darkest divas from Hollywood's past, and the makeup they loved.

A CHANCE IN HELL:
AN AVA EDISON HEIST
by Marcus Cook

Many words can describe Ava Edison: ex-Navy Seal, guilt-ridden widow, fiercely overprotective mother, and professional thief.

Whether it's submitting herself to time spent in a women's prison, or fending off foreign goons en route to the Gates of Hell, Ava and her cocky ghostly partner, Mary, believe no heist is too small.

The question is, can Ava utilize past experiences in order to help her return from a place no one has ever escaped to steal a mysterious item?

THE VERMIN SLEEP
by James M. Watjen

Haunted by a traumatic childhood with an abusive father and a mother's death, Alex Fulmer, struggles to find his footing in life while targeting pedophiles scattered throughout Chicago. Alex eventually lands the job of his dreams as a set builder on a children's television show. Everything seems to be going great until he discovers a director's sinister intentions towards a child actor and becomes entangled in a dangerous game of vigilante justice – a game that could lead him into the horrors he knew as a child, and into the pit of the vermin he despises.

IN DORMANCY, THEY SLEEP
by D.G. Sutter

While vacationing in Gloucester, Massachusetts with his wife, a journalist named Paul stumbles upon the big break he's been seeking. On a kayaking trip just off New England's infamous North Shore, Paul hears the story of young Daniel Fogle – the boy who went missing years ago while exploring underground caverns.

Paul becomes obsessed with unraveling Fogle's mysterious disappearance: A case the town of Gloucester has long kept a secret. Tracing the aged footsteps the boy left behind, Paul finds himself in the same lair that changed young Daniel's life, encountering an otherworldly horror he could never have imagined, and placing him in a fight for his life, the town of Gloucester, and the very fabric of our world.

From the mythical Dogtown to Hammond Castle, to the breakwater and Eastern Point Lighthouse, *In Dormancy, They Sleep* is a modern folktale about fabricated myths, torn relationships, and conspiracy, with plenty of classic creature terror!

For more about Nightmare Press, visit:

-Nightmare Press Facebook page
-Nightmare Press Fans & Authors Facebook group
-The Nightmare Press Network on YouTube

We are also on X and Instagram.

Read More Nightmare Press!!!

Made in the USA
Columbia, SC
27 May 2025

58526884R00171